UNBALANCED

A NOVEL

JASON PARENT

Unbalanced
Red Adept Publishing, LLC
104 Bugenfield Court
Garner, NC 27529

https://RedAdeptPublishing.com/

---

1. http://StreetlightGraphics.com

CHAPTER 1

Detective Sergeant Asante Royo stared at the bound stacks of hundreds, thinking how easy it would be for a guy in his line of work to go crooked. But he never would. Sure, morals had something to do with it, but mostly, he couldn't think of anything he wanted or needed so badly that it would be worth obtaining through criminal means. Maybe if he had a brother in need of a heart transplant, a partner dying from cancer, or a kid who desperately wanted to go to Harvard and had the brains to get in, he would consider it, but probably not. He was a man of few means and fewer needs, always in the black by a conservative margin.

He had no financial complications and no vices either—no gambling debt, no drug habit, no drinking problem, no gold-digging boyfriend, no spoiled-rotten children, no nothing except a Rottweiler who tore up his sofa every time he stayed out too late and a part-time lover, Rickie, whose purple Lycra pants and affected lisp made him just a little too flaming to take seriously.

Royo was a cop, plain and simple—a man who'd been called only by his last name for so long that he no longer went by his first. But he tried not to let that complete his identity.

God, I'm so boring.

His stomach roiled at the thought of the too many guys on the force who would sell out their grandmothers for a doughnut. Some even flaunted it, coming into work with shiny new Rolexes or living like rock stars in four-bedroom condos in high-rises comfortably away from the dirty streets they patrolled. Crime was rampant in Fall River, Massachusetts, because too many cops were on the take, living large.

So easy to take a roll in the mud. Royo had never liked things that came easily.

But he couldn't do anything about the corruption. Ratting on fellow officers went against the unwritten code: blue bled blue, or some other cliché that turned out to be not only true but also a way of life. Besides, the crooked could buy IA just as easily as the rest of the lot. He'd learned long ago in his nearly twenty years on the job that enforcing the law with everyday citizens was hard enough, as it was a task open to heavy scrutiny and infinite interpretations—more shades of gray than a winter sky full of clouds.

Royo shrugged. The body on the couch was simpler, an absolute set against a sparsely furnished backdrop. An entertainment center sat to his left, and a loveseat and a bookcase were pushed against the far wall, under a window. A mostly tan rug, threadbare and stained, and a brown couch with an accompanying black coffee table lay to his right along with a dead body. A person was either alive or dead, as simple as that, not counting an afterlife or some other spiritual concoction—and Royo did not believe.

Standing at the doorway into the apartment, he studied the dead woman's round face. Black mascara ran down her rosy cheeks. Her eyes were open, and her lips parted, as if she had a story to tell but didn't know how to start. Royo wished she could.

But asking a corpse to do his job for him was unfair to the deceased. In truth, he wouldn't have found much thrill in his work if it did. Solving crimes was like solving puzzles, as much fun in the process as in the solution. The dead all talked eventually, in their own way. Royo just had to learn their language and decipher the clues they'd left behind.

Clearing his mind of everyday clutter, he prepared to enter the crime scene. Before he'd finished gloving his hands and bagging his shoes, someone had already collected and tagged the money, at least a few grand, and twenty or so tablets of Molly found in the bedroom. Royo wouldn't check to see if it made it to the evidence locker.

He ran his hand down the doorframe of apartment 315 as he waited for the officer inside to snap his final pictures, forever chronicling her at her most exposed.

"Any signs of forced entry?" he asked no one in particular as he made his own assessment.

He winced as a splinter dug into his forefinger. As he pulled out the half-inch-long wooden spike, a drop of blood swelled from the wound like a balloon under a slow stream of helium. Then he pulled off the glove, shoved it into his pocket, and sucked the finger dry.

"I didn't see any, sir," Officer Megan Costa, a bright new recruit he remembered from a class he'd taught at the academy, answered.

She stood at attention to his right, her uniform pressed and clean and her shoes all sparkle and shine... underneath the plastic booties anyway. The camera hanging from her neck was a clear sign she'd been assigned to compile photographic evidence. A smile lifted her cheeks, and she blushed, too young and fresh to be burdened by the endless death the gears of their city churned out.

Soon enough. Royo sighed. Costa couldn't have been much younger than the dead woman. They had the same gray-free long hair, the same unwrinkled skin, and all the trappings of youth. Yet one had no time left while the other was blessed with it in abundance. *Or cursed.*

Somewhere between forty and forty-five, depending on who was asking, Royo sometimes thought he might be happier in a new career or perhaps taking a slower pace in a smaller town, one without a thriving drug trade and many more bad sections than good. But he would never change. He supposed he had some sort of sordid love triangle with degeneracy and heartache and was uniquely qualified to keep doing what he was doing.

But what turns one woman into a bright-eyed rookie and the other into a glassy-eyed ruin? Royo wondered what might have been going through the woman's mind as she died, staring up at nothing but that cold, empty field of cracked and peeling paint.

After donning a fresh glove, he examined the frame more closely: cheap, unsanded, poorly crafted wood. The lock was intact, the door whole and on its hinges. If he was dealing with a homicide, the murderer must have been someone the dead woman knew, who had a key to the apartment, entered through an unlocked door, or was let in by the victim.

He glanced back at the dead woman. Her head rested on a throw pillow, her torso flat against the cushions with her arms tucked at her sides and her feet resting on the arm of the couch. He mentally tabulated her statistics. Even though most of the details would prove inconsequential, they would help him build the story that was her life if not give meaning to its ending.

The woman—late twenties to early thirties, blond hair, green eyes, a small scar on her left cheek, and a chunk of her right earlobe missing—wore a Metallica T-shirt and jeans, purple socks, and tied Reebok sneakers, one hanging half off. Her sock was bunched around her heel. Royo's eyes narrowed at the dangling shoe. Something was odd about it, though exactly what eluded him.

An upended bottle of vodka and an empty pill container lay beside the dead woman on a splinter-edged coffee table. He leaned in to read the prescription label. *Oxy*. The pills didn't belong to the girl on the couch, unless her name was Edward Fletcher, and she lived elsewhere in the building. Costa held out a plastic evidence bag, and he dropped the pill bottle in.

Next to the pill container were over a dozen broken extended-release capsules. If she'd taken their contents simultaneously, it would have been enough to shut down her heart, her lungs, and her entire central nervous system.

Royo had been to many a similar crime scene. The cause of death seemed obvious: overdose of oxycodone, self-inflicted. But that was up to the ME to determine.

Still...

Royo's eyes once again fell upon the woman's sneakers.

"Not much to suggest a struggle either," Costa continued.

"Huh?" Royo blinked and regained his focus. "No, not much, but..." His gaze landed back on the dead woman's feet. "Let me ask you something. If you were going to lie down on your couch and put your feet up, would you take off your sneakers first?"

Officer Costa chuckled. "Yeah, I would, but I'm not sure this girl would have cared much about dirtying her couch, if she was planning on killing herself. Also, sometimes I get on the couch then kick off my shoes." Costa straightened and wiped the goofy grin from her face. "Sir."

But you wouldn't leave one half-on. He shook his head and cleared his throat. "Not our job to speculate. Just take down the facts."

Neither the table nor the floor had anything on them except the pill bottle and empty capsules, the vodka, and a television remote. Nothing was broken or damaged except the scratches on the table's surface and the furniture's legs and the burn marks and wine stains on the rug.

All in all, the scene did *look* like a suicide, despite what that nagging feeling in his gut suggested. More often than not, in his line of work, things were exactly as they seemed.

Yet...

"No evidence of purging." He spread the woman's lips, exposing her teeth. "Some discoloration and abrasions on her lips and gums." He pointed at a small cut over the woman's molar, his mind drifting into the land of speculation. "Could mean nothing. Maybe she brushes too hard."

"Awfully clean for an overdose?" Costa asked. The young officer seemed too eager to egg him on.

"Exactly." He tapped his chin. "You said not much here suggested a struggle. What's the 'not much'?"

Costa pointed at a bruise the size and shape of a grape on the dead woman's face, just over her jaw. "Looks like a thumbprint, like maybe someone squeezed her cheek so hard that he bruised it. There's a smaller one on the other side. Maybe someone held her down... or her mouth open."

"That it?" Royo raised an eyebrow. The second mark was barely a mark at all, bigger than a pimple and too indistinct for Royo to analyze by eye. Perhaps it was a splotch of makeup, grease, ink or even something she'd eaten. That first mark, though... Costa had described it perfectly. The discolored area was about the size of the pad of his thumb. It definitely looked like a bruise, but it could have gotten there any number of ways. It might have even been a hickey. But when taken with the mark on the other side, it made him wonder.

"Well," Costa said, "it's weird she didn't spill any of the oxys. Her makeup is all over her face, so we know she was crying, clearly shaken, but she didn't spill any of the capsules as she broke them open and dumped them into her mouth?"

Royo scratched his chin, deciding he liked the young officer despite her youthful vigor. She'd already learned to expect the worst from people.

He turned the woman's arm to expose the inside of her elbow, looking for tracks, but found none. "Did you notice this?" He pointed at a perfect dime-sized circle of scar tissue halfway up the forearm.

Costa crouched for a better look. "Looks like a burn. And there are smaller ones up the arm. Looks like someone used her for an ashtray at some point."

"Or she did it to herself. She has cuts and more burns up her other arm too." Royo scratched his head. "If she *didn't* do that to herself, I'd be mighty curious to find out who did."

"You liking the boyfriend?"

Royo shrugged. "Not really. These marks are old. I'm betting the ME will find a lot more markings when they strip her. Likely a history of abuse messed her up. Points to suicide. Plus, we've got a nearly empty bottle of booze and a completely empty bottle of painkillers right here on the coffee table. That's a Dr. Kevorkian cocktail if I ever saw one."

"Who?"

"Never mind. My point is if this isn't suicide, someone was very careful to make it look like she killed herself. Other than perhaps her mouth and that bruise, she has no other recent injuries I can see without removing her clothes or turning her over, and the room doesn't look like the site of a wrestling match. But again, maybe we should stop trying to do the examiner's job for her."

Officer Costa bounced on her toes. "Maybe the struggle took place elsewhere, and she was carried here."

Royo chuckled, deciding to humor her and at the same time satisfy his spinning wheels. "Okay, but where? Any signs of a struggle elsewhere in the apartment? In the hallway? Do you see any defensive wounds or bruising other than those you already pointed out? Can you find even an ounce of evidence that suggests anyone else was here at the time of death?"

Costa frowned, and her gaze fell to her feet. "Not yet," she muttered. "But that doesn't mean it doesn't exist. I mean... look at her. Doesn't she look... I don't know..."

"Staged?"

Costa nodded.

She reminded him of himself from a long, long time ago, when he actually thought he was doing the city some good by putting away its bad guys—before he learned they sprouted like weeds in the sidewalk. He thought about telling her to get out while she still could, move somewhere sunnier, and raise alpacas or something before she turned out as jaded and cynical as he'd become. But she would have to learn that on her own.

"It ain't much, but it *is* something. Take point on witness statements. Find out if anyone was seen coming or going from this apartment today or yesterday, since we don't yet know time of death. I'm no doctor, and you aren't, either, so we wait until we get the examiner's report, and treat this as a murder until we know otherwise. Sound good to you, Officer?"

Costa rose on her toes. "Yes, sir!"

"Start with that guy I saw on my way in. The boyfriend you were referring to, I'm guessing?"

"Yes, he found the body. Called 911."

"The way he looked... as white as a ghost, face all twisted up like he was screaming, but nothing was coming out of his mouth. Kinda gave me the creeps. But get a tape of that 911 call. You know the stats as well as I do. Far more often than not, when a woman gets murdered, it's the spouse, boyfriend, or ex who's done it or is behind it. Bring him in as a person of interest."

Costa nodded.

Royo pulled the lapels of his coat tighter, bracing for the cold winter night. He smiled at the young officer. "Good work here, Officer Costa. See you back at the station?"

"Yes, sir."

CHAPTER 2

Eight months later.

As Jaden Sanders entered the hallway, he spotted a paper taped to his door and sighed then wiped his sweaty palms on his jeans. The third floor of his apartment complex was muggy, thick with stale sweat and moist, tasteable spores. The heat was stifling, and even his laptop bag seemed suddenly overladen, like gravity had randomly decided to work double upon it.

He walked down the hallway to his apartment, and the weight of the air grew heavier as he considered the meaning of the notice tacked to his door. The single sheet of paper was folded twice, as if to fit an envelope, and Scotch-taped directly below the numbers 314.

He chuckled nervously and, having the neck-hair-raising feeling of being watched, checked the hallway for onlookers but saw no one. *What is it this time? Snow-removal instructions? Fire-alarm testing? Stop putting tampons in the laundry machines? Time schedule for toilet unclogging?*

Apartment complexes had rules. He got that. But he'd become tired of reading them every time the landlord had a gripe with one person. He was pretty sure he'd never put a tampon in any of the machines in the basement, and if flushable wipes weren't really flushable, they shouldn't call them that.

Common sense told him not to get bothered by the memoranda, as the faceless Prospero Property Management staff liked to call their typo-riddled nonsense. In the year and a half he'd lived at the apartment complex, he'd received dozens of them. Yet every time he found one posted to his door or slipped under it, he wanted to crumple it in his fist and shove it so far up the property manager's ass that people would think him a ventriloquist.

In his midthirties, Jaden had already become set in his ways. He lived alone for a reason: he didn't like people telling him what to

9

do. He got enough of that at work, where he processed contracts for a Fortune Six consulting firm and wasted his law degree while doing what the real lawyers in the contracts department told him to do and should probably have been doing themselves. Admittedly, they'd been taking it a little easier on him the last several months, and perhaps he'd been taking it a little easier himself. A quiet suspicion had formed in his mind that they wanted him out. In the end, he was just a pencil pusher, speed and volume more important to his 7:00-a.m.-to-7:00 p.m. no-mobility career than cunning or even a law degree.

Living at the mercy of a snooze button, Jaden dragged his feet from one end of the day to the next. His friends had all married, his remaining family members were few, and his life was small. Its emptiness kept him mellow. His apartment was his place of refuge and his warm, soft bed, his escape from a bad dream. And once he closed the door behind him, shuffling into the apartment's silent embrace, he became master of his domain.

Cass had changed all that. But she wasn't around nearly as much as he would have liked or in the capacity he still craved. He supposed they were working on different planes. Dr. Clemson didn't think his pining for her was healthy. Jaden had a sneaking suspicion that at least one of his meds, all of which kept him limper than cooked spaghetti, was the doctor's way of stopping him from seeing Cass. But he was seeing her despite the drugs, and she was present when he needed her most. He never wanted to give that up.

Otherwise, he was mostly alone. Alone was easy, without waves. Solitude, though not ideal, was constant, one of the few things he could count on: an end to the noise. He just needed to escape the world and make it through his door unscathed.

But he had another note to contend with—another infraction of the comfort of life's monotony. He'd received so many notes but none like the first, the one that had forever changed him.

Staring at his feet, he walked the remaining few yards to his door, letting a long exhalation whistle through his nose. Pursing his lips, he raised his head, as calm as he was ever going to be.

He studied the paper long and hard, hesitant to touch it, for fear that doing so would be to take ownership of it. A well-defined crease, like someone had run the fold between fingernails, formed the paper into a perfectly symmetrical rectangle. It hung from a stamp-sized square of tape without frayed edges, as if it had been cut from the spool in lieu of using the serrated teeth on the dispenser.

Exactly like the first one.

But that couldn't be right. He was confusing things again. Dr. Clemson had said to pause, close his eyes, and concentrate on breathing when he got confused or angry. That usually worked.

But the note had him entranced. *Could it be from her?* Sweat trickled down his sides. One of his eyes twitched, and he closed them, fighting back the headache forming. After several long, slow breaths, he opened them, gritted his teeth, and tore the note from the door.

His key shook in his hand, and he dropped it as he tried to push it into the keyhole. Cursing, he bent to pick it up, gaze darting everywhere but to the note. A whiff of that sweet Chanel—*her* perfume—floated up his nostrils, and he relaxed, even smiled, then grabbed his key from the floor and stood. The aroma had vanished, if it had ever truly been there in the first place.

Hand still trembling but less so, he fumbled his key into the knob, turned it, and stepped inside. After setting his laptop bag against the wall and his keys on the counter, he placed the note on top of a stack of bills.

He tried to walk away and ignore it. He really did. The note couldn't have been from *her*. He considered calling Dr. Clemson. *For what? Because you got a note?* He knew the note wasn't from her, but he wanted so badly to be proven wrong.

Regardless of who'd taped it there, notes on Jaden's door were one of those things that got under his skin, like beer helmets, grandma mobs, and people who did karaoke to Jimmy Buffet or Garth Brooks tunes. He couldn't walk away knowing it was sitting on his counter unread, even though he was sure it would sadden or anger him.

He huffed then laughed off his uneasiness. *You're being silly. It's nothing. Might as well get it over with.* Jaden took one step, tripped, and almost fell on his face. With his heart leaping into his throat, he threw out his arms to balance himself.

"Rascal," he snapped, looking down at the mackerel tabby cat weaving in and out of the space between his legs, tail up and motor running.

Despite his near fall, Jaden couldn't suppress a smile. He nudged the cat with his shin, which only encouraged more kitty kisses. "All right, all right!" He picked up Rascal and scratched him under his chin. "Knock it off before I sell you to a bad Chinese restaurant."

A pang hit him deep in his chest. He sniffled, his eyes watering, but quickly choked back the tears. Jaden felt like a loser who couldn't stop losing. His heart had been broken beyond repair, a miserable thing that puttered along like a cantankerous old mower. He wondered how much more damage it could sustain before it gave its last putts.

He pressed his cheek against Rascal's and grinned shakily. *Something to live for.* Though Rascal didn't have long to live. The cat had feline leukemia. Jaden had adopted him at the same time he moved into the apartment. The shelter had given him a clean bill of health, but Rascal had been an indoor cat ever since, so Jaden figured he must have caught the virus sometime shortly before adoption. That, or the shelter had dumped the cat on him. It didn't matter. He wouldn't have traded Rascal for the healthiest kitten. He hadn't learned of the cat's sickness until a few months ago, when Rascal's weight loss and lack of appetite spurred an emergency vet visit. The doctor had given the cat anywhere from three months to a year.

Jaden put Rascal on the counter and kissed the cat's forehead. He smiled into his furry friend's eyes but cringed at the reek of the cat's breath, the pungent stench of infection, which was a symptom of the decay racking the poor beast.

He paused, closed his eyes, and concentrated on breathing. Not the least bit hungry, he nevertheless comforted himself with the routine of ordering dinner. "Heh, how does Chinese sound?" He rifled through the mess of menus and flyers littering his counter, shuffling his mail and the note into the pile and temporarily pushing it to the back of his mind.

He dialed the number on the front of Golden Star's menu, wondering how many times he would have to call it before he'd committed it to memory. If he were smart, he would add it to speed dial among the few spots already taken by Rob, his best friend, who was married and largely out of the picture, Mom, Cass, and Tara, his sister and only true remaining friend. He ordered the number-nine combo for himself and some fried shrimp for his cat.

Absently stroking Rascal, he stared at the clutter on his counter. "Most of these coupons are probably expired. I really ought to clean."

His eyes fell upon the folded sheet of paper, and his mood, which had barely started to elevate after a long, terrible day and thoughts of his beloved pet's premature demise, took another downturn.

Dr. Clemson said his meds were supposed to keep him level. *Dr. Clemson doesn't know—wait. Did I take them today?* He grimaced as if he'd stepped in a heaping pile of dog crap and had to scrape it off with a stick.

Rascal purred as Jaden petted him above his tail, where he liked it best. "One cat doesn't make me a cat lady, does it, boy? Well..." He slapped his thighs, pantomiming exasperation for the sake of an animal who wouldn't understand it. "Should we see what we've been barred from doing now? I hope for your sake it's not coughing up fur balls."

He picked up the letter and turned it in his clammy hands. It had no marks of any kind on the portions he could see. He unfolded it and pressed it flat against the counter.

Rascal walked across it to his dish. Jaden narrowed his gaze on the tiny print. The paper held one paragraph in a standard font—Times New Roman, he thought. The memorandum, if that was what it was, had none of the trappings of Prospero Property Management memo—no letterhead with the bold, obnoxious logo, no watermark, and no air of condescension.

You're the reason she's gone.

It had a smiley face at the end.

Jaden gasped, jerking his arms back and releasing the paper as if it had burst into flames. He squeezed his eyes shut and focused on his breathing, which hitched.

He slid the note in front of him and read again.

Howdy, neighbor!

Please remember not to let your door slam closed when you leave your apartment. It is very disturbing to the rest of us in the hall. This is my second request, and I hope you'll take it to heart this time.

Much obliged!

Jaden's heart thudded. He must have imagined what he'd read the first time—his eyes had been playing tricks on him. But that was a heck of nasty trick.

He tried to put it out of his mind and focus on the real words in front of him. *Second time?* Jaden turned it over in his head, but concentrating on it so hard made his skull feel as if it were imploding, shards of bone stabbing into his brain. On its face, the note didn't seem like much, yet it filled Jaden with dread for reasons he couldn't explain. He sensed the menace behind the words, the threat between the lines. Right or wrong, it filled him with a tempest of grief, fear, and hate.

Dr. Clemson's mantra—pause, eyes shut, breathe—came too late. He rocked, catching the counter with his hand just in time before he face-planted against it.

For a moment, he didn't know who, where, or even *when* he was. He was surrounded by quiet, except for a soft tone ringing in his ears. His mind went blank.

He blinked and tried to focus on anything. *Counter. Cat. Rascal. Dying.*

A hollow feeling panged in his stomach. He was holding a crumpled paper, squeezing it in his white-knuckled grip.

Jaden blinked away his teary blur and read the words anew. *Second time?* He couldn't remember a first time. Yet he felt déjà vu. *Have I seen a note like that before?* His mind was in shambles, and he couldn't focus.

Focus! The door? Slamming?

True, when his hands were full or he couldn't catch the door in time, it sometimes slammed. The hinges were like mousetraps snapping shut on the unwary. That wasn't his fault but his curse. He'd locked himself out of the apartment on two occasions already.

Or has it been more than that? It would have been more, had a neighbor not taught him how easily he could break in by sliding a credit card between the frame and the lock. He'd thought that trick only worked in movies, but it was surprisingly simple. He wondered if someone had gotten in every time he lost a sock and thanked God when he remembered to lock the dead bolt.

He tossed the note onto the counter and sneered. *Complain to management, asshole.* "Second time?" *Why does that seem wrong yet right?*

With his eyes blurring over again, he smacked himself in the forehead. "Focus." He held in his breath, closed his eyes, then let out a long, deep exhalation. *Why is remembering so important?* He might have thrown away the first note without even looking at it. He was a good neighbor, the *best* neighbor, always quiet and keeping to himself. *Why would anyone have a problem with me?*

"Howdy, neighbor!" he mocked in his best Western drawl. "What? Do I live next door to a fucking cowboy?" He sniggered, but heat rose in his cheeks. *Just let it go, man. Let it go! Dr. Clemson says you need to stay level. Another outburst, and you'll have to go to those classes.*

Jaden groaned. "Why should I let it go? I did nothing wrong."

The note got under his skin, like it was twisting a knife in some old wound over and over, never letting it heal, and that had to be intentional. And the more he dwelled on it, the more his shoulders heaved—a liability of his condition, Dr. Clemson would say. Anger could get him into trouble if he wasn't careful.

Recognize the irrational and adjust accordingly. Inject logic into your emotions. Jaden grumbled, "As if it were that simple."

His head was starting to throb all over again, and his face radiated heat. Slamming his hand down on the letter, he shouted at his door, "You're not my fucking boss!"

He grabbed his phone and texted his sister. A single mother of two, holding down a full-time job while fighting breast cancer, Tara was Jaden's big sis despite being two years younger. Even with a hundred problems of her own, she made time for his. He didn't know what he would have done had she not been there for him that one time.

He laughed uneasily, denying the memory. He'd had something of a breakdown one night, gone a little too deep into his cups, and might have held a blade to his wrist for far too long to be considered a fleeting thought. But thanks to Tara, he was doing better, seeing Dr. Clemson, and regularly taking antidepressants and off-label prescriptions that were supposed to keep him if not happy, at least subdued. No more anger and bitterness, no more pained existence, only the dull hum of life.

For a time, he persisted, the anger and hurt not truly gone but buried. Either his tolerance was growing, or his inconsistency in taking his pills was. His spotty memory was another liability of his condition, so sayeth the esteemed Dr. Clemson. He couldn't even pronounce the new drug—*Haliperdol? Helloperidoll?*—which Jaden thought had done nothing yet and might have been even making things worse.

Funny, at that moment, he couldn't recall why he had so badly wished to die. With his brow furrowed, he focused on composing his text. *Do you believe this? My neighbor just left a note on my door telling me not to slam it.*

The phone rang, and he picked up. "Hello?"

"You got another note?"

Tara sighed into the phone, causing static to crinkle through Jaden's receiver. He didn't respond, wondering what she knew about previous notes but unable to form the words to ask.

"You okay? Talk to me, Jaden."

Jaden huffed. "The jerk didn't even sign it. I should knock on his door and tell him if he leaves another fucking note on mine, I'll break his goddamn fingers."

"Calm down. Maybe we should call Dr. Clemson. You're getting all worked up again. Focus on your breathing. I'll come by when

Matthew gets home and can watch Damien, and we'll handle it together."

Jaden knew his sister was right, but it didn't make him any less angry. "Why should my night be ruined by some asshole, while he gets to go on enjoying his?" He paced the length of his kitchen. Rascal followed him back and forth along the counter.

"Are you sleeping all right? Are you taking your meds?"

Jaden's nephew called for his mommy. Tara shushed him, but the calls became more insistent.

"I-I gotta go. I'm sorry, Jaden. I'll be by as soon as I can. In the meantime, please call Dr. Clemson. And promise me you won't do anything stupid."

"Stupid? Ugh!" Jaden slammed down his phone and pulled at his hair. He paced faster and faster, his face flushing. *The nerve of some people.* He wanted to grab something, some*one*, around the neck and squeeze, squeeze, squeeze until all his frustration exuded through his fingertips.

He snatched up the note and stormed into the hall. Turning around, he started back inside, then he turned around again. Smacking the note against the door across from his, the note's most likely point of origin, he yelled, "Keep your fucking notes to yourself!"

"Shit." He'd forgotten his door. As he turned, it was inches from slamming shut. He lunged forward with his foot and barely caught the door with the toe of his shoe a half second before locking himself out.

He let out a breath and straightened, sure his forward split had pulled something in his groin. The note unstuck from his neighbor's door, slid down, and landed on the carpet. Leaving it where it lay, he stepped back into his apartment and slammed the door.

That was stupid. He was calmer, sure, but he resumed pacing and didn't feel better. He'd never met his neighbor or even seen him. And he'd assumed it was a *he,* though he had no evidence to back that assumption. *Not a very gentlemanly way to treat a lady.*

He stopped. *It hadn't been a he the first time.*

The thought came out of nowhere and hit him like a punch to the gut. His lower lip quivered. "First time?" He tittered then shook his head so quickly that his eyes couldn't keep up with motion. The wall streaked across his vision.

Dizzy, he swayed and ran a hand down his face. "Forget the first time. What does it matter? Probably some old jerk with nothing better to do than harass his neighbors."

He sighed, picturing a centenarian breathing through an oxygen mask and having a heart attack because some temperamental asshole couldn't take his simple request for common decency. The room loomed larger, and he felt small then smaller still, shrinking out of existence. He was nothing—except maybe an angry jerk.

I'm not that guy. At least, he didn't want to be. He was, putting it mildly, socially awkward. But his heart was good and mostly in the right place. *Isn't it?* His chin dipped against his chest.

Had to go yelling and screaming at her door, didn't you? Way to make friends.

He shook his head. He considered apologizing but quickly reconsidered, thinking that would make him look insane. Sure, he had his meds, but he'd never actually tried to harm anyone before—only himself.

So no, he wouldn't apologize. The damage was already done, and the last thing he wanted to do was make things worse. He hoped one day soon to catch that neighbor in the hall and maybe help her with her groceries or something.

Unlikely. Apartment living wasn't like in the sitcoms he'd watched growing up: everyone friendly and supportive, sharing sugar and coffee and getting into crazy, comedic situations that always worked out for everyone in the end. He barely saw any of his neighbors, except when someone was wheeled out on a stretcher or police came to investigate a noise complaint. Then they came out in droves, noses in the air, sniffing out someone else's misfortune. He remembered one time when they all came out, ogling him. *Fucking busybodies.*

He exhaled loudly. *Pause. Eyes shut. Breathe.*

No, his neighbors mostly kept to themselves.

Except when they put condescending notes on their neighbors' doors.

Jaden grumbled then chuckled, already beginning to put the matter behind him. He pulled a beer from his fridge, pried off the cap, and took a swig.

His cell phone lit up on the counter—Tara.

"Sorry. Had to feed the boys," she said, a clanging of silverware in the background. "Are you doing any better? Matthew's here now, so I can—"

"I'm fine." When she didn't respond, Jaden added, "Really."

"So?"

"So what?"

"You didn't do anything stupid, did you?"

"Nah. Just knocked on her door, and—" He thought long and hard before finishing the statement. "Politely asked her to stop pinning her fucking shit on my fucking door."

Tara breathed a heavy sigh. "Couldn't let it go, huh? You worry me, you know. Anyway, are you okay now? I mean... really okay?"

"Yeah, I'm fine. Thank you."

"All right, but call me if you need me, no matter the time."

"I will. Thanks." He hung up.

As he tossed his phone onto the counter, it vibrated. *Fuck it.*

He opened cabinets, half-heartedly looking for snacks, while his real focus remained on his phone. Like notes left on or slid under his door, Jaden could leave no email or text unread once he knew it was there.

Tara had called it OCD. But if he accepted that label, he would have to accept that he had yet another problem. Besides, Dr. Clemson hadn't made that diagnosis, so at least Jaden had that going for him. He was just... particular or maybe anal retentive.

He rolled his eyes and picked up his phone again, unable to resist the urge to clear that little red number one signaling the unread text. He scowled as he opened it.

You have to learn to let things go. You're too wound up. I worry about you all the time.

Jaden snorted then smiled. It was nice, sort of, knowing someone cared enough to worry for him.

His phone buzzed again. *You have to let her—*

Jaden threw his phone across the room, where it bounced off the couch unharmed. He had no idea why he'd thrown it. He'd reacted as if the phone had turned into a giant centipede wriggling in his hand, and he needed it away from him as quickly as possible. But as soon as it was out of his hands, he felt foolish.

Still, a lingering uneasiness kept him from walking over and picking it up from the floor. He took another long swig of his beer and rested his palms against the countertop. His stomach gurgled, and Rascal tiptoed over his hand.

"Okay, Rascal. Sit tight." Jaden grabbed his wallet and his keys. "I'll be right back with your shrimp."

The cat meowed, and Jaden leaned in to accept the head butt he knew was coming. Rascal didn't let him down.

Grinning, that bit of ugliness with the note beginning to fade, Jaden backed out into the hallway. He heard a faint click, the sound of a door closing—but not his door.

He eased his door shut, being careful not to catch Rascal in it, then locked the bolt and turned. He glared so hard at the door across from him that he thought his gaze might bore holes in it. The note he'd left at its base was gone.

CHAPTER 3

As Royo studied the young Latino in a gray button-down tucked into his grass-stained jeans, he wondered again if he might be wasting the department's time. Even when cause of death had been stamped a suicide, months of investigation inevitably followed when illegal drugs were the means to a tragic end. *Still, the maintenance guy?* Royo put the odds at about thirty to one that he would play the *no hablo* card. Unfortunately for him, Royo spoke fluent Spanish—just not the same Spanish.

A label across the man's chest read Prospero Property Management: Manuel, which told Royo exactly nothing about where he might be from. Deciphering his dialect was as difficult as understanding his thickly accented English. But Royo pressed on in English for Officer Costa's benefit.

"How long did you say you've been a maintenance man here?"

Manuel held up three fingers. "*Tres* years."

"And in that time, I've bet you've seen a lot of what goes on here. No one ever notices the maintenance guy."

Manuel nodded as he chewed a thumbnail. He shuffled his feet, and Royo studied him closer. Maintenance staff were sometimes valuable witnesses when willing to talk. He hadn't been lying when he said no one noticed the guy fixing a doorknob down the hall, changing a light bulb or unclogging the toilet in the apartment next door, or mowing the lawn. They blended in to the scenery as if a natural part of it. But Manuel wasn't volunteering a thing.

In the death of the woman several months prior, the medical examiner's report had deemed suicide most likely, though she conceded that the woman's blemishes might have been sustained through forced ingestion or any of countless other ways. Royo and Costa had exhaustively questioned the boyfriend, the neighbors, and everyone else they could find at the complex, but no one could shed much light on why Cassidy Branigan would kill herself. She'd certainly had a difficult upbringing as a foster child and had been moved from home to home with a brother as her only constant connection, but she had no rap sheet or chronicled history of substance abuse. They'd researched police reports pertaining to the property, ranging from domestic violence to prostitution to many drug-related offenses.

Having found no additional evidence of foul play with respect to Branigan's death, they still had the drug angle to follow up on. Obviously, Royo wouldn't slap a charge of possession with intent to distribute on Branigan, but her possession of oxys prescribed to someone else left several unanswered questions.

The crime was small-time, not exactly beneath him, but Royo had bigger predators to catch. Still, Costa had taken to the case with a tenacity and ethic he just didn't see much anymore. She wanted to take another look at the apartment to find any hidden drug caches or anything else they might have missed, convinced the case had more to it than what the ME believed. In the last eight months, Royo had become a sort of mentor by happenstance, and he wanted to see it through to the end with her, no matter how unfulfilling that end might be.

Costa pointed at the door to his right, apartment 315. "Did you know the woman who lived here?"

Manuel smiled, wringing his hands as he looked down. "I just fix doorknobs. Trim hedges. These things, you know?"

"So you didn't know the woman who lived here?" Royo asked.

Manuel shook his head so hard that he almost looked cartoonish. "No, sir." He shuffled his feet again and looked past them.

Royo guessed the man wanted to be anywhere else. Being a minority and maybe not long in the country, the man probably didn't trust police or other authority figures and never would.

"All right. Thank you. We'll just need about ten minutes, then we'll lock up on our way out."

"*Si.*" Manuel grabbed a keyring attached by a lanyard to his belt, but as he started to unlock the door, it creaked open.

Royo rested his hand on his gun. "Is that supposed to be unlocked?"

Manuel stepped back slowly, his eyes wide as he stared at Royo's weapon. He shook his head.

Costa waved the maintenance man back, and he scuttled behind her. Royo pushed in the door. Darkness swallowed the room inside.

Stepping in, Royo fumbled along the wall for the light switch. Something swiped against his leg, and he stiffened, but his heart settled as he glanced back at the door to see a cat trot past Costa and Manuel, who crouched to pet it.

Royo found the switch and flicked on the light. The room was empty. He nodded to Costa, who moved through the rest of the apartment while he examined the kitchen. She cleared the other rooms quickly and returned.

"Everything's gone." Her shoulders drooped. "Cleaned out. I doubt we'll find anything now."

"It was a long shot anyway." Royo sniffed. "Whose cat was that? Damn thing nearly gave me a heart attack."

Manuel filled the threshold. "I return him to his home. He gets out sometime."

"Why's it smell like—"

"Paint." Manuel pointed at the walls. "Probably they leave the door."

"Why did it take Prospero so long to have the apartment repainted?"

Raising two fingers, Manuel replied, "Second time." He walked into the room and spread his fingers over a section of the wall that separated the living room and the bedroom. "Someone destroy here. Plastered."

"There was a hole in the wall here?"

"Si."

He narrowed his eyes at Costa. "Do you recall any evidence being taken from here?'

She shook her head. "I don't recall any hole there either."

Royo turned to Manuel. "When was the wall... *destroyed*?"

Manuel shrugged. "Maybe... three, four weeks ago." He pointed out the door. "I say he do it probably, but..." His eyes widened again, and he clamped his lips shut.

"The guy across the hall?" Costa halved the distance between herself and Manuel, her poise and eagerness causing the man to shrink back. "You think he did this?"

Manuel nodded. "S-Si, si. He... how you say..." He twirled a finger beside his temple. "*Loco.*"

"Did you actually see him come in here and break the wall?"

"No."

"Have you ever seen him in here after the woman who lived here passed away?"

"No, but just today, he comes out into the hall and yells at himself or at the door. One time, he smash a paper on it. He no see me, but I see him. No damage, but... you know... *loco.*" Manuel smiled awkwardly. "But he nice to cat."

CHAPTER 4

Jaden's head totters on his neck, and his shirt is covered in drool. He's sweating profusely, but he's shivering, his teeth chattering, and he can't focus. The room spins, a blur of white hospital linens. "No," he slurs. But he is back there, at Brentworth.

A knock comes at the door. "Oh, Jaden," a man says in a singsong. "Looks like we gave you the wrong pills again."

Jaden lunges toward the door and tries to block it, but whatever they have given him has made him loopy. He stumbles and falls, barely missing the door with his head as it crashes open. The orderly wears his faded blue scrubs and is surrounded by a corona of light at the threshold. He stares down at Jaden with the sadistic zeal of one who has joined the healthcare profession to hurt.

An older male patient stands behind him, his fat belly jiggling as he laughs. His slightly lazy eye is the only one not glaring at Jaden. He squeezes and tugs the front of his pants like a child who needs to urinate. A smell like hot-dog water emits from one of the two intruders.

"Oh, sorry, buddy," the orderly says. "But we can't let you OD. Then we'd have no one to play with."

As Jaden plants his palms to push himself up, the man kicks his arms out from under him. Jaden slams down on his side then rolls onto his back, stunned. Before he can recover, a knee is on his chest, pressing down hard. He wheezes as he sucks in air.

Something with a wooden taste jabs him in the back of his throat, and he heaves. He bites down on the object, but it remains lodged inside him, causing him to heave again and again. He cannot breathe between lurches. Bile burns as it rises up Jaden's esophagus. He's suffocating and starts to choke. The vomit bubbles over his lips and slides down his chin and cheeks, though some goes back down his throat. The weight lifts from his chest, and he rolls onto his side, sputtering and coughing. A tongue depressor floats beside Jaden in a puddle of his puke.

He's kicked onto his stomach, and the weight returns to his back.

"Get his pants," the orderly says.

The giggling man-boy circles Jaden, who tries to shake the orderly off his back, but he can barely breathe, and the vomiting, though sobering him a little, has made him weak.

"Time for a cavity search." The orderly's voice is low and menacing but rife with excitement. "We don't want you to smuggle any contraband in or out of here, buddy. You know, hide pills you might use to take your own life. We've gotta be thorough with you. I know you understand."

Something cold and hard like metal enters Jaden, and he cries out in agony. Tears burst from his eyes. He bites his hand until the pain turns to rage, then he bucks like a bronco. Whatever was in him is removed, and a forearm or an elbow thumps the back of his head. More weight covers his back and legs, pinning him down.

"Do it," the orderly says, urgency in his tone.

Giggling follows, and something else enters Jaden, something warm. The patient is writhing on top of him, knees knocking against the ground. Knock, knock, knock. Knock, knock, knock.

***

Jaden lurched upright in bed. The room was black. His mind was groggy, and his eyes were slow to adjust. He swiped a hand across his sheets, their familiar smooth softness an anchor to slow his swiftly beating heart.

His bed was otherwise empty. Neither Cass nor Rascal lay beside him. But their missing warmth wasn't responsible for his chills.

Something had wrenched him from sleep. *Bad dream?* If so, he didn't want to remember it. Peace ran into panic faster than a muscle car going from zero to sixty. His heart beat like a frenzied beast battering at the bars of a wicker cage. His comforter lay in a heap at the foot of his bed, kicked off in his tossing and turning. The air conditioner hummed loudly as it blasted frigid air, cooling the sweat on his back and forehead.

In the silence of night and the wakefulness of a conscious mind, his panic eased almost as quickly as it had come. All he could remember was a loud banging, like a hammer against wood.

Jaden's pillowcase was wet. Sweat congealed on his forehead. His alarm clock blinked on the nightstand, stuck at 2:47. He wondered if he'd lost power. He thought he'd heard thunder and listened for raindrops against his window, but the night remained quiet.

He let out a breath and rested his head back on the pillow. He would have to reset his clock, or the alarm wouldn't wake him for work, but he didn't want to move. Closing his eyes, he just wanted to go back to sleep.

Knock, knock, knock.

Jaden's eyes burst open. He unraveled the sheet tying up his leg. *Someone at the door? Now?* He searched for reasons he would have a visitor so late.

A fire? He heard no alarms. *Police? Someone hurt?* No one, not even his family, would visit him unannounced, especially not at some time after 2:47 a.m. on a Thursday. *Unless...*

"Cass?" *A booty call?* Jaden didn't consider himself a stud or anything—not even close. He was an average man of average height and average build and, if he was being honest, a little more than average weight, such that no matter how many times he patted his stomach and told himself he was just bloated that day, that bloated look and feeling remained the next day. Middle age was just around the corner, and his body didn't shake off the weight like it used to. He became winded if he ate too fast, and he worked so much that his cardio regimen consisted of the flight of stairs to get to and from the cafeteria. More often than not, he took the elevator at his apartment complex.

Jaden was at the point in his life when, as cool as it was that someone wanted to use him for sex, he would rather just get some sleep. Still, if Cass was already there, he wasn't going to turn her away. She hadn't been around, and he'd missed her a lot lately. As much as they loved each other, they both still had lives to live.

He chuckled, the notion striking him as peculiarly funny. For some reason, he felt like crying. Startled from sleep, he wasn't thinking straight. The dull thump of an always-active headache threatened to erupt into something infinitely more painful. He cupped his hand over his mouth and blew into it. His breath reeked of stale coffee mixed with something akin to Rascal's litterbox.

Where is Rascal? He scanned his bed for the little fur ball, but the cat hadn't joined him that evening. He looked on the floor but didn't see the animal anywhere. *Probably drinking out of the toilet again.* Maybe, but when the animal's sickness hit hard, Rascal could usually be found lying in the bathtub or on the kitchen's tile floor, as if the cold could numb his pain.

Jaden stumbled out of his bedroom and into the bathroom, but the tub was empty. He shrugged and swigged from the bottle of mouthwash on the sink.

As he swished the liquid around in his mouth, his nostrils flared in reaction to the burn. A hardened, waxy booger clung to a nose hair curled around his nostril. Gripping the hair between his thumb and forefinger, he tore it out. The sting made him yelp, and he swallowed some of the mouthwash.

The rest he spit into the sink, then he stared into the mirror at his white, blotchy skin and spaced-out eyes rimmed by deep-purple lines.

Knock, knock, knock, knock.

A shudder ran through his body as he jerked alert. "I'm coming. I'm coming," he muttered. He plucked the crust from the corners of his eyes and smoothed his dark widow's peak to one side then the other before ruffling it to cover as much hairline as possible.

Returning to his bedroom, he threw a bathrobe on over a fresh T-shirt after checking it for yellow stains under the armpits then buttoned his boxers. The robe's belt hung untied at his sides as Jaden shuffled toward his apartment door, flicking on the hall light as he passed. Out of habit, he peeked through the eyehole as he reached for the knob.

"Who the heck?"

Jaden froze, hand outstretched. A skinny white man or maybe a light-skinned Hispanic with a head full of stubble stood with his arms crossed over a thickly stuffed green coat. August was way too hot for him to be wearing that, even so early in the morning. The coat was unzipped to reveal fat gold chains and a yellow T-shirt. He looked like some gangsta four decades past his sell-by date. One of the chains had a giant *K* swinging like it was the only letter in the alphabet that mattered. The man—and Jaden was hesitant to call him that, since he doubted the guy was more than twenty—dug at a single gold canine with a bubble-gum-pink tongue, the action making his lip curl into a snarl.

As if sensing he was being watched, the man ran his tongue across his top row of teeth and puffed out his upper lip. The stubble over it was the same length as that on his head and jawline.

Jaden straightened. He scratched his chin, trying to puzzle out who the man was and what he could possibly want with a contract analyst with no life, overdrawn credit cards, and empty bank accounts. The man was wearing a lot of green and yellow. *Are those gang colors? A Brazilian gang? Green Bay Packers fan?*

But what if...

Jaden shook off the thought before it could take hold. No one from the hospital could get to him, not in his home. Regardless, whoever Gold Tooth was, Jaden had no intention of opening the door for him. The neighborhood was fairly quiet, with nobody having much worth stealing, but break-ins still happened at least every other month, though typically the apartments weren't occupied at the time of the crime.

Jaden was home, and he wasn't about to hand over what little he had to a burglar, if that was what the guy was. He stepped backward, and the floorboard made a fart-like sound under his heel. Though the sound was way too soft for anyone outside to hear, he froze, held his breath, and prayed the crackhead or gangbanger or moron who had the wrong address or whoever Gold Tooth was would just leave.

Jaden clenched up tighter than a dead mussel when the banging came again, its rapid-fire beat racing against that of his heart. He ran a hand through his hair. *I don't fucking need this shit right now.* He began to sweat. The man didn't look like any of the orderlies. *Maybe a patient?* Jaden was having greater difficulty pushing away the thought that those horrid people had found him. His breathing shortened, whistling through his gritted teeth. *Just go away, asshole. Leave me alone.* His breath hitched. *Please... just leave me alone.*

"Come on, man," Gold Tooth called. "I know you're in there. I just wanna talk to you for a second."

Jaden opened his mouth to tell the man he had no business there and to just go away so that Jaden could go back to sleep. But he thought better of it. *Maybe if I just shut up, he'll think I'm not here or just give up and go home.*

"Look, man. I know you're in there. I tried to do this all civil-like, you know, and have a man-to-man with you, but if you don't open this door in three seconds... well, then, civility and shit goes right out the fucking window. And let me tell you, it's a long drop out your window, motherfucker. Won't kill you or nothing, but it'll hurt like a son of a bitch."

Jaden's lower lip trembled. In a pitch an octave higher than normal, he stuttered, "W-W-Who are you? W-What do you want?" He moved closer to the door and leaned down to peek through the peephole.

Just Gold Tooth, scrawny necked but stony eyed, stood there. He had no weapons Jaden could see. Still, Jaden couldn't be sure who or what might be hiding just outside his view.

Gold Tooth leaned into the door, his head ballooning in the eyehole. "Like I said, man. I just want to talk."

Jaden took a deep breath, summoning his nerve. "We're talking right now. What do you want?"

"Come on, man. Just open the door."

"I think you should leave. I'll... I'll call the cops!" Jaden glanced around the kitchen for his phone, but it was on his nightstand, where he put it every night before bed, charging.

A single slam of a palm against wood came from the door. "Oh, you fucked up, man. You fucked up. What did you think, huh? You could just do what you did, and there wouldn't be no consequences? There's always consequences!" With every word came another pound. The door rattled. The cheap panel hollow inside was barely stronger than cardboard.

Jaden clenched his jaw. His mind raced until at last enough sense returned to spur him into action. *It's them! It's gotta be them! Need to defend myself. Need to hide!* He dashed about the kitchen, hands trembling as he pulled open drawers. He pushed aside spatulas and salad tongs until he found an open but never-used three-knife set. The plastic caps were still on their tips.

He grabbed the butcher knife, started to move, then reached back in with his free hand for the paring knife and popped off their caps. The bathrobe lay tight against his neck on his right but drooped off his left shoulder. The cuff hung past his wrist, hiding his hand and the smaller blade.

With a loud crash, the door splintered around the dead bolt. Another hit like that, and Gold Tooth would be inside. Jaden sprinted for the bedroom, hitting the light switch as he passed, cloaking the apartment in darkness.

He had no time to grab his phone and dial 911, and he didn't want to let go of the knives to do so. They were his lifelines, feeding him the little strength he had. Breathing so fast that it hurt, he squeezed into a ball between his bed and the nightstand. As ridiculous as part of him knew it was, he tried to make himself small and unseen. He wouldn't let them touch him or do those things to him ever again. A tear spilled down his cheek. "Go away!"

His bedroom light flicked on. Gold Tooth stormed in, followed by two other man-boys who must have been waiting beyond the sight of the peephole. They spotted Jaden immediately, stopped, and laughed. No, Gold Tooth giggled. He sounded so much like that filthy, fat man that had been on top of Jaden. The hot-dog-water smell came back to him.

Something inside Jaden snapped. He stayed where he was, horrible memories playing out behind his eyes. His bathrobe still billowed over one hand, hiding the paring knife while the butcher knife rested in his hand against the floor. He'd been shaking with fear, and while that remained, rage amplified his trembling.

"I'll let you in on a secret," Gold Tooth said. "We never intended on doing this civilly." He gave a grin that flashed the gold on one tooth and saliva-laced wickedness on all the others. Turning to one of his compatriots—a short, stocky black kid, barely nineteen and shaped like a safe but not as solid—Gold Tooth said, "Pull him out of there, Tubbs."

Even in his frantically jumbled thoughts, Jaden couldn't help wondering if the third guy was named Crockett—not that any of them were old enough to get the reference. Tubbs came toward him, hands reaching. Adrenaline shot through Jaden's body, clearing his mind and setting his teeth to grinding. *What right do they have to be in* my *apartment? What right do they have to lay hands on me?* His fear was draining, the anger and indignation fueling his every muscle.

Tubbs grabbed his lapels.

Flexing his fingers around the butcher knife's handle, Jaden didn't resist as Tubbs pulled him to his feet. "Never again!" he shouted, as he punched the butcher knife into Tubbs's stomach.

With all the pent-up anger, frustration, and pain he'd lived with since Brentworth, he jackhammered that sucker in and out of Tubbs so fast that his attacker was filled with more holes than a pincushion. And the expression on Tubbs's face—aghast, pale, mouth agape—was art in motion. As the blade pulled free with one final squish, hot blood dripping from it like rain from an eave, Tubbs slumped over the bed, if not already dead then close to it.

Jaden stared at the knife, his breath escaping him as he tried to process what he'd just done. *I defended myself.* As shocked as he was by his action, a sense of pride wormed its way through him. But two more Brentworth jerks remained. *If they would just leave and never come back...*

Brandishing the weapon, Jaden turned toward Gold Tooth, who stood at the end of the bed with his hands near his face, staring in wide-eyed disbelief. His other cohort, a ginger kid with a boxer's broken nose and a crooked grimace, circled to the other side of the bed. They weren't laughing anymore. Jaden watched them as a rivulet of blood slid down the upright blade and snaked slowly over his hand.

"What the fuck, man?" Gold Tooth sputtered, finding his voice. "What the fuck!" He moved erratically, jerking or feinting in every direction, apparently unsure whether he should stay or go.

His ginger crony had more balls. With a cold look of determination, he moved to Jaden's flank, ripping the reading lamp from the nightstand. As Jaden flicked the knife his way, blood speckling the sheets, Ginger hopped onto the bed and swung the lamp down. Jaden squealed as the metallic base *thunked* against his wrist, and he dropped the butcher knife.

Ginger's momentum sent him careening over the bed, dropping the lamp, and falling on top of Jaden. He cocked back his fist, but his face went ashen as Jaden pulled the paring knife free from the newly made hole in Ginger's side. Jaden didn't know if his subconscious or dumb luck had done that work for him, but the result was the same. Ginger's hands moved to plug the leak, but he remained on top of Jaden.

The weight of his attacker caused bile to rise in Jaden's throat. "Get off," he muttered. "Get off, get off, *get off*!" He stabbed wildly and cringed when he saw he'd plunged the blade into his attacker's eye. The man collapsed sideways onto his still-twitching partner.

Jaden's heart pounded, but he felt relieved to be out from underneath that disgusting man. He picked up the butcher knife and pointed it at Gold Tooth.

"N-No-No, man." Gold Tooth threw his hands up in defeat. "I'm good." He backed away, deeper into the room.

Jaden stepped between him and the door, slashing the air between them. "Why did you come here? Why couldn't you just leave me alone?"

"Bro," Gold Tooth said, taking a step closer and keeping his hands up high, where Jaden could see them. "I-I-I'm sorry. You win. It's over."

But Jaden didn't lower the knife, nor did he let him pass. He couldn't let him come back. He couldn't be hurt like that again.

"I-I'm sorry, bro." Gold Tooth took another step. "I fucked up. You don't gotta do that."

"Bro?" Jaden was practically snarling, wrath and adrenaline manifesting like rabies in an already-aggressive dog. "The last thing I am is your bro, asshole."

"Dude, if-if-if you'll just let me get by, you'll never see me again. I swear."

"You should never have come here in the first place."

"Please..." Gold Tooth eased forward.

Jaden raised the knife, and Gold Tooth juked to the right. Then Jaden slashed.

Gold Tooth jumped back, his jacket holding a deep gash exposing white insulation. "Please, man, just let me by."

The would-be home invader made a break for it. He'd almost made it past Jaden when a hard shoulder spun him around. They stumbled out into the short hallway leading to the shattered remains of the apartment door, but before Gold Tooth could escape, Jaden grabbed the back of his jacket with one hand, raising the blood-soaked kitchen knife with the other.

"Please... don't..." Gold Tooth whimpered, spinning to face Jaden, hands up in defense.

Jaden drove the knife down. "Who fucked up now, asshole? Huh? Who fucked up now?"

Gold Tooth blocked it with his arms and screamed.

Jaden grabbed the front of the slashed jacket and pulled the intruder toward him as he hammer-swung again and again. Gold Tooth sacrificed his arms to shield his head and body, jerking wildly to get free. All the while, the man screamed for help. Blood spattered everywhere, turning the white kitchen linoleum into a Jackson Pollack.

On the fourth swing, Jaden faked high then stabbed low, his attempts to bury his blade becoming like a game. His mind was otherwise a blank page. He felt nothing beyond a desire to hurt the man who would have hurt him and no doubt others—and in fouler ways—had he had the chance. Metal slid through flesh as easily as it would a perfectly cooked filet. Angling the knife up under Gold Tooth's ribs, Jaden buried it to its grip. He twisted it and pulled it free. Blood gurgled from a mouth beneath eyes huge with the terror of one who knew he was about to die.

The impact caused the man to spasm violently, breaking Jaden's hold on his jacket. He fell backward onto his buttocks, and Jaden fell on top of him, still stabbing wherever the blade could find purchase.

Crying, Gold Tooth bucked. Jaden banged against the wall, dropping the butcher knife.

Gold Tooth turned onto his stomach and crawled over the remains of Jaden's front door. Jaden watched the home invader slither like a slug through the ooze of his own blood. He moved slower and slower. His blood loss was enough to fill a milk jug. He collapsed just outside the door, breathing shallowly and smearing the old carpet with his cheek.

Jaden picked up his knife, stepped over the splintered wood, straddled what was left of the man, then plunged the blade deep into the center of Gold Tooth's back. The intruder's body tensed and hitched before going limp.

As Jaden stood with his knife dripping onto the carpet, neighbors crowded the hallway, gaping with hands over their mouths. The ruckus must have summoned them from their beds. But they kept their distance, neither crawling back into their dens nor stepping forward to assist. Sirens sounded in the distance.

As his mind began to slow and his muscles to relax, Jaden made peace with the fact that part of him had enjoyed the release. He had pent up so much that had needed to come out, and the three criminals had given him a means to vent the likes of which he could never have imagined—righteous vengeance.

But the ramifications of what he'd done were starting to take root in his mind. Looking both ways down the hall, he saw a corridor lined with open doors. Someone ran toward him. The door across the hall remained closed, but Jaden sensed a presence behind it. Feet made shadows through the gap at its base.

"Drop it!" someone on his left yelled.

The knife fell from his grip, thudding to the floor. Jaden's eyes remained fixated on the door across the hall, his gaze only breaking when someone tackled him to the ground.

He barely felt the blow or noticed the rough hands pulling his arms behind his back, clasping cold metal around his wrists. He couldn't guess how long he'd been laughing and crying before he realized he was.

Still, that door remained closed.

"Did you like that?" Jaden screamed at it. "Did I slam it loudly enough for you?"

CHAPTER 5

Royo couldn't believe what the witness had told him. Apartment 314 looked like a war zone. Two men had already been pronounced dead. One of them was missing an eye, and the other had been carved up like a turkey dinner. A third, who looked even worse than the first two, was clinging to life by the proverbial thread. And the guy coated with their blood, Royo had immediately pegged for a homicidal maniac.

"You're saying he lives here, and the three injured or dead individuals are the perpetrators?"

"Yes, sir," Norma Templeton said. The eighty-something-year-old woman lived in 307, and she had bluish cotton-candy hair that matched her robe and slippers.

"I was eating my Grape Nuts when I heard those fellers—those *dead* fellers," she amended as four EMTs carried off one of the alleged burglars, "who'd been pounding on that nice young man's door."

She pointed at Jaden Sanders, an unassuming-looking average Joe. As far as Royo could tell, he'd just single-handedly taken out three would-be home invaders without receiving so much as a scratch.

The man was unrecognizable, cloaked in viscera. He appeared to be in his thirties. His hair was starting to thin on top, his waist thickening at the sides, and bushy black hair covered his legs and exposed portions of his chest. His feet were bare, treading soundlessly over the faded green carpet as an officer led him toward Royo.

"Jaden Sanders?" Royo asked. He and Costa had interviewed him with respect to his neighbor-girlfriend's death, and he'd seemed as meek as a mouse.

"Yes, sir," Norma said. "I just watched through a crack in my door, wanting to know what all the hooting and hollering was about, but when that feller in the green coat started kicking in the door, well, that's when I knew I had to call the police."

"You made the 911 call?"

"Sure did." Norma nodded. "With his wearing a jacket like that in the dead of summer, well, I figured he must be one of those gangbangers, hiding his needle marks or a weapon. Probably both. I watch all the *Law and Order* shows. So I can recognize trouble when I see it. I'm sure you know the type. Must see them every day in your line of work."

"Did you see them come out of the apartment?"

"Yes, sir. That feller in the green jacket crawled out on his hands and knees, and the feller that lives there followed him and stabbed him right in the back."

"You saw the man who lives in 314 stab the man in the green jacket in the back?"

"Sure did, and if you ask me, that feller got what he had coming. I've been living here now some twenty..."

Not really listening, Royo drew a row of tally marks on his notepad then flipped it shut. "Thank you, Miss..."

"It's Norma, handsome." She ran her fingers down his arm.

He chuckled awkwardly and walked away. "Stravenski," he called to the burly, surly officer guarding the broken shambles of a door.

Stravenski looked his way. "Sir?"

Royo marched up to him. "Aren't you usually on days? How'd you pull this shift?"

"Got in early. Samson's relief. The day's about to start, so here I am. Just lucky, I guess."

"Yeah, you and me both. I was actually here yesterday, checking into the apartment across the hall. Unrelated case."

Royo stepped back and tugged on Stravenski's shirt. "Look out."

Two more EMTs exited the apartment, carrying another black-bagged body on a stretcher.

"Man," Royo said, "I wouldn't have believed it if I hadn't walked the scene. That guy, *that* nerdy-looking, never-seen-the-inside-of-a-gym slug of a man—Mr. Office Depot or some shit—took out three perps trying to rob him?"

Stravenski grunted. "All the witnesses confirm it. Quiet guy. Keeps to himself. Helps out during snowstorms, shoveling out some of the older residents. No priors. Only complaint about the guy is that he sometimes lets his door slam shut."

"Yeah, I know. Quiet guy, keeps to himself. Isn't that what the neighbors always say about serial killers?" Royo snorted. "Anyway, I looked into him with relation to a suicide that happened in the apartment across from his." Royo prodded the splintered wood with his foot. "Well, he won't be getting those slammed-door complaints for a little while." He stared at the pool of blood just past the en-tranceway.

"A lot of blood for just one guy," Stravenski said.

"You haven't been inside? Forensics have already done their thing. Half the department has already paraded through. I took in the scene then went to hear what the good, upstanding citizens of our great city and residents of this apartment complex had to say." He snorted. "Everyone's saying the same thing: the three going to the hospital or the morgue started the chaos. Sanders finished it."

"Stabbing a man in the back while he's already bleeding to death does kind of put the period on the end of a statement," Stravenski said through a yawn, stretching. His hat slid back on his shaved head.

"Yeah." Royo scratched his stubble. "Lot of the residents here heard someone screaming for help, but no one seems to know if it was Sanders or one of his attackers." He waved a hand over the con-gealing blood. "Anyway, that ain't nothing. That's from the one who's still breathing. The bedroom looks like a bomb went off in there. Mr. Office Depot stabbed the shit out of those other two... vics? Perps?

Shit, I don't know whether to arrest the guy or give him a goddamn medal."

Stravenski shrugged. "What would be the charge?"

"Voluntary manslaughter. Excessive force, but man, that's some bullshit. Three guys break into Sanders's apartment, so of course he's in fear for his life. What's a guy to do? Get his ass beat, maybe killed, and his place robbed, or defend himself?"

Stravenski puffed out his cheeks as he blew out a breath. "He did stab the one guy in the back, out here in the hall. Sure seems like the initial perp was trying to get away."

"They attacked a man in his own home. I know what I would've done, but at least I own a gun. You and I both know that if this were Florida or Texas, we wouldn't even be having this conversation. But because we live in a state where burglars who trip can sue homeowners for negligence, we've gotta cuff the man for defending himself and what's his. Why? Because it was knives against fists? That's—" He shook his head. "That's just bullshit. It was also three against one."

Stravenski nodded. "Preaching to the choir, Detective. Surrounded by tree-hugging, rainbow-loving—" The officer's face went slack. "Wait, I..."

Royo scoffed. He'd seen that look a thousand times, every time someone said something remotely conservative, like they were afraid being pro-death penalty made them seem somehow bigoted, antigay, anti-Hispanic, or anti-gay Hispanic. "Oh, for fuck's sake, Stravenski. I'm gay, not a snowflake."

With all the time he'd spent on the force, Royo never ceased to be amazed by how his sexual orientation could send his straight colleagues dancing over eggshells. He'd dealt with bigotry in all its forms over the years and never once reported it. Times had changed, and what once was tolerated by few had become accepted by many, but those many still failed to see that treating him delicately—treating him *differently*—was still just another form of bigotry, even if a well-meaning form.

He swept the awkwardness under the rug along with the conversation itself. "You know what? Cut him loose. I'm not arresting him."

"You sure? I mean, uh, not to question you or anything, but in his state... You know, he might be dangerous."

"Yeah, I'm sure, and I'll take full responsibility. He's a blank sheet right now, no use to anyone. Whatever fire lit him up has all but burned itself out. It won't do him or us any good to bring him downtown. Did you see his face? The poor guy's in shock. His eyes as vacant as a ghost town." *But the violence it must have taken... One thing's for certain: there's more to Sanders than we thought.*

He cleared his throat. "We'll have him come in for a statement in a day or two. For now, send him to the hospital. We should be doing that anyway. So much blood on him—you sure none of it's his?"

Stravenski grunted. "EMTs gave him a clean bill of health."

"Yeah, but they weren't looking at his brain. The hospital will bring in a mental health specialist. I'm guessing he's gonna need one. Besides, he can't stay here tonight, and if he's got nowhere else to go, the hospital is seven thousand steps above lockup."

"Can't argue with that."

"Just make sure he gets word to come down to the station later tomorrow or whenever he's released."

Stravenski started down the hall then stopped. "Wait. So... no arrests?"

Royo tugged at his stubble. "Well, if that one guy lives, we've got him on B and E, assault, attempted burglary, and who knows what else."

"If he lives."

"Our guys got anything on him?"

Stravenski consulted his notepad. "Yeah, Burnetts's seen him before. Got priors for possession with intent to distribute and solicitation, nothing violent. Low-level drug pusher. Seems out of his league here."

"Name?"

"Morton Tresser. Goes by the nickname M.T. Clip."

"Yeah, I'm not calling him that. Tresser able to talk at all? Give any kind of statement?"

"Pretty much out of it by the time first responders got to him. He'd already lost a lot of blood. I'm betting it's gonna be Sanders's story against no one else's." He took a heavy breath. "But one of the paramedics did get a sentence out of him: 'I tried to get away, but he wouldn't let me.'"

Royo whistled. "Well, that could complicate things." He rubbed his forehead. "I don't know."

When he lowered his hand, he caught sight of a young Latino man in a gray button-down, jeans, and work boots loitering at the top of the stairs. He seemed to be watching Royo and the officer as they spoke.

"Who's that?" Royo pointed at the man then remembered. He was the maintenance man who'd let him into Branigan's apartment. Facing Stravenski, he asked, "Did anyone take his statement?"

Stravenski looked where Royo was pointing and frowned. "Who?"

When Royo looked again, the man was gone. "The maintenance guy. He was right there a second ago."

"I didn't take a statement from anyone on staff. I can check with the other—"

"No, no. Never mind."

The man unnerved Royo. The guilty sometimes hung around the scene of their dirty work to try to pick up whatever information police were gathering. But he had his perps and victims all accounted for, each on the way to the hospital or an early grave. *What interest could the maintenance guy—Manuel, was it?—have in this mess?*

He rolled it off his shoulders. "Probably just another gawker hoping to see a dead body." *Or maybe he just wants to know what he'll have to fix.* Royo focused instead on the alleged statement made by Tresser. *I tried to get away, but he wouldn't let me.*

"We're in agreement that if three guys bust in your door and attack you, they deserve what they get, correct?"

Stravenski nodded. "One hundred percent." He pointed with a thumb over his shoulder. "I won't be shedding any tears for those guys."

Royo grunted his agreement. "Well, we'll wait to see what the rest of the evidence tells us, but like I said, I'm in no hurry to press charges or pass judgment. Let's leave that to the DA and a grand jury to decide." He stroked his chin. "There's little need to investigate the three perps, if none of them live long enough to be charged. Even so, I want to know what they were doing here. Question all witnesses, family, and known associates, whether they've seen them here before, who with, et cetera. You know the drill. Get some other officers to help, and get me as much background on the three as you can. Somebody living must know what those boys were up to tonight."

Stravenski nodded and headed off. Royo stepped over the broken door for another look at the crime scene, letting the witness testimony he and his fellow officers had gathered and the blood spatters paint a picture of what had unfolded. Looking down at the blood curdling at his feet, he spotted what looked like pencil shavings amid the debris. He'd first assumed they were from the damaged door. He crouched for a better look and found more of the thin flakes of wood beyond the carnage then picked one up. *Sawdust?*

Royo shrugged and headed toward the bedroom, not finding any more flakes on the way. He would need to talk to Sanders to get a fuller understanding of what had gone down, from start to finish. Staring at the stained sheets and dappled walls, he sighed. *What a mess.*

Evaluating the scene, he was sure of one thing: Sanders had been through one hell of an ordeal. It would be up to the Commonwealth of Massachusetts to determine whether that ordeal was over or just beginning.

***

An officer, a white guy with a power lifter's physique and a square jaw like a Bond villain, pulled Jaden from the back seat of a cruiser. He couldn't remember how he'd gotten there or where all the blood had come from.

Pause. He couldn't pause. His mind was racing, and his heartbeat thumped in his ears, drowning out all other sound. And his headache felt like a thousand woodpeckers hammering in unison, each eager to bore out his termites.

He closed his eyes, trying to shut out the pain from the light. Behind his eyelids, he saw her. "Cass?" He tried to bring his hands up to his face and wipe his tears, only to find them cuffed behind his back.

"Just hold on a second, Mr. Sanders," the officer said, "and we'll get you uncuffed."

"What... What happened?" He looked down at his robe. "What is this... this... Is that blood? Is she safe?"

"Is who safe, Mr. Sanders?" the officer asked.

But Jaden hardly heard him. He couldn't make sense of what was happening. *Am I being arrested?* Fragments of the night flashed through his brain. *A break-in? Who? Something about a note... or Brentworth. Is Cass okay? Where is Rascal? Yes, a break-in. Three of them. Who were they? And why? Were they really from Brentworth?* He shook his head feverishly, but the answers to his many questions wouldn't reveal themselves.

"Hold still now," the officer said softly.

Couldn't have been about a note, could it? No, they were from Brentworth. No one else would do what they did. But... they didn't look like anyone from the hospital.

A million thoughts played through Jaden's mind as if spliced together from a random selection of scenes from an equally random selection of films. Past and present whirled like tornados through his thought patterns, whenever he could establish one. People were dead.

He blinked rapidly then attempted to focus on his surroundings. He was outside his apartment complex. His cuffs were off. He was standing. In all directions, police lights whirled, blinding him with every spin. A young man he didn't know, a neighbor perhaps, leered at him from the parking lot. At the front door, Cass talked with an officer. He stepped toward her, but the cop who'd let him out of the cruiser grabbed his arm.

Jaden freaked. He tugged and jerked, but the officer held him fast and pulled him away from Cass. He faced the policeman and ripped his arm free then turned back to the front door. But Cass was gone. The officer who'd been speaking with her was talking to the old lady from 307.

With a tug of his sleeve, Jaden was being led away again. A blanket had been draped over his shoulders, though he couldn't recall when. That same officer was leading him. *To where?*

More flashing red lights blinded him. *An ambulance? Was I hurt?* He couldn't remember.

"The door!"

He struggled against the officer, but the man was too strong, and he was so weak and tired, and his head pounded so dizzyingly loudly. He just wanted to lie down to rest.

But the door! "The door is broken! Rascal! My cat! My cat will get out!"

Pause. Close eyes. Breathe.

The night was a blur slowly coming into focus. He stood at the back of an ambulance. Some people he'd never seen before had broken their way into his apartment. *Then what?* He'd stabbed one of them. *At least one.*

But wasn't the guy trying to hurt me? And Cass? No... she wasn't there. She was safe. Those men, they were there, in his home, unwanted. *And for what? Yes, to hurt me. To kill me.*

"Why?" he muttered.

"I'm sorry?" the paramedic helping him into the back of the ambulance asked.

"N-Nothing." Jaden tried again to shake off his confusion. "Did I say something? I don't remember. God, I barely remember anything after..."

After grabbing the knives.

He leaned to his left and hurled. Remnants of supper spattered the ground at the paramedic's feet.

"Gross." The twenty-something moaned. He was tall and fit and wearing a short-sleeved white dress shirt tucked into black pants. He lifted his foot and peered down at it, his mouth contorting into a frown. "You got it on my sneaker."

"Sorry," Jaden managed after spitting out the last bits of sweet-and-sour pork. He climbed into the back of the ambulance, sat on a stretcher, and crashed onto his side.

"I killed those guys."

"Two of them anyway, yeah," the paramedic said.

Jaden hadn't realized he'd spoken aloud. He looked up at the man and studied his face. It seemed a kindly face, with stoner eyes and a broad nose. His name tag read Guilmette. "Who are you? What's happening?"

"My name's Joey. We're taking you to Charlton. You don't appear to have any physical wounds, but procedure says to have you fully checked out. Do you hurt anywhere?"

Jaden took an inventory of his body, and for the first time since he'd found himself in that police car, he noticed tenderness in his wrist. He held up his right arm. "Here."

Joey pushed back the sleeve of Jaden's bathrobe and pressed down on his wrist. Jaden winced.

"It's a little puffy. Definitely swollen and bruising." After a few more seconds of pressing fingertips, he said, "Nothing appears to be broken, but wrists are tricky. Eight small bones. You'll want an X-ray. Any other complaints?"

"I... I don't think so. My head really hurts, but... on the inside."

"I'll get you something for that. Just lie back and relax. You've obviously been through a lot. The doctors at Charlton will fix you up right."

"Right. Doctors." Jaden laid his head back on a pillow. "But my cat," he mumbled as his eyelids fluttered. *Something important... to remember. Stay... awake.* He had to do something before he could let his mind drift—something to do with his cat. *Or was it about Cass?*

But his mind had gone through enough that night. Staying awake no longer remained an option. He drifted into sleep, struggling to remember what needed to be done, and entered the dream of a woman calling him into her warm embrace.

Her arms grew cold.

CHAPTER 6

Royo sat behind his assemble-by-number desk in an office barely bigger than the average bathroom, staring down at the rap sheet of one Morton Tresser, aka M.T. Clip.

What a stupid name. He ran down the litany of arrests and convictions. *Charged with possession of a Class D substance; possession of a class A substance—convicted; aggravated assault and violation of probation—plead out to a lesser charge; possession of Class D substance—guilty plea entered; possession of Class D substance with intent to distribute? A business man, I see. Pled out to a lesser charge. Solicitation—DA declined to prosecute. Four more possession charges with no convictions. Domestic violence—charge dismissed. Latest charge: possession with intent to distribute, charges dismissed after allowance of motion to suppress. I wonder who screwed that up.*

Officer Stravenski had compiled quite a bit of information on the three perps involved in the break-in, but he and the other officers had recovered no link between the three and Jaden Sanders. A few witnesses thought they'd seen one or two of the perps at the complex before, but they couldn't confirm whether they'd been with Sanders or another resident. Most were confident that they'd never seen any of them with Sanders. Tresser's two compadres, Grady and Malden, had similar rap sheets, but conversations with family members of the three revealed no insight into their motives. Most denied any knowledge of their relative's activities or refused to speak with police altogether.

But the file showed enough alienation among parents, siblings, and exes to suggest what Royo already suspected and their rap sheets confirmed: users. *Bottom-feeders, all of them, but not as bad as the scum who fed them.*

He riffled through the papers to his left, turning his attention to the RMV records he'd pulled for Jaden Sanders. *Speeding, seventy-*

five in a fifty-five, fifteen plus years ago. Illegal U-turn. He looked up Sanders's name in the department's database and got a hit, the one he'd anticipated, but no others.

Royo leaned forward and scanned a report from eight months ago, authored by Officer Megan Costa. Sanders had been taken into custody. He'd been despondent and confrontational, refusing to allow officers to escort him from the scene, but had not been charged. After he calmed to the point of nonresponsiveness, he was released into the care of his sister, Tara Morrison.

Folding his hands behind his head, Royo rocked back in his chair. He stared at the wall, which he'd never bothered to decorate. The room, his desk, his outward persona—all were as nondescript as he could make them. Few knew the real Detective Asante Royo, and he liked to keep it that way.

That suicide... Could this be somehow related? He couldn't immediately see a connection or even speculate as to how they could be connected, but he also wasn't one to dismiss anything as coincidence. Sanders had been an incoherent mess after that had happened, only to show up eight months later as a knife-wielding killer. The man obviously had sides to his personality not easily explained by what one saw on the surface. *I'll have to follow up with Officer Costa.*

Royo chewed the end of his pen. Still, Sanders was squeaky-clean on paper. "No priors, no suggestion of a history of violence, yet three guys down. You're just a regular badass, aren't you, Mr. Sanders?"

A knock came at his open door. Officer Wilcox from the front desk cleared his throat. "Detective Royo, Jaden Sanders is here to see you, sir."

Royo stared at the man standing beside Wilcox. His second impression of Sanders wasn't any better than his first. To be fair, his first impression had been in passing, since Officer Costa had run with the interview eight months earlier. The man who'd fought off three attackers wasn't exactly the embodiment of masculinity. With a stom-

ach resting about an inch over his waistline, Sanders wasn't exactly fat but soft, lumpy, and lacking muscle tone. *Probably not on the
heavy regimen of kale smoothies Rickie has me drinking—great for a
slim figure and a loose colon.* Royo frowned. *I almost envy him for that.*

Worse still, the man was in shambles. With a wrinkled shirt, tou-
sled hair, and an uneven beard in which the gray hairs had grown
out longer than the brown, Sanders looked like a slob. But that was
all understandable after the harrowing ordeal he'd just been through,
and Royo thought himself uncharitable for the derision. Sanders had
been attacked in his home and had been forced to kill his assailants.
Well, two of them, anyway. The jury was still out on the third. Even
having had a weekend to recharge, Sanders looked as if he might
drop dead on the spot. He probably hadn't slept a wink since he'd left
the hospital.

Still, the man had found strength when he'd needed it most.
Royo doubted Sanders himself knew he had it. It took a crisis to truly
determine the measure of a man. But violence like that didn't come
out of nowhere. Sanders's meek exterior belied an inner savagery, one
that was both powerful and primal. He carried himself with an air of
boring normalcy—the kind of guy who thought putting extra crou-
tons on his salad was living dangerously. His posture was that of a
monkey carrying her young on her back, nothing militant or confident about it. Yet he did look a sight better and more collected without all the blood on him. And his eyes had lost their vacancy, re-
placed with a sort of cold emptiness.

"Pleasure to meet you, Detective," Sanders said as he stepped
over the threshold. He extended his hand in warm greeting, but the
smile on his face projected nothing but ice.

Royo stood and shook it then hurriedly closed all the folders in
front of him and exited the database on his monitor. When his desk
was moderately organized, a blank legal pad and chewed pen laid out

dead center, he motioned for Sanders to take a seat in the single guest chair sitting in the corner.

Sanders carried the aluminum folding chair over and planted it down so close to the front of the desk that Royo thought he would have difficulty squeezing into it. Yet somehow he managed to do so with grace.

Royo smiled, though he didn't feel it stretch to his eyes. "Thank you for coming in, Mr. Sanders."

Sanders smiled back. His grin didn't reach his eyes either. "Not a problem, Detective, though I'm not sure how I can help. I must have given my statement to half the precinct already." He shifted in his chair, his smile turning into something cannibalistic as he gnawed on his fingernails. His whole body vibrated, as if he couldn't shake a chill.

Royo tented his fingers and leaned forward. "You can relax, Mr. Sanders. It seems clear to us all what happened Thursday morning. Hell, every witness told the same story, so this is pretty much just a formality. We just need to take your full statement on the record, then we can send you on your way."

"Should I have a lawyer present?"

"If you'd like, but this is just filling in some blanks so that we can close out the case file. I don't think there's a single soul in this building who doesn't think you a hero for what you did."

Sanders blushed. He folded his hands in his lap. His knee bounced, but the rest of him was less jittery. "Well, I don't know about all that."

"Well, I do," Royo said a little too exuberantly. He cleared his throat. "Anyway, first order of business, I wanted to let you know that we ran into that manager from Prospero and told him he needs to get your door fixed ASAP. Likely it will be fixed real soon, if it isn't already."

Sanders pursed his lips. "I doubt it."

"I'm sorry?"

"Nothing. Sorry. The company that owns the property, they're quick to bitch but slow to fix. I'll probably be ducking under caution tape for the next month." He gulped. "But that doesn't stop them from barging in whenever they feel like it, whether I'm home or not. This one maintenance guy is always lingering. Creeps me the hell out." Sanders grimaced and looked away. "You know, I haven't seen my cat since that night."

"I see. Well, I think he's got a guy on the door already, so your things should be safe. As for the cat, I'm sure he'll turn up." Royo offered a smile that he hoped at least appeared genuine. As insensitive as it was, he didn't give a rat's ass about Sanders's cat.

"He's dying. Leukemia."

Royo softened. *And just like that, I do care.* He pursed his lips, nodding slowly. "I'll check with animal control to see if anyone's brought a cat in recently or reported a stray in the vicinity of your apartment complex." He curled his lips into his teeth and sighed. "I truly am sorry, Mr. Sanders."

Sanders's eyes watered. "Let's... Let's just get this over with, okay?"

"Sure." Royo stiffened. He drew open his desk drawer and removed a tape recorder, which he turned on and placed at the edge of the desk. "Do you mind if I record this?"

"I don't know. Should I?"

"Again, it's just a formality. Normally, I'd use one of the digital cameras in the interview rooms, but I'm feeling old-school." He chuckled. "Besides, it really messes up the young interns when I ask them to transcribe it. They don't know diddly about anything predating Blu-ray." Royo hoped his joke would set Sanders at ease, but the vibe he was getting from his disheveled visitor was humorless and unwavering.

He let out a breath. "Believe it or not, Mr. Sanders, I'm on your side here."

Sanders nodded.

"Your responses must be verbal. The machine can't hear a head nod. So let me ask again, just so there's no confusion on the record: do you mind if I record this?"

"Yes." Sanders shifted again in his seat. "No, I don't mind."

"Can you scoot your chair over just a bit, please? I try to keep the recorder directly between us so that it can pick up both question and answer clearly. These old things hardly work half the time, as it is." He swung his arm wide. "And the acoustics in here are crazy, despite the room being no bigger than a broom closet."

Sanders snorted and scooted his chair to his right so that he and Royo sat face-to-face with only the width of the desk between them. "Yeah, a lot like my cubicle at work."

"Where's that again?"

"DSC, the corporate offices, but it's not nearly as fancy as it sounds. I negotiate contracts all day. Sometimes they get done. Sometimes they don't."

"Must be tough work, though. Shit, DSC? They're like Fortune Ten or something, aren't they? Those must be some contracts. I bet you're dealing with millions and millions every day. More than we'll ever see. Am I right?"

"Try billions. We're Fortune Six. But you're right. I don't see a dime of it either." Sanders frowned. "We probably won't even get our bonuses next year."

Royo eased into the conversation. The topic of one's employment usually loosened tongues—everyone liked to gripe about work. He hoped to establish a dialogue before he asked the relevant questions. "How long have you been there?"

Sanders's eyes searched the ceiling. "Oh, close to five years."

"Any enemies at work?"

"You mean anyone who might want to kick in my door and try to kill me?" He sat back. "No. You saw those guys. Did they look like they worked for DSC?"

"Well, I don't like to stereotype, but I see your point. Do you do any drugs?"

"Illegal drugs? No, but how many times have you gotten a yes to that question?"

Royo snickered. "True. Just trying to cover all our bases. How about prescriptions?"

"Yeah, I've got a few of those. But you already know that, since your people have been through all my stuff."

Royo did know. He was particularly interested in an antipsychotic Sanders was taking and the reason why it had been prescribed. The man had been dealt a heavy loss that could easily explain his antidepressants. *But Haldol?*

Sanders's hostility to the question suggested going further down that line would close him up. Royo leaned forward, arms out and palms upturned, doing his best to convey the feeling that they were just two guys talking, sharing secrets. The task was made difficult by the tape recorder capturing their every word. "Look, why don't we just take a step back and start over. No one's on trial here. I'm just trying to figure out why someone might choose your door at five-something in the morning over a complex full of potentially easier targets. That is, assuming burglary was their motive."

Sanders scratched his temple. His hand was shaking. "I didn't say I thought burglary was their motive."

Royo sat up. "You know why you were attacked?"

"I didn't say that either." He licked his lips and swallowed, a tremble running through his whole body. "I thought maybe they might have been from..." He swallowed again. "The hospital, but thinking back, they didn't look like anyone I saw there."

"The hospital? Brentworth, where you were admitted after—"

Sanders nodded then looked away.

"Why would you think they might be from Brentworth?"

Sanders shook his head. "There are... It's a terrible place."

Royo made a mental note to look deeper into Sanders's stay at Brentworth, should it appear relevant. What the vic wasn't saying spoke volumes and his body language, volumes more. Sanders was terrified of that place. He had not come out of it healed.

But Sanders was right: the three perps had no known ties to Brentworth, and that line of questioning seemed to have no bearing on the case at hand. "But you still don't think it was a burglary? Why not?"

"It could have had something to do with the note."

"Note?" Royo leaned farther forward, his elbows flat against the desk. In all the evidence they had collected—two kitchen knives of differing lengths, a metallic lamp base, splinters from Tresser's shoe and pants, a substance that appeared to be sawdust, blood samples, lots and lots of photographs, and an anthology's worth of witness statements—they had uncovered no note or anything pointing to the existence of a note. True, Royo still had medical records and autopsy reports to acquire and review, but he doubted either would shed light on the new clue. He was practically salivating when he asked, "What note?"

Sanders took a deep breath. "When I came home from work that night, I found a note taped to my door. I think it was from my neighbor across the hall, but... I'm not a hundred percent. But who else could it be from?"

"What did it say?" Royo asked, hovering over his desk.

"Basically, it told me not to slam my door."

Royo's shoulders drooped, and he sighed. Disputes between neighbors—even violent disputes—were commonplace and as old as time. One didn't need to search far to find Hatfields and McCoys in any part of the city. But Sanders's neighbors had been questioned, and the landlord confirmed that, though still under lease, apartment 315 had not been occupied since the woman's suicide. And a complaint about door slamming was a long way off from B and E and felonious assault, not to mention the fact that none of the perps lived in apartment 315, in the same complex, or even within ten miles of it.

Sanders crossed his arms. "I know what you're thinking, but listen. The note... it wasn't the first one I got, and I—I reacted to it."

"How so?"

"I slammed it against my neighbor's door, yelling that she should keep her frigging notes to herself. Only I didn't say frigging."

"Himself."

"Huh?'

"*He* should keep his frigging notes to *himself*."

"What are you—"

"Your neighbors all say they haven't seen anyone enter that apartment in months. Well, except one neighbor, who claimed to see a gentleman one time, but she may have been mistaken, or that could have just been maintenance, a painter, or someone else hired by Prospero." He fell back in his chair. "That said, I will make a note to check into who is leasing the apartment, but that really seems like a dead end. If I remember correctly, the woman who—" He checked himself. "Ms. Branigan had it through the end of the year." He tapped his pen on the desk. "Maybe we should start from the point of contact with your assailants."

"Okay." Sanders rubbed his temples. His knee bounced faster. "I-I'm sorry, Detective. I'm a little anxious. Where should I begin?"

"At the beginning."

Chewing his thumbnail, Sanders nodded. "Okay." He took a deep breath and massaged his forehead. Squinting, he appeared to be in pain. "I was in bed when I heard a bang. At first, I thought I had dreamed it. But when it came again, I put on my bathrobe and went to see who it was."

"Did you think it might be anyone in particular?"

"Like I said, I thought they might have been from the hospital—"

"When you heard the knocking?"

"Oh, at that point, I thought maybe it was Cass. She's my... girlfriend?" He grimaced then scratched his forehead. "You know how it is."

"Not really. Is she your only girlfriend?" Royo paused, wondering if he would be able to move on to another relationship if Rickie were to cheat on him. He shuddered at the thought.

"Oh, yes, of course." Sanders laughed and closed his eyes. Tears formed at their corners. "I mean, I'm not really sure what our status is. It's complicated."

"You okay?"

Sanders looked up. "Yeah. Yeah. Sorry." Cringing, he rubbed his temples. "I get these headaches sometimes."

Royo pressed on. "So, she doesn't live with you?"

"No."

"Did you have some sort of bad breakup? Do you fight a lot?"

Sanders grimaced and blinked repeatedly. "No. Not really. I'm pretty sure she had nothing to do with what happened, if that's what you're getting at."

"You're sure of that?"

Sanders closed his eyes and started breathing as if he were deep into a Lamaze class. After a moment, he opened his eyes again. "I'm pretty sure."

"Do you know where she was last night?"

"Home, probably. I'm not sure. But I really think you're barking up the wrong tree there. I mean, there had been a first note, I think, but this note—"

"What's her full name? Just so we can clear her."

"Cassidy Branigan."

Royo froze. His lips parted, but he worked hard to compose his disbelief. In all his years on the job, that was a first. He'd handled crazies before—violent criminals so high on drugs that they laughed as they pulled out their own teeth or carved themselves and others with rusted sawblades—but he'd never been seated across from someone who seemed so lucid in all respects except one. He'd seen a mother unwilling to give up her deceased daughter's blanket, grief making her hysterical to the point that she believed doing so would be to admit her daughter was dead. Grief drove people nuts, for sure, but Sanders's grief seemed to be keeping him outwardly sane if not deluded.

But maybe it wasn't grief. Maybe it was guilt. Royo stared at his interviewee with suspicion and curiosity. Eventually, he realized his recording was filling with empty silence. Clearing his throat, he ventured back into territory within his expertise and resolved to explore the Brentworth angle a bit further, if confidentiality commitments didn't block his attempt.

"So you hop out of bed, get dressed, and go to the door." Royo refocused, cutting out the tangential. That could come later, but first, he must have the facts. "What do you do next?"

"Well, I flicked on the light and looked out. All three of them must have been out there, but I only saw the one with the gold tooth."

"His name is Tresser. Morton Tresser. That name ring a bell?"

Sanders's brow furrowed. Again, he closed his eyes and let out a long breath. After opening them again, he spent a moment staring at the ceiling then said, "Nope, not at all."

Royo was almost embarrassed to ask. "How about M.T. Clip? Know anyone by that name?"

Sanders just shook his head.

Royo was content to leave the record silent on that point. "And was his face familiar to you? Had you seen him around the complex before?"

"No, I don't think so."

"How about Leonard Malden?"

"The film critic? Isn't he dead?"

"I don't think so, and anyway, that's Mal*tin*. But no, one of the other assailants. Black guy."

"Nope, never heard of him either." Sanders held up a finger. "And before you ask, no, I've never seen him before."

"Kealan Grady?"

"Nope and nope. Irish-sounding name. I assume he was the red-head?"

"You got it."

Royo studied Sanders's face as he answered each question. He seemed to fluctuate between a nervous wreck and a smooth-sailing ship. Talking about potential motives had rattled him somehow, but talking about what had happened, what he'd had to do to those three men, seemed as easy as breathing. He almost seemed pleased with himself.

"Did you open the door? Did you say something to him?"

"No. Not at first. I stayed quiet, knowing something wasn't right as soon as I saw him. But he wouldn't leave. Said he knew I was home and kept on pounding on my door."

"Wait." Royo straightened. "Did he call you by name?"

"No, but he sure seemed to know who I was. He said he just wanted to talk, but he got more and more aggressive while I stayed quiet. Started threatening to bash the door in."

"Hmm." Royo scratched his chin. "I'm still not seeing how he indicated he knew you. Did he say what he wanted to talk about?"

"No, but before he kicked in the door, I caved and asked him what he wanted. He started screaming for me to open the door. He said there were consequences for what I had done earlier, and the only thing I could think of that might have upset anyone was how I reacted to that stupid note."

Again with the note. Royo tried to keep his expression flat. "Did you have any confrontations at work or, um, with your girlfriend in the last week?"

"Nothing out of the ordinary."

"Any within the ordinary?"

"No."

"Any arguments with family, friends, neighbors, mailmen, people in lines, or any other strangers or acquaintances?"

"None. I don't talk to a lot of people." Sanders shifted then reshifted, his fidgeting returning at the line of questioning. "Again, I really think this all has to do with my neighbor and—"

"The note? Forget it, Mr. Sanders. Your other nearby neighbors are twice your age and don't seem likely to be the type to hire folks to break down doors. As for 315, that apartment is empty." He watched Sanders closely and asked, "Do you think someone lives there?"

Sanders studied the wall to his left and chewed his thumbnail. He blinked several times and rubbed his temples. "I... I don't know."

Royo pushed a little harder, being mindful of a clearly delicate, possibly dangerous psyche. "Hasn't been anyone in there since that woman committed suicide. Miss... What was her name again? Not to sound callous, but you were in a relationship with her, weren't you?"

Sanders trembled and covered his mouth. He did not answer the question.

Royo already knew that answer, so he moved on to a question he couldn't yet answer. "Could the men who attacked you have been motivated by anything relating to that suicide?"

Sanders's face contorted into a mask of torment. He squeezed his eyes shut and clenched his jaw, scrunching everything. "I-I'm sorry," he said, stroking his temples and blowing out breaths. "I'm having trouble thinking straight, like there's a drill boring holes into my skull." He blinked his eyes clear, air whooshing through his puckered lips.

Royo gave him a minute to compose himself. Sanders's pain appeared genuine. Royo could easily break the man, but he wasn't ready to do so if no one could put him back together again. He was convinced Sanders had been a victim in the home invasion scenario and deserved to be treated as such. Certainly, more than a gut feeling with respect to Sanders and Branigan's suicide would be needed to explore that further.

A tear spilled from Sanders's eye. Royo was about to ask if he needed a doctor when the anguish vanished from Sanders's face, and he looked up with eyes full of quiet but immeasurable hate. Royo gasped.

"I don't know what they wanted, Detective," he snapped. "Isn't that your job to tell me?"

"That's what I'm trying to figure out here."

Royo leaned back and studied him. Sanders's pain had dissipated, or he was biting it back, to the point that only the wrinkles around his eyes and the redness where he'd rubbed lingered as reminders. If it had all been an act, he knew how to fabricate a migraine. *But what would he have to gain in pretending?* "Maybe we should finish this some other time."

"No, I—"

The intercom light on Royo's phone blinked. He pushed a button and hovered over the speaker. "Hold on a second." Before the person on the other end could speak, he said, "I'm finishing up taking a statement. Give me five more minutes."

He grunted. He had no idea who wanted what, but he hated being interrupted. It made him lose his train of thought. "Anyway, where were we?"

"M-M-My..." Sanders huffed. "My neighbor—"

"Oh yeah." Royo sat up. "So Tresser's pounding on your door. Did he say anything else?"

"No, not that I can remember."

"Either Grady or Malden say anything?"

"I don't remember either of them ever saying anything. Gold Tooth, er, Tresser, did all the talking."

"So what happened next?"

More Lamaze breathing. "I heard the door breaking, and I panicked. I don't remember much after that. I know I grabbed the knives from the kitchen, turned off the lights, and ran into the bedroom to hide. The next thing I remember, the black guy was pulling me up to my feet, and I... I stabbed him."

Royo pursed his lips and nodded. "A few times, by the look of it."

Sanders frowned and crossed his arms. "So? I was afraid for my life. Those guys were trying to kill me."

"I hear you. Like I said, I'm your friend here." Royo raised an eyebrow, a practiced look meant to issue a response. He wasn't sure why he was about to provoke Sanders again. A nagging itch was all the provocation he needed. "I must say, though... you killed two people, Mr. Sanders. Probably three when all is said and done. But you don't seem all that shaken up about it."

Sanders scowled. "Why should I be? Those assholes broke into my house and tried to kill me!" He jumped to his feet and slammed his palms against the desk as if to emphasize the tail end of his sentence. Then he froze, closed his eyes, and let out a breath. He took several more deep breaths and paced the length of the office before sitting back down. The redness in his face had already started to vanish. "I'm sorry. I don't mean that toward you. I guess I'm still angry that they violated my home." He shivered. "They put their filthy hands on me."

Royo couldn't help himself. "Is that what you were? Angry?"

"I was scared out of my freaking mind! After I stabbed that one guy, then..." He paused again, glaring coldly at Royo, then clammed up. "It's all a blur. I don't remember much between then and when a doctor shoved a flashlight into my eyes at Charlton."

"Well, we can pretty much paint the scene from there," Royo said with all the sympathy he could muster, trying to reestablish their rapport. "Are you sure there was nothing else said? Nothing else that could help us to determine motive? Tresser was no saint, but this wasn't his usual MO."

Sanders sat straight and confident, as still as a statue, as composure returned as if by the flick of a switch. He looked defiant and maybe proud of what he'd done. "I can't think of anything else right now, but if I think of something, I'll certainly let you know."

Royo took a business card from a dwindling stack on his desk. "Here. Please do." He started to click off the tape recorder but halted with his finger on the stop button. "Oh, one more thing. At any point, did Tresser try to run?"

"What?" Sanders hesitated. The corner of his eye twitched, and a reddish hue returned to his face. "Of course not! The three of them were all over me. They were trying to hurt me. I did what I had to do. That's it."

"I thought you said you didn't remember anything after stabbing the first guy."

Sanders's jaw clenched. He did that eye shutting-breathing thing again, which Royo assumed to be some sort of hippy anger management technique. He would have to check into that too.

He didn't know what to make of Sanders. Clearly, the man had some sort of emotional or psychological issue. Maybe he'd provoked the attack somehow. But nothing changed the fact that three men had burst down his door and tried to hurt him. In Royo's eyes, that was black and white. *You do that, and you deserve what you get.*

"I remember them coming at me and wanting to hurt me."

"You stabbed one of them in the back."

"I... I don't remember that. I only remember being afraid and feeling like I had to kill them, or they were going to kill me. I didn't *want* to kill them. I *had* to."

Royo crossed his arms and nodded slowly. The tape recorder was still rolling. "Good. Don't deviate from that."

"I won't, 'cause it's the truth." Sanders stood. "Is that it? Am I free to go?"

"You were never required to stay. Like I said, this is just a formality, as far as I'm concerned."

"As far as *you're* concerned?"

"Yeah, I'm not arresting you. What the DA—"

Sanders leaned over Royo's desk, color returning to his cheeks. "Wait. You're not arresting me? Why the hell would anyone even think about arresting me?"

"Well, an argument could be made—and again, I'm not making it—that you gained the upper hand and attacked Tresser or, alternatively, that you used excessive force in defending yourself—"

"That's ridiculous! I was attacked by three men!"

"Mr. Sanders, calm down." Royo stood, once again placing himself eye to eye with Sanders. "Please, sit down." He relaxed his stance. Noticing the machine was still recording, he clicked it off. "Listen to me. I agree with you. I'm just telling you that the DA *could* file charges, if she wanted to, but I doubt she will. Some of the evidence... Well, it's not even worth getting into 'cause it's so unlikely."

Sanders ran a hand down his face. "This is unbelievable! And you had me sitting here this whole time, telling you everything that happened, thinking I was helping you out. Without telling me that I could and should have an attorney present? Without even explaining my rights?" He raised his arms, his palms up and his eyes wide with disbelief. He shoved a finger in Royo's face. "In fact, you expressly told me that I didn't need to have an attorney here because

I wasn't in any trouble. Meanwhile, your friends at the prosecutor's office are debating whether to bend me over a barrel for defending myself. Un-*fucking*-believable! You rotten pigs are all the same. God-damn crooks, every last one of you!"

Royo had never liked the farm animal comparison people were quick to make of members of his profession. Sanders's last statement hit him like a slap from a giant. Still, he bit back his anger. "Mr. Sanders," he said, his voice low and gritty. He prided himself on keeping his cool, and a part of him could understand Sanders's anger, as excessive and perhaps misdirected as it was. "Like I've said, I'm on your side—"

"You pigs are on no one's side but your own." With that, Jaden Sanders stormed out of the office, leaving Royo agitated and without an outlet.

CHAPTER 7

Prosecutor Heather Laughton put all the evidence she had before the grand jury. She fiddled with her platinum necklace, the scales of justice inlaid with four carats of diamonds. It had been a law school graduation gift along with a brand-new Lexus from Daddy, whose income would unbalance any scale. She applauded herself for giving Jaden Sanders a fair shake. Certainly, she'd stressed those facts that favored her point of view: that Sanders had committed a crime for which he should be punished. But she didn't hide that Morton Tresser and his cronies had broken into Sanders's apartment with unknown though undoubtedly criminal intent. Nevertheless, attacking a fleeing person, even a *criminal,* with the intent to kill him was attempted murder by any sense of the term, a crime for which she honestly believed Sanders must be held accountable. The law of the Commonwealth needed a clear line that such conduct, so-called vigilante justice made not only approvable but enticing by an onslaught of comic books, movies, and comic book movies, was inexcusable no matter the circumstances.

Of course, if the case jettisoned her into the public eye and progressed her career or furthered her political ambitions, well, that was just an added bonus. She'd been on a hot streak, taking only winners to trial, but they'd all been duds in a star-making sense, lacking sensationalism and devoid of any media attention. They'd even been boring to her.

But Sanders's case, *that* had mainstream appeal, something for the pundits to pundit. The issues involved ran the gamut across black-letter law and social justice, right through the court of public opinion. Though the case posed a risk of failure, she could see no downside. Even if public opinion wasn't, Massachusetts law was on her side. If she won, her skills would be lauded, while a loss would only go to show what twelve jurors thought the law should be. Either way, her face would be in all the papers, flashing her perfect smile. *Maybe I'll even get interviewed by Nancy Grace.*

So, Heather dressed in her posh Gucci suit, presenting herself as much as the case she intended to build, with full understanding of the psychology of being liked. She showed those fine, upstanding members of the grand jury her photographs of Morton Tresser hooked up to every machine imaginable and clinging to life. She magnified the defensive wounds on Tresser's arms, which could only have been caused by a knife coming down on them again and again as Tresser shielded himself from a brutal attack. She pointed out the location, away from the deaths of his partners in crime and near the only way out of the apartment, which she suggested was further evidence of Tresser's attempt to flee. All corroborated that final stab to his back, witnessed by several of Sanders's neighbors, and the single, drug-hazy statement Detective Royo had taken from a paramedic caring for the likely soon-to-be-dead drug peddler: "I tried to get away, but he wouldn't let me."

She sighed and glanced at her ring finger, the only one of the four *not* ringed. *If only Royo didn't smoke the pole. Kinda cute for an older man.* Heather quickly dismissed the thought. Time for relationships would come later, when she was done standing on her own. *At the top.*

She walked the courtroom with a lion's confidence and a gazelle's grace, every word out of her mouth and every gesture of her hands and body practiced and calculated to influence in a work of performance art. Always cognizant not to overplay her hand, Heather crafted a story the jurors could not only understand but also swallow—the hunter becoming the hunted, a man enraged by bloodlust and the need for revenge. She did exactly what she would do if she had the chance at trial: she laid out the law, plain and simple, and showed the jury how it was broken. A violent man had chased down a fleeing and defenseless man and stabbed him in the back while he lay helpless and pleading for his life. At a bare minimum, the facts constituted voluntary manslaughter—meeting reasonable force with excessive force, like a push to get by met with slicing and dicing—but Heather bumped it up to murder in the second degree.

Jaden Sanders was an animal in need of a cage.

She smirked. *Cold, unyielding, black-letter law—the skeletal frame that holds society together. Shakily.* She shrugged. *Where would we be without it?*

The first two kills were the extraordinary results of a home invasion, one man getting lucky against three people who, as far as she could tell, had no motive or good reason to be there. Sanders was fighting for his life, no doubt about it. At least as cornered as he was, Heather saw no way to make a credible case otherwise. So she focused on the third kill. Only time would tell.

Under Massachusetts law, whether in one's home or not, murder was murder. While a victim of a home invasion was free to protect himself from death or serious bodily injury by any reasonable means necessary—which, even in the Commonwealth, meant just about any means necessary—once the defense was over, he was not then free to go on the offensive and slaughter a fleeing instigator. If Sanders had blocked Tresser's path as he attempted to flee for the sole purpose of stabbing the crap out of him, then Sanders was guilty of attempted murder. The warm-blooded kind of murder, in the heat of passion, was okay, but no one should get away with killing someone in flight. The stab wound to Tresser's back was her ace in the hole.

Unless Sanders's dumb enough to take the stand. Heather didn't know much about Sanders beyond what she'd read on paper, which were personal statistics mostly. He had plenty of book smarts, but she had nothing to evaluate the often-underestimated trait called common sense. And he didn't seem to have much in the way of friends or family, which meant fewer people to raise a fuss, cry foul, or miss him if he went away. As she listened along with the grand jury to Sanders's recorded statement, she heard the voice of a petty, soulless man with a chip on his shoulder one would have to be the captain of the *Titanic* not to notice. He wasn't likeable and sounded remorseless.

She aimed her perfect smile at the jurors, slowly batted her long eyelashes—flirtatiously but just once—and left them to their decision, confident they would come back with a finding of probable cause so that she could order Sanders's arrest.

The nearly immediate speed of their response bolstered her confidence. She left the courtroom beaming.

"You sure you can win this one?" District Attorney Selena Harris asked, wearing her perpetual scowl as she bulled her way through the hall toward Heather.

"Piece of cake," Heather answered without hesitation, hiding her discomfort at her boss's sudden appearance and the loaded question she'd brought with her.

"The best you're going to get here is manslaughter." DA Harris huffed, her bulldog jowls quivering with the expelling of air. "Murder two? How are you going to prove malice aforethought?"

Heather maintained her composure. "Sanders straddled Tresser and planted a knife in his back. Surely a reasonable juror can infer that he formed an intent to kill before doing that."

"Perhaps, but mutual combat? Reasonable provocation? The defense has several weapons to take this down to manslaughter or maybe even self-defense."

"The jury will be instructed on manslaughter as a lesser included offense." She smoothed out the tails of her suit. "Either way, Sanders should go down for something."

Harris grunted. "While I don't share your confidence, I won't stand in your way. But if this goes to trial, it had better not be because our office failed to offer Sanders a reasonable opt out."

Heather scowled but only on the inside, her poker face remaining intact. A plea deal meant no press and no celebrity. Though a plea might be in both Sanders's and the Commonwealth's best interests, it was not in hers. Nevertheless, she nodded her assent.

"Okay, then," Harris replied. "But, Laughton, if this goes south somehow, it's on you."

CHAPTER 8

Barely a week had passed, and Royo and two uniformed officers were back at 300 North Street, heading up the stairs to Jaden Sanders's apartment building. In the daylight, the complex's pale gray walls, white shutters, and wooden steps with accompanying ramp looked about as innocuous as Sanders, yet both had seen their fair share of tragedy and violence in the last several months.

He opened the door and stepped into a small alcove, where a second, locked door blocked his entry. Rather than call the office for someone to let him in, he waited patiently for someone to exit.

After a few minutes, Royo hit three buttons to request someone buzz them in. As someone responded through the intercom, he spotted Ms. Templeton coming up a flight of stairs, her hands trembling as she carried a load of laundry. He smiled and waved then waited as she painstakingly put down the basket at a snail's pace. Before she could walk to the door, a buzz sounded, and Royo pulled it open.

"Good morning, Ms. Templeton." He picked up her laundry basket, which weighed only a few pounds but was undoubtedly hard to carry for someone with her knobby, arthritic fingers. "Please, allow me."

"Oh," she said, tittering and stroking his arm. "Handsome and a gentleman. They don't make them like you anymore."

She took his arm as they plodded up the stairs. The two officers followed quietly.

"What brings you back here, Detective?" Her eyes lit up. "Has there been another break-in? Everyone here has been so worried, but I think I would have heard about it."

"No. No." Royo smiled. He didn't want to share the reason for their visit with the old gossip, though he had no doubt she would find out sooner or later. "Just following up with something related to what happened the other night."

"Oh, I hope that Sanders boy isn't in any more trouble. Poor boy's been through a lot." She leaned in closer. Her breath reeked of what smelled like rubbing alcohol. "You know, he was seeing that—"

"Yes, we know all about it. So sad, what happened," Royo said, reaching the landing for the third floor.

Two men, one of whom was wearing scrubs, stood talking there. With a glance at Royo and likely the two uniforms behind him, they drifted down the hall. He shifted the basket under one arm.

"And so young." Ms. Templeton let go of his arm and crept ahead to her apartment door, which she had kept unlocked.

Not too worried about a break-in. Royo smirked. As he turned to enter her apartment, he caught sight of another person coming up the stairs: a man in his early- to midtwenties, whistling a familiar Spanish lullaby. The young man was carrying a scrawny creature that had brownish-black fur and was so thin that Royo might have mistaken it for a weasel if not for the distinctive M-shaped stripes of a tabby painted on its forehead.

The man froze and stopped whistling, staring with wide eyes at the backs of the officers. Slowly, he turned and headed back down the stairs.

"Wait!" Royo called, but the man disappeared. Officer Burton, the larger of the two mammoth officers, turned to see whom Royo had addressed, but the man was gone.

"Just put that in here," Ms. Templeton called from somewhere inside her apartment.

He dropped the laundry basket just inside the doorway. "Did either of you see that person?"

Burton shrugged. Beast officer number two, Sergeant Rollins, replied with a "No, sir."

"He looked familiar." Royo scanned his memory. "Yes! Manuel, the maintenance guy. I saw him the night of the break-in. I don't think anyone ever got his statement."

"You want one of us to go get it now?" Rollins asked.

"No."

But Royo wasn't so sure. Twice, the man had vanished at the sight of police. And he'd been highly anxious the one time Royo had had the chance to talk with him. That wasn't uncommon, but he recognized Manuel's expression, something far more than suspicion or worry: it had been nothing short of terror. A trail of sand-colored flakes lay in the man's wake. Royo crouched and picked one up. *Sawdust?*

"No. Let's just do what we came here to do."

He led the officers down the hall to apartment 314, hating himself for being there. He didn't have to be. He could have let the officers do it alone. Nothing compelled him there other than his own integrity.

"Nice to see they got the door fixed," he muttered, raising a hand to knock.

Before his fist could land, the door swung open. Jaden Sanders stood on the other side of it, looking sad and pitiful in a stained T-shirt and gym shorts, though Royo knew he was about to look a whole lot sadder and infinitely more pitiable, if not pitiful.

"Yes?" Sanders asked with obvious trouble getting the word out. His gaze fell to the carpet and stayed there.

Royo stood tall. He didn't like what he was about to do, but he felt he owed it to those he was supposed to be protecting and serving to always comport himself with dignity, even when he thought his compelled action undignified. "Jaden Sanders, we have a warrant for your arrest for the murder of Morton Tresser." He turned to Burton, who, along with Sergeant Rollins, Royo liked to use when taking felony suspects into custody. In addition to being a pleasure to look at, the two bodybuilders usually ensured a smooth arrest without serious incident, even when the suspect wanted to make it difficult. "Cuff him."

Sanders took a step back. "Can I get dressed first?"

Royo looked at Burton. The officer shrugged as if to say, "It's your call." And it was. But Sanders's reaction or maybe his *lack* of reaction made Royo sweat. He'd expected a scene—a rehashing of the temper Sanders had shown back at his office. Instead, Sanders just stared at some indistinct spot near Royo's shoes.

He certainly hadn't expected a cool and collected question. He grunted. "Okay." He tilted his head toward Burton. "But he goes with you. And, Sanders, believe me when I say you won't be doing yourself any favors if you try anything stupid."

Sanders turned, took one step toward his bedroom, then sprinted into it and slammed the door in the face of Officer Burton, who'd been one step too many behind. Royo pushed past Burton and turned the knob, but the door was locked. He wondered if the bedroom lock was something new, since he hadn't noticed it, and Sanders hadn't used it the night Sanders was attacked. Not that the flimsy plywood would offer much protection as he slept at night.

Nor would it protect him from Officer Burton. Royo gave him a curt nod, and with a thrust of his shoulder, Burton knocked the door off its hinges. The scent of long-unwashed sheets hit Royo with the draft from the falling door. Royo and Rollins found Sanders with his hand over his mouth, knocking his head back as if downing a shot.

"Stop him!" Royo shouted, though he was first to act. He grabbed Sanders's arm and swung it against the dresser. A rust-colored vial fell from Sanders's hand as he cried out in pain. Small round white tablets shot from his mouth.

Rollins secured Sanders's other arm and slammed him onto the bed, then he pulled his arms behind him and cuffed him. As Rollins stood him back up, Royo picked up the pill bottle.

"What is it?" Burton asked.

Royo read the label. "Wellbutrin. It's an antidepressant. Bottle holds up to ninety." Looking around his feet and at those left in the bottle, Royo estimated about twenty pills remained, but he had no way of telling how many had been in the bottle to begin with. He spotted another pill bottle between the pillows at the head of the queen-sized bed. He hurried to pick it up, expecting the worst.

No, no, no, no, no.

He read the label: *Endocet.* Unlike the Wellbutrin, the prescription on that bottle wasn't made out to Sanders.

Seething with anger, more for his short-sightedness than for anything else, he grabbed Sanders by his chin, pushing his face so close that they could Eskimo kiss. "How many did you take, huh? How many did you take?"

Teary-eyed, Sanders just shrugged.

"This is a crime, you know. How did you get these? From your girlfriend?"

"Sir—" Rollins began.

But Royo's rant wasn't over. "I expected something from you. More fight and anger directed at me for arresting you after I said I wouldn't, at the blanket unfairness of it all." He paced, trying to calm himself. "That, I would get, but... But I didn't expect this!" He whipped the vial against the wall.

"What should we do with him?" Rollins asked.

The officer already had that answer and was just being polite enough to wait for his command.

"Get him down to Charlton. I have no idea what effect an overdose of Wellbutrin might have, possibly with Endocet. Maybe nothing, or maybe he's already dead. So let's move."

Already responsible for unnecessary delay, Royo didn't bother calling an ambulance, opting for a speeding cruiser instead. He stepped out of the officers' way then followed as they hurried Sanders out of the apartment complex to the back of a squad car.

"Keep him cuffed and an eye on him at all times," Royo said as Rollins guided Sanders's head under the roof. "Remove his shoelaces and the tie for his shorts. Full suicide watch."

The door slammed, and Rollins got in the passenger seat. Burton was already waiting behind the wheel.

"Use your lights," Royo said. "Get there fast. I'll be right behind you." He moved away but quickly turned back. "On the way over, be sure to read him his rights."

CHAPTER 9

Dehydrated and with his stomach cramping after having been pumped dry, Jaden got out of the hospital. The courts were closed, so he spent the night in Ash Street, a real prison with real criminals doing hard time. They weren't people like him. They were animals—killers and rapists.

Filled with the worst people on earth. He grunted. *Sounds like a Snapple commercial.*

One night was all he needed to know he could never make it long-term in a place like that, where his cellmate might not think twice before slitting his throat for a pack of cigarettes. Not that he smoked, which was one item on a short list of things he had going for him. And he'd already made it through a worse place, one that made prison seem like a rainbow after the rain.

Even though any place had to be better than that psych ward, Jaden lacked the fortitude and the mental and physical composition to handle real time. He would have to keep his head down and his nose out of the various aboveboard and underground operations of the general population. But his fellow prisoners weren't his primary concern. He didn't buy into the sausage-and-sodomy party that all movies made prison life seem to be to. Sure, he would always be looking over his shoulder, but if he kept to himself, most people would leave him that way: alone and with too much time to think.

And thinking was bad. It led to dwelling, which led to more pills. They would still have to give him his pills. He couldn't stomach himself enough to be alone for so long with only his thoughts to distract him. His keepers would regulate his meds so that he couldn't repeat what he'd tried when he was arrested. If not for Dr. Clemson's intervention, he might have ended up right back in Brentworth.

Though his meds didn't seem to do much of anything. He'd downed at least fifteen of the tablets with a handful of oxys and felt

no effects beyond a minute-long bellyache followed by explosive di-
arrhea and cotton mouth, as if he'd spent a week in the desert.

And he'd gotten a lot of sleep—blissful, unconscious escapism.
Why did it ever have to end?

He woke with a clearer mind than he'd had in months. Tara
would have called what he'd done selfish, and her disapproval hurt
worst of all. She'd been through so much. If he could just resolve his
legal issues and get out of his own way, he would try to be a better
brother. She deserved that and so much more, if he could only find it
in himself to try. Trying meant living.

He took a deep breath. *But first I've got to get through this.*

As he was being transported from the New Bedford prison to the
Fall River courthouse, Jaden thought back to the previous evening,
which he'd spent alone in a cell that made his cubicle look like the
Ritz Carlton. For whatever reason, the correctional officers had giv-
en him his own room, an all-white interior with no soft surfaces—a
padded cell without the padding. It had closed in around him like a
coffin.

Yet he'd slept easily. His accommodations were harder but a sight
better than an actual padded cell. After his minor breakdown—*okay,
full-on mental break*—he'd spent a few weeks in a nuthouse. If he'd
had suicidal tendencies when he stepped into that place, he would
have been stark raving mad to end it all by the time he got out.
The stigma associated with mental illness and asylums loaded him
with overwhelming depression and anxiety. If he admitted he needed to be there, he admitted he was broken. Fixing his kind of broken
seemed impossible. The best he could do was shore up the cracks
with super glue and patch the holes with duct tape.

And that place! Thinking about Brentworth even at his calmest
and most collected threatened to throw him back into the abyss.
He couldn't understand why he'd been so mistreated, misused, and
abused like a mouse under a cat's paw. Hospitals were supposed to

be places of healing, but the psych ward in which he'd been dumped had a widely divergent effect on his psyche. He went in because he'd tried to kill himself. Each day inside those kennel-like confines made him wish he'd succeeded. Not until the signs of physical abuse had become too obvious to be ignored and too flagrant to have been self-inflicted was he transferred into the care of Dr. Horace Clemson, where the much-deeper-running mental abuse could be explored.

He had enough wits about him to know he couldn't let the doctors get even a whiff of his true thoughts, so he strained every muscle in his body to stay calm, repressing every thought before it could manifest, on the assumption it would lead to disaster. His deception was so strong, his repression so deep, that he managed to deceive not only the institution's staff but himself as well.

Dr. Clemson had been helping him with that too—private sessions three times a week, away from the hospital—helping him sift through his life to see what was real and face it. Continued treatment had been a condition of his release, and if he was being honest with himself, Jaden probably wouldn't have made it without Dr. Clemson. But every time he made forward strides, it seemed the universe conspired to set him back. Another note, the break-in, Rascal's disappearance—he couldn't heal. He would never heal in prison, and he would surely find a way to kill himself if sent back to an asylum.

Screw that. I would die before going back there. Jaden dug his nails into his palms. *The other patients... When the lights went out... That orderly... I won't go back there. I can't. I just can't.*

His body trembled, and a single tear ran down his cheek. *Pause.* He sucked in a breath and stilled, holding it. *Eyes shut.* He let his eyelids slide down. *Breathe.* He let out the breath.

Jaden's heart and mind slowed. *Why am I thinking this way?* He forced a smile. "They're not going to find me guilty. Hell, this probably won't even go to trial. All just a mix-up that will be over and done with soon, then I'll be back on my couch, drinking hot coffee and watching a good flick with—"

Rascal. He snapped his mouth shut before an anguished scream could escape. What came out was more like a growl that hissed through his teeth. His cat still hadn't returned. He wondered where Rascal could have gone and why he hadn't come back yet. He'd gotten loose before but always stayed somewhere close, meowing until Jaden found him and carried him back home to safety and warmth.

Jaden hoped he'd remembered to leave food out in the hall for Rascal, though the landlord frowned on that. *Fuck the landlord.* If the complex had better security, maybe Rascal wouldn't be out there somewhere, all alone and slowly dying. *Poor guy must be going crazy without me.*

A dull thud hit him in the back, and he staggered forward. The chains around his wrists and waist rattled.

"Move your ass," the prisoner behind him on the daisy chain grunted.

The man's breath caressed the back of Jaden's neck. Again, he had to stifle the fear and rage. It always started with something small, a nudge just big enough to trigger a memory. He paused, shut his eyes, and resumed his shuffle through a back hallway at the Fall River Judicial Complex.

After a moment, he opened his eyes and stared at the back of an orange jumpsuit. *Just like me.* He wasn't even supposed to be in the garb of a criminal, but that had been his own fault. His head had spun so badly that he threw up all over himself. A CO was kind enough to provide him with a change of clothes, the only kindness he'd thus far received.

He took a deep breath. *Temporarily. Relax, dammit.*

A sheriff's deputy led Jaden and two other detainees through a doorway into a corral with two rows of wooden benches. A raised dais stood to his right. The pews where those lucky enough to have been arrested sat were to his left, inside what the deputy referred to as "the pen."

A cage for animals. A pen for pigs.

The pen was claustrophobic, like having that fat, sweaty pig on top of him. His head reeled, the thumping in his skull mind-crushingly loud. His eyes glazed over, and he closed them. His breaths were fast and shallow.

When he opened his eyes again, a woman with hair so bright and blond that it was almost platinum sat among the crowd of spectators. Many held notepads or recording devices, and a full camera crew was set up in the corner. *Journalists.* With the woman's presence came breath. She shone like a star in the darkness of space and wore a long cream-colored jacket and a hot-pink scarf he'd always teased her for owning. The flat line of her mouth and dark circles around her eyes—abysmal pits in a canvas of pale white—exposed genuine concern for him. Jaden wondered how many times she'd tried to get ahold of him since the break-in.

She offered him a hesitant wave and mouthed something he couldn't understand. He tried to wave back, but the jingle of metal chains reminded him he couldn't. Her being there brought a pang to his stomach and wetness to his eyes. He had to look away, as his mind was a whirlwind of love, shame, and an overwhelming sense of loss he couldn't comprehend. And he hadn't even used his phone call to try to reach her.

He longed to talk to her but assumed someone there—the court officer standing by the door at the back of the room or perhaps either of the two deputies who'd led him in—would gag or beat him for breaking the stifling cold silence. The atmosphere was more dismal than a funeral's, more solemn than an empty church's. But *she* had come for him and was there to prop him up, though he hadn't always been there for her, at least not when it mattered most.

Jaden straightened his back and composed himself. No, he'd used his one phone call to leave a message on his boss's voicemail to say he would be out sick. Maybe the news stations had overlooked the incident. *A triple homicide?* He glanced at the reporters, only one or two of whom seemed to be looking his way. The rest were scratching notes on paper. *They can't be here for me.* He grimaced, a seed of doubt blossoming. The way people gossiped, only one person at work needed to find out about his arrest. Then everyone would know. He studied the journalists again, praying for his boss's blissful ignorance. He wasn't so naive as to think his prayer would be answered, but he wanted to keep his job, no matter how much he hated it.

Especially now that I have to pay for a lawyer. He huffed. *I should have found one already.*

But Jaden didn't know any defense attorneys. He didn't want to burden his elderly mother with what he hoped would be a frightening but soon-corrected error. And Tara, God, he had asked too much of her already. She was always there for him at a moment's notice. *And what have I ever done for her?*

He looked at Cass, who sat examining her hair for split ends, something she always did when nervous. *I should have called her.*

The rustle of papers broke the silence. Jaden raised his head to see some college kid, a baby face with a crooked tie, speed reading through three rust-colored folders on a table set just to the right of the room's center. To its left was an identical table, where a young lady sat straight backed with her hands folded in front of her. Her face was stern, and she was poised and ready for action, her materials organized neatly on the desk.

God, I hope she's the public defender.

The baby face tripped over a chair leg as he gathered his folders and approached.

Shit.

"H-Hey, guys," the attorney stammered. "My name's Patrick Wells. I know at least one of you has requested a court-appointed attorney for today's hearing. Well, that's me. Don't worry. I'm not as young as I look and have plenty of experience. I just wish they'd given us a bit more time. Anyway, do any of you already have a lawyer?"

"Fuck you," the man to Jaden's right said. His left eye was a mess of scar tissue and covered with a milky-white film. A little muscle over his bottom jaw twitched in a spasm of someone perpetually angry. He was the same one who'd pushed Jaden a few minutes earlier. Jaden smirked, happy to see that his anger wasn't solely aimed toward him.

"O... kay..." Patrick moved his fattest folder to the top. "I'm guessing you're Roman Carver?"

"What's it to you?" Roman snarled. "Fuck off."

Ignoring the foul-mouthed criminal and trying to play it cool as beads of sweat formed at his hairline, Patrick moved between Jaden and the young man to his left. The criminal's chains tapped against the wood at the same tempo his knee bounced. His hands, locked liked Jaden's at the wrists, hovered below a cleft lip as he chewed off the broken end of a nail. His eyes were big, brown powder kegs. The fuse behind them was so short that Jaden thought at any moment the young prisoner might go off... or let his bowels loose, which in such close quarters seemed an even less desirable possibility.

"Antoine Adams?" Patrick asked.

The man's knee stopped bouncing just long enough for Antoine to nod. No sooner had he made the acknowledgement than the *tap-tap-tapping* started anew.

"Felony assault," Patrick began. His face darkened. "Sexual..." His Adam's apple jumped as he gulped. "To a minor." The words oozed from his lips with all the uncertainty of an Alzheimer's sufferer.

"I didn't touch that little boy," Antoine blurted. "His parents be lying."

Patrick grimaced. Jaden shifted in his seat a little to his right.

"The fuck?" Roman said, half standing, but settled back down as the deputy took a step toward him.

Jaden stiffened but relaxed when he saw that Roman was looking past him.

"You a motherfucking pee-pee toucher?"

"I-I-I didn't do it!" Antoine shrank into the bench. "The kid's lying. I'm innocent."

Roman snarled. "Ain't nobody innocent here, dead man."

"Guys, we can talk about the details of your cases later, in private. Right now, I'm just reading the charges and determining how you'll be pleading to them." Patrick buttoned his jacket then unbuttoned it, leaning closer to Antoine. "So, you'll be pleading not guilty. Here's how it will go. The judge is going to ask you some questions. He'll state the charge and ask you how you plead. You'll say, 'Not guilty.'"

"I know how this works." Antoine said, still full of jitters. "I seen Judge Caprio."

"Well, this is a little—"

"All rise!" a court officer announced.

A hunched old white man in a black robe entered through the door behind the bench. With his deep-set eyes, his pointed witchy nose, and his horseshoe of hair wrapped around a liver-spotted head, he reminded Jaden of Montgomery Burns from *The Simpsons*.

"The Honorable Judge Raymond Cullen presiding," the court officer finished.

Excellent, Jaden thought as the deputy signaled for them to stand.

While the courtroom stood, awaiting permission to sit, a rail-thin man in his late twenties wearing a white button-down, a black tie, and black dress pants hustled in from the judge's chambers. His arms were laden with expandable file folders stuffed to their brims. He carried them to the empty jury box, plopped them onto the bench, and took a seat, his chest rising and falling rapidly as he caught his breath. His face, gaunt and full of sharp edges, made him look weaselly, and Jaden imagined the nasally voice his hooked beak of a nose must produce—something from a late-nineties boy band. He gave Jaden a slight nod as he caught his stare, and Jaden hurriedly looked away, warmth creeping up his neck.

"Please be seated," the judge said as he sat behind the bench.

The crowd obeyed like good little dogs.

"Never mind," Patrick said, organizing the folders in his hands. "You." He pointed at Jaden then at the accused diddler. "Just watch him, and do as he does." He hurried back to his desk.

A stenographer sat perched below the judge with some kind of black cup over her mouth. Beside her sat another man in a dusty-brown suit. His gaze was lowered to his desk, his forehead resting on his hand as if he might be sleeping.

"Tom, what do we have on the docket?" Judge Cullen asked.

The brown-suited man blinked. "Arraignments." He pointed at the pen. "Just those three."

"Good." The judge smiled. "We can all get out of here early. Well, except for those three." Some people chuckled at that, and the judge smirked. "Well? Who's first?"

"Jaden Sanders, Your Honor." The clerk handed Judge Cullen a file.

"Mr. Sanders?" The judge looked Jaden's way. "Please stand."

Jaden froze. When he saw Patrick waving his arm up, he stood.

The judge peered into a file. Without raising his head, he said, "Says here you were involved in an incident that occurred at—" He turned toward the gaunt man in the jury box, who was dressed like a Jehovah's Witness. "Isn't that where—"

"Same complex, Your Honor," the man said, smiling, and turned Jaden's way. "Never met him though, Your Honor. But I can tell you: he's sure made parking difficult the last few days."

The judge grunted, dismissing the joke. "Do you know this man?" he asked Jaden. "Anthony Marinelli, my law clerk?"

Jaden studied the younger man. With his clean-cut, emaciated-Clark Kent look, right down to his thick-rimmed glasses, he probably wouldn't have stood out in a crowd. If Jaden had seen him before, he couldn't remember it. Still, something was familiar about the clerk's toothy grin. Nevertheless, Jaden shook his head.

"You must answer audibly, Mr. Sanders." Judge Cullen glared at Patrick. "Hasn't this all been explained to you?"

"N-No..." After a moment's pause, Jaden added, "Your Honor. Th-Th-That is, no, I've never met your law clerk. Anthony, is it?"

The judge sighed. "Do you or your attorney have any objection to his presence here today?"

Jaden glanced at Patrick, who shook his head. "N-No... Your Honor."

"Great. Let's begin, then. Tom?"

The session clerk cleared his throat. "Mr. Jaden Sanders of 300 North Street, Apartment 314, Fall River, Massachusetts, has been charged with one count of murder in the second degree."

The young woman in the creaseless black suit rose. She looked like a Barbie doll straight out of the package. "The charges stem from a break-in that occurred on August 11, 2022, at the defendant's address by one Morton Tresser of Tiverton, Rhode Island. It is alleged that Tresser, unarmed, entered the defendant's apartment and, upon discovering it occupied, attempted to flee. At which time, the defendant stabbed Mr. Tresser, such wounds resulting in Mr. Tresser's death."

"Thank you, Ms. Laughton." The judge's face was like a tombstone, cold and solemn, as he stared at Jaden with impassive eyes. "Mr. Sanders, do you understand the charge as read by the session clerk? That you have been charged with second-degree murder?"

Jaden jumped at his chance to speak. "But, Your Honor, they didn't even mention the other two guys who—"

Judge Cullen rapped his gavel. "Mr. Sanders, this is not the time to try your case. That time will come soon enough. Right now, I simply wish to hear one or two words from you. To the sole charge of murder in the second degree, Mr. Sanders, how do you plead?"

Jaden straightened and hesitated only briefly. "Not guilty."

"Very well. A plea of not guilty will be entered on your behalf." The judge's gaze shifted to the baby-faced attorney. "Has bail been discussed?"

Patrick stood. "No, Your Honor."

"What is the Commonwealth's position?"

The prosecutor stood. "Given the severity of the crime and the excessively violent manner in which it was enacted, bail should be set at no less than one hundred thousand dollars."

Jaden gasped. "That's—"

The judge cut him off. "Counsel for the defendant?"

"Your Honor," Patrick began, projecting more confidence, "my client has no priors and no record of violence. His roots are in southern New England, and he has no intention of leaving the state. His neighbors will all testify that he was quiet and never troublesome. Three men kicked in his door, and he was forced to defend himself. My client—"

"Is not on trial yet, Counsel," the judge said, raising an eyebrow.

"Given all that, we believe bail should be much lower. My client is not wealthy, nor is he a flight risk. He will need his minimal savings to hire an attorney, should he not elect to proceed with court-appointed representation. For these reasons, bail should be set at no more than ten thousand dollars."

"Bail will be set at fifty thousand." Judge Cullen banged his gavel before Patrick could utter the response Jaden saw poised between his open lips.

Jaden retreated within himself. *Fifty thousand? That's everything I've got. How the hell will I be able to afford an attorney?*

"Mr. Sanders?"

"Huh?" Jaden looked up to see the judge glaring at him.

"I asked if you understood that failure to pay the amount set for bail will result in your continued incarceration until trial can resolve the matter, one way or another."

He nodded, but upon noticing the judge's continuing glare, he blurted, "I-I-I understand."

Judge Cullen offered him a smug grin. "Good. Who's next?"

With his head still hurting, Jaden sat down, vaguely aware of the two other defendants as they pleaded to their charges. He assumed not guilty. Even if no one there was innocent, as his fellow inmate had so poetically stated, he doubted anyone ever pleaded guilty. He didn't think he was guilty. But thinking and feeling didn't always share the same bed.

He turned toward Cass, shame welling up from his heart. She stared back, smiling warmly, her eyes wet. *I didn't mean to make such a mess of everything.* His heart was bursting. *How did everything go so wrong, so fast?* His thoughts were everywhere. He wanted to go to her, but his circumstances made even a paltry showing of sentiment impossible. He needed to pause, close his eyes, and breathe.

So he tried. He'd been trying so hard to do just that so much lately.

The court adjourned, and the deputy ordered his charges to rise. Jaden jumped to his feet. "Patrick!"

He looked around as if some other Patrick might have been hailed. When his eyes met Jaden's, he hurried over. The deputy grunted his impatience, but he held Roman at the end of the corral.

"Can you get a message to the lady in the second row with the pink scarf?"

Patrick shrugged. "What's the message?"

"Tell her to get my sister to post bail and to hire me a real attorney. I mean, I—"

"I know what you mean." Patrick rolled his eyes. "Don't sweat it. I get that all the time. But you were really lucky on bail. The judge has discretion but rarely grants it in second-degree-murder cases. That was a sure signal to the ADA that he thinks the charges are trumped up. A good sign!" He turned toward the audience area. "Anyway, who's the message for?"

Jaden followed Patrick's gaze. The sitting area was empty, and the door swung shut behind a ghost in heels.

CHAPTER 10

Royo took in Officer Costa standing at attention in his office and thought she was probably a bit much in large doses. He bet she was the kind of kid who raised her hand to answer every question in school. Yet that kind of enthusiasm was rare and strangely infective, if he would let it affect him. Energy and optimism exuded from the boisterous officer like heat from the sun, so much so that even an older cynic like him had a hard time not being swept up in it. Squinting, he thought he spotted a wrinkle in Costa's uniform and gave a mirthless grin. *Ah, the first chink in her armor has appeared.*

He stood and waved toward the empty chair. "Please, have a seat."

Costa pulled back the chair and delicately sat upon it, smoothing out her pants legs. She pressed her knees together, folded her arms across her lap, and smiled as she looked him straight in the eye.

Royo admired her confidence and fearlessness. He hoped she would never see the day when either or both were permanently wounded. Looking out his window, he saw a precinct floor awash with the drawn faces of people grown jaded by internal and defense-lawyer criticisms painting them as the bad guys for putting away the bad guys. Costa's odds of becoming like the rest of them—becoming like him—were high, so long as she was set on building a career at the FRPD. He might have tried to talk her out of that path, had the department not so desperately needed more like her.

He grabbed an evidence bag from his desk and tossed it to Costa. "You recognize that?"

Costa turned the bag, studying the prescription drug bottle inside it. "Endocet. Belonging to Edward Fletcher. Of course I recognize it."

She continued to pore over the information on the bottle's label before moving on to the information on the bag itself. Royo watched her eyes—the eyes of a future detective, he thought—roam over every detail then widen when the mystery revealed itself to her.

Furrowing her brow, she said, "This looks like the bottle we found at Cassidy Branigan's apartment. She or her dealer illegally procured it—whether freely given or stolen—from an elderly resident of the same building. Fletcher denies knowledge of ever receiving the oxys, never mind their theft, so it could be some mail-order scam or maybe a PCA or someone else signing for the drugs on his behalf. If I remember correctly, Fletcher was largely bedridden."

"Okay." Royo offered a sly grin. "So why do you look like someone just ran over your dog?"

"Because either you've found another bottle and are digging deeper into the source of the drug sales, or this is the same bottle we found, and it has been mislabeled. The name, case, and file numbers are all wrong."

Costa leaned forward and placed the bag gently on Royo's desk. Slowly, she sat back in her chair as she let out a breath, likely considering what she should say next. "Detective Royo, with all due respect, if you think I mislabeled evidence in the Branigan case, I can assure you I did not."

Royo laughed. "Relax, Officer Costa. This is evidence in a whole new case I'd like to bring you in on." As Costa's eyes lit up and her overzealous smile returned, Royo almost regretted the offer. Their pairing was like Tigger and Eeyore. But it had been made.

"The name on this bag is Jaden Sanders. Do you recognize it?"

Costa tilted her head like a dog hearing a far-off sound. "Wasn't he the boyfriend who found the body? We released him as a person of interest when the autopsy confirmed Branigan's death was a suicide. You don't think the ME got it wrong, do you?"

Royo shrugged. "I don't know. Remember that marking you thought looked like a fingerprint? It was barely even mentioned in the examiner's report. And she found no other evidence of a struggle—no foreign DNA under her nails, no other fresh bruises, cuts, et cetera." He sighed. "A second pill bottle being stolen from the same man doesn't suggest foul play in the Branigan case."

But Royo knew the ME's conclusion had never sat well with Costa, and dangling the bait in front of her worked as he'd anticipated.

She leaned forward. "But what about the scars we saw?"

"Yes, the report listed a whole litany of old wounds, from scars to burns to broken bones. She must have been either a victim of abuse or extremely accident-prone." He crossed his arms. "But back to Sanders. When I arrested him for another matter—I'll get to that—he tried to kill himself with the exact same illegally obtained oxys that Branigan offed herself with. Doesn't that seem odd to you?"

Costa scrunched up her mouth on one side. She raised a finger and opened her mouth to speak then deflated like a bouncy house with a hole in it. "I don't know, sir. That might mean any number of things: that she left a bottle at his place; that they both got pills from the same dealer; that he'd gotten a bottle from her; or..." Her face lit up like a fireworks display. "Or-or-or maybe he's the dealer! You think he may be the one using Fletcher to stock up on oxys?"

"The thought had crossed my mind." Royo held up his hands. "Again, I don't know, but it certainly seems worth looking into."

"And the girl's death?"

"Couldn't hurt to take another look while we're at it." He thought back to the dead woman's shoes, the markings on her face, and all the older wounds. "Not an official reopening, mind you. Just a quiet follow-up, you and me. Something always bothered me about that crime scene, and I know it bothered you too. Too perfect. Too staged. Not the last actions of a tortured soul. That's why I want to bring you in on this with me. You interested in doing some vice work with a side of homicide?"

"Yes, sir!"

"Well, right now, we already have Sanders on possession and might be able to make intent to distribute stick. But like I said, let's keep our inquiries quiet for the time being. Sanders is about to be tried for murder regarding a break-in at his apartment—which is directly across the hall from Ms. Branigan's former apartment."

Costa raised an eyebrow. "Small world."

"Ain't it, though?" Royo chuckled. "Or incestuous. This is Fall River, after all. Anyway, you know how I feel about coincidences."

He handed her the file on the Sanders break-in. "Read up. I've been trying to wrap my head around why three low-level douchebags would break into Sanders's apartment. Drugs seem such an obvious motive now that this evidence has come to light. All three thugs had rap sheets filled with drug-related offenses—mostly misdemeanor possession charges but drug-related all the same. In any event, there's more going on here than Sanders is letting on... or perhaps more than he knows."

Costa took the folder and stood at attention, waiting to be dismissed.

"Once you're all caught up, get me everything you can on Sanders, Tresser, Grady, Malden, Branigan, and Fletcher. We also need to track these pills from their origin through delivery. I have a feeling these seemingly random events are linked, and I want to know how. You up for it?"

Costa beamed like an Olympian on the podium. "Yes, sir."

With her optimism infecting him, Royo chuckled and nodded. "Dismissed."

CHAPTER 11

Out on bail for the last two days thanks to his sister's help, Jaden frayed the edge of a spiral notepad with his fingernail as he waited in an otherwise-empty hallway for Giles Blount, attorney-at-law. Ugly beige wallpaper cloaked the hall in obnoxious boredom. Instead of classing up the room, the antique furniture had lost its elegance to time, neglect, and a thousand scratches. The smell of cheap cigars bombarded his nose and clung to his clothes. The only sounds were the *clickity-clack* of the receptionist's large fake nails over her keyboard in the small office across from him and the hum of a filtration unit for an octagonal fish tank propped in a corner beside a jungle-sized fern.

I should have gone to that hotshot lawyer who's always in the news for sticking it to the man. He closed his eyes, trying to recall the lawyer's name. *Adrienne... Belvedere? Beaudelaire?* His head thumped back against the wall. *Something like that.*

A bus terminal ad showing a chiseled-jawed man in a stately suit with his head held high and his eyes staring skyward with a gaze of steely determination had led Jaden to Blount's New Bedford criminal defense firm. A toilet flushed somewhere in the building, followed by the groan and clanging of old pipes. For some reason, the sounds drew his attention to the fish tank. A sorry-looking angelfish hung suspended in the water, so still that Jaden thought it might be fake. He got up and tapped the glass. The fish didn't so much as flinch.

"Are you all alone in there?" Jaden couldn't see any other fish, but they could have been hiding among the pirate booty, plastic plants, and faux coral. He checked the glass for those fish who suck the gunk off it, figuring every fish tank had at least one. *Except this tank, apparently.*

"Just like me, huh, buddy? All alone. Well, at least we got each other." Jaden thought the fish might have been the saddest thing he'd seen since Simba's dad died in *The Lion King* then wondered if he might be projecting. "Can you project emotions onto a fish?" he asked the fish.

The fish didn't answer. Jaden straightened, remembering that his childhood fish tank had always started out well populated, but he inevitably bought a species that cannibalized the rest.

"Humph. Is that what you did? Killed all your friends?" Jaden laughed, but it jerked on his tear ducts. "Maybe we aren't so different."

"That's Benji," a man behind him said. "You like him?"

Jaden turned to face a tall, handsome man with eye-magnifying bifocals. He wore a neatly pressed gray suit, wing-tipped black shoes polished to a fine shine, a white button-down, but no tie. He was the man from the ad, except there, he hadn't been wearing the goggles. His fine moussed-in-place hair and long-toothed smile radiated energy unbefitting of the hallway's stagnancy.

"Benji?" Jaden asked. "Wasn't that a dog?"

"That's the joke. There used to be a Rover, a Max, a Rin Tin Tin, a Lassie, and a Clifford, but one by one, they each went missing while Benji here got fatter and fatter."

Jaden looked again at the angelfish, which wasn't fat at all but as flat as a pancake, albeit a saucer-sized pancake. *You little devil.*

The suit extended his hand. "Giles Blount. Sorry to keep you waiting, Mr. Sanders. I was tied up with another matter."

"Jaden's fine."

The attorney swung his arm toward a door opposite the receptionist's office. "Why don't we step in here, and you can tell me what brings you in to see me today."

Giles opened the door and led Jaden to a pair of plush velvety chairs facing each other with a small round table between them. On it was an enormous ceramic ashtray filled with peppery remains.

Jaden sat and took in the spacious office. Giles had positioned them at what appeared to be the recreational end of the room. The other half was all business. A giant oak desk stood before massive, ornately trimmed windows. Sunlight filtered in through open blinds, illuminating files stacked orderly on a side table, while writing instruments, stationery, business cards, and all sorts of legal knickknacks formed a horizontal line across the front of the desktop. Diplomas, awards, and various photographs of Giles with D-list celebrities, local politicians, businessmen, and a few others of more serious note populated the walls on each side of the desk.

Jaden squinted. "Is that Jeb Bush?"

"Sure is." Giles laughed and walked over to a photo of himself with the former Florida governor and two others Jaden didn't recognize. All were dressed in the too-embarrassing-to-wear-elsewhere checkered Polo and jockey attire of the eighteen-hole champion. "You've got a good eye. Myrtle Beach... eh, about six years ago. Nice guy. Paid for the entire round." He slapped his thighs and plopped down in the chair across from Jaden. "So, Mr. Sanders... hell of a mess you've gotten yourself into, isn't it?"

Jaden rubbed his temples and sighed. "Sure is. How much do you already know?"

"Enough. The papers took quite an interest in you. And I know the law you're up against, the defense you should make, and the verdict you should obtain." He threw up a palm. "Now, there are no guarantees in this business. No one can predict what twelve morons on a jury will do with one hundred percent accuracy. But I'd say you've come to the right place. My practice consists almost entirely of criminal defense, and I've been doing it for, eh, close to twenty years now. When you leave here today, talk to anyone in the field, and they can and will vouch for my track record. With me at your side, we should have this matter resolved and behind you in no time. And that's not just my ego talking, though confidence goes a long way in front of a judge or jury." He winked and smiled, evidently pleased with himself. "Like I said, I get results. My record speaks for itself."

Jaden didn't trust lawyers, but to be fair, he didn't trust anyone. Giles was saying all the right things, which, instead of putting Jaden at ease, put him further on guard because it threatened to give him hope. Hope was a dangerous thing when it came to such a serious gamble.

"Will we have to go to trial?"

Giles scrunched his face up in thought. "I couldn't tell you. Depends on whether we can talk some sense into the prosecutor. I'll definitely be starting with a motion to dismiss. That much is a given." He frowned. "It's peculiar that the commonwealth wants to pursue this at all, if you ask me. A verdict in your favor could set a precedent the state doesn't want to set. Maybe those meatheads at the DA's office are blinding themselves with their ambitions. Maybe they think they've got an ace in the hole. Without seeing all the evidence, I can't really comment. But bottom line—what a jury's going to hear, if we go that far—is that three scumbags with criminal records broke into your home, and you didn't let them bend you over a barrel. That's heroic, red-blooded American, even. Something to be honored, not punished."

Jaden smiled. He was sold. Giles was his man, his champion, and a voice to guide him through the darkness.

"Of course, my time isn't free, though I wish it could be. My regular hourly rate is six hundred."

Jaden's jaw dropped. It had taken him years of grinding to obtain a weekly salary that netted more than that after the federal and two state governments fleeced him for their shares.

"Too much? I can see it is, but no worries, my friend. Your case is high-profile and will likely garner me some considerable free publicity. The more the publicity, the more the exposure, both of which equate to more quality, bill-paying clients. So I'm offering you my *celebrity* rate: half price."

"Th—Three hundred an hour?" Somehow, Jaden still didn't think he was getting a bargain. *After all, why should I have to drain all my savings, including my retirement fund, to defend myself for defending myself?* The whole justice system was poisoned fruit with a rotted, worm-riddled pit at its core.

"Yes, sir." Giles flashed his easy smile. "And I'll need fifty thousand for a retainer."

"Fifty thousand! I put up that much in bail, and I had to borrow some of it from my sister!"

"Oh, not all right away. I'll give you some time to come up with it—say a couple of weeks? Give me what you have now, and we can get started. Of course, whatever's not used will be returned to you at the end of my representation."

Jaden's shoulders drooped, and he gazed at the floor.

Giles's voice softened. "We're going to get through this, Jaden, but I'd be lying if I said you didn't need a good lawyer. When it comes to criminal defense, I'm one of the best outside of Boston—"

"So why don't I get one from Boston?"

Giles didn't flinch. His smile didn't so much as twitch. "If that's the route you want to take, I can refer you to several reputable folks. They'll cost you, though. I'm charging half as much as they would." He paused while Jaden processed. "So... do we have a deal?"

"I... I guess."

They shook hands.

"Great. I'll have Mary draw up a fee agreement before you leave." Giles picked up a legal pad and a pen from the table between them. "For now, tell me everything that happened from the morning leading up to the break-in to the moment you stepped into this office, sparing no details or leaving out any conversations, and feel free to include any other events outside that time frame that you feel have bearing on your case."

Giles glanced at his watch. Jaden assumed the clock had just started. After a long breath, he leaned forward and told his tale as completely and as quickly as he could.

CHAPTER 12

Detective Royo didn't care for courthouses, with their wooden benches and altars for worshiping a man in a robe. They reminded him of churches, and he despised those even more. His father's church, the Church of the Holy Grace, had condemned his lifestyle and turned him against Royo. *But good ol' Dad's dead and buried next to that damn church, so to hell with them both.*

He shifted on the pew and sneered. *So much for separation of church and state.*

Unlike his father's church, the courthouse was a necessary evil. The former was just plain evil. He'd been to more than a hundred preliminary hearings over the course of his career. Some were motions to dismiss based on allegations he'd done his job wrong. Others said he'd violated some fictional constitutional right of some criminal lowlife who'd blown up a Chick-fil-A or gunned down a school bus. Those people didn't deserve to live. They'd taken innocent lives and tried to squirm their way out of watered-down justice when Hammurabi's Code should have reigned supreme. Original sin: now there was a church-inspired concept he could swallow. Man, at his core, was evil. Goodness came from the conscious choice to rise above one's inherent nature.

In those hundred-plus hearings to which he'd been summoned, only one defendant had been successful. And that was Royo's fault. He'd been green and sloppy, a newly made detective, and had his suspect dead to rights but couldn't wait for a warrant to nail him to the wall. Royo had kicked down the lowlife's door with no exigent circumstances to color his play and without so much as a knock and announce. Cowboy *shit.*

Well, he'd learned his lesson when that same criminal, back out on the street because of Royo's mistake, got together with his buddies and ran a train on a passed-out drunk college girl the very next week.

Royo nailed him right for that, but he always wondered whether, if not for his impatience, he might have prevented the young woman's life from being destroyed. He never made the same mistake again.

He'd kept tabs on the poor victim, and she killed herself a year later. He still needed a drink now and then to smooth over the wrinkle that had left on his conscience.

So dismissals on Fourth Amendment violations or some other procedural error were rare. Cops made mistakes, but usually additional evidence piled up high enough to make an arrest stick even without the so-called fruits of the poisonous tree.

He scoffed. *Fucking courts and their Biblical themes. Church. And. State.*

But that day, Royo faced a moral dilemma. He was serving as a prosecution witness with the expectation of helping to put a bad guy away but had no real desire to send Sanders to prison, at least not for killing Tresser. Sure, he'd found drugs unlawfully in Sanders's possession, but thus far, his investigation into Sanders had revealed no connections to the three individuals and no ties to the local drug trade. He couldn't shed his moral code, not even as an officer of the law, and testify in a way that suggested Sanders had committed a crime.

He would tell the truth, plain and simple. He patted the folder on the bench beside him, which held all the truth he would need.

Sanders, on the other hand, could use a little luck. He sat in the front row with his attorney—Giles Blount, a competent choice—whispering to him. Sanders glanced sideways more than once at Royo, whose collar tightened as their hushed conversation tingled like ants on his skin. The scowl on Sanders's face spoke volumes, not to mention the way he'd stormed out of the interview a couple of weeks ago. The anger was back, and although it was directed at him, Royo absorbed it better than the feeling that the suicidal Sanders had left him with.

Can I really blame him? I did tell him I wasn't pressing charges. Royo snorted like a bull preparing to charge. *And I didn't, nor did I push for it. I can't be blamed for this.*

Yet he did feel responsible. The whole arrest and prosecution made him feel unclean, like the law was being used in a way it wasn't meant to be. He wanted no part of it. Even if Sanders was bad news—into drugs or worse—he hadn't murdered Morton Tresser. No court or jury would ever convince him otherwise.

What's the difference? A bad man going away for the wrong crime or the right one is still one less bad man on the streets. Royo huffed as the unanswered questions surrounding Sanders's character became exasperating.

Still, the looks Sanders sent Royo's way were getting on his nerves. Calling him out for a Fourth Amendment violation and dragging him into court after a shift when he could have been sleeping or mowing down a bacon, egg, and cheese sandwich... *that* actually didn't bother him. *Every asshole's gotta try. But those looks...* Royo buried his face in his hands, avoiding the stare and scrubbing away the sleep.

"Are you here to help me or to help me go down?"

Royo looked up from his inner sanctum. Sanders had draped his arms over the back of his bench, apparently waiting for a response.

"I have no axe to grind, Mr. Sanders. If you somehow get your case dismissed today, it won't be over my"—he made air quotes—"'shoddy police work.' That said, I'm not here to make sure you go down either."

Sanders slapped his attorney on the arm. "What's he mean, '*somehow*,' Giles? I thought this was a sure thing."

Blount's flat expression didn't waver, and he didn't miss a beat. "Like I told you when you hired me, there are no sure things."

Sanders's eyes widened. "But you said *this* was a given."

"Please keep your voice down. I said that *having to make this motion* is a given. Though almost nobody wins them, you need to make all your procedural arguments at or before trial in order to preserve them for appeal."

"Or to run up the bill," Sanders muttered.

"If you're not happy with my representation—"

"No. No, no. Sorry. I'm just frustrated. I was hoping to get this over and done with today, and now it feels like a complete waste of time."

"We have a strong argument." Blount moved closer to his client.

Royo leaned back in his pew, pretending not to listen.

"It all hangs on how the detective testifies."

Over Sanders's shoulder, Royo caught another pair of eyes watching the attorney-client-privileged discourse. They belonged to Judge Cullen's law clerk, a clean-cut white boy with the look of future prosecutor written all over him. But he had a sense of edginess in his gaze and a gleam as sharp as the edge of a knife. Royo felt as if he'd seen the clerk recently but couldn't quite place where.

"All rise!" a court officer boomed.

Royo stood, took his cell phone out of his pocket, and powered it down. Civilians weren't allowed to have cell phones in the courtroom, but he wasn't a civilian. Still, he'd seen more than one judge berate and humiliate an attorney who'd forgotten to shut off his phone. Sometimes they even took the phones away. Once, Royo had even seen a judge answer the call. Like most cops he knew, judges didn't have much by way of a sense of humor.

The judge was an ancient codger, a white male like all the old ones were, and had a shrill voice and a mug that reminded Royo of one of the two hecklers in the balcony on *The Muppet Show*.

After only twenty minutes of testimony from Officers Stravenski and Silva relating to the chain of custody of a sneaker allegedly responsible for a footprint in a pile of dog crap at the scene of a B and E, Royo drifted into a state of mindless oblivion.

The rap of a gavel against wood snapped him back to reality. Sanders and his attorney were across the fence, standing before a table. The prosecutor—Laughton, he was pretty sure, though all he could see was her back—stood at their right.

She's trying the case? Royo frowned. The commonwealth must be taking Sanders's prosecution seriously. Laughton was a dog after a bone, a tenacious litigator, and the best on the DA's squad. *They must really want this ruling on the books and in their favor.* He pursed his lips. *I wonder if they're even offering a plea.*

He cursed silently, trying to convince himself it wasn't his problem. But going after Sanders like that would weigh on his conscience, even though he wasn't the one doing it.

It won't change anything. You are who you are. He would still get up on that stand and answer all questions with the truth and nothing but.

"Mr. Blount," the judge said. "It's your motion."

"Yes, Your Honor." Sanders's attorney cleared his throat. "My client, Jaden Sanders, moves this court to dismiss the charge of murder in the second degree and any lesser offenses that the commonwealth may argue stem from the same set of unlawfully obtained evidence—namely, statements taken from my client from the point of arrest, which we assert to have been the morning of August 11, 2022, through Detective Royo's interview of my client at his office and those statements taken at all times thereafter. These statements, which provide the crux of the commonwealth's charge against my client, were obtained without first informing Mr. Sanders of his Miranda rights."

Blount crossed his hands behind his back. "My client further moves for dismissal on public policy grounds as well as justification, meaning that my client, as the victim of a brutal attack by three dangerous individuals with felonious intent, was justified in defending himself in the manner in which he did."

"Counsel, isn't that an issue of fact more appropriate for trial?" The judge wore a look of interest, not skepticism, and Royo had a glimmer of hope that he might not need to testify that day at all.

"Usually, Your Honor," Blount continued. "But here, there is a compelling public policy concern—"

The judge waved a hand dismissively. "Save it. Let's hear what you have on the Miranda violation."

"But, Your Honor, allowing this case to proceed has the potential to make criminals out of innocent victims. Women who don't just lie down to be raped in their own beds, the elderly and the frail who lack the strength in their muscles to resist those who would abuse them, and good people, like Jaden Sanders, who make quick decisions and use the only means available to them to save themselves from the very real threat of serious harm or death."

"Noted." The judge grunted, his eyes cold and unyielding. "Motion denied on those grounds. I assume you wish to prevent evidence on the procedural due process claim."

Royo raised an eyebrow. Laughton had won half the argument without saying a single word. She sat still, as quiet as a breezeless night, wise enough to keep her mouth shut while she was ahead.

"Yes, Your Honor." Sanders's attorney's neck reddened, and he looked down at the desk. After shuffling some papers, he said, "The defense would like to call Detective Asante Royo to the stand."

"Proceed," Judge Cullen muttered.

Here we go. Royo let out a breath and stood. He walked to the center aisle and through the gate held open by a court officer, who led him to the witness box. Though he could have found his way there blindfolded. He sat, raised his hand up to his shoulder, and waited.

"Please swear in the witness," the judge said.

The court officer, Jerry Something-or-Other, raised his right hand. "Do you swear that the testimony you are about to give is the truth, the whole truth, and nothing but the truth?"

"I do." Royo sighed. *Are we married now?*

Sanders's attorney approached, all clean and as smooth as polished wood. His somewhat tone form filled out his tailored suit nicely—solid navy, not too flashy. But he was a little too type A for Royo's tastes. Besides, Royo had sworn off lawyers since the last relationship he'd had with one ended when Royo arrested him for driving over their mailbox while high on cocaine. He'd really liked that mailbox.

"Good morning, Detective Royo," the attorney said warmly enough.

"Good morning."

"My name is Giles Blount, and I represent the defendant, Jaden Sanders, with respect to the criminal charges brought against him being discussed here today." Blount hooked his thumbs through his belt loops. "Could you please state your full name for the record?"

"Asante Avillo Royo."

"And what do you do for a living?"

"I'm a detective with the Fall River Police Department."

Blount clasped his hands behind his back and began to pace. "And how long have you been a detective?"

"Approximately fifteen years."

"All with the FRPD?"

"Yes, sir."

"And before that?"

"I was an officer. For four years."

"Also with the Fall River Police Department?"

"Yes, sir."

"And how many cases have you investigated as an officer then detective with the FRPD?"

Royo stared up at the ceiling, trying to estimate how many cases he handled a year. "I don't know."

"Ballpark?"

"Hundreds."

"And with all your years and experience with the FRPD, would you say you've become an expert on police procedure?"

Royo shrugged. "I'd say I know as much as anyone else with my exper—"

Laughton jumped to her feet. "Objection! Detective Royo is here as a fact witness, not to offer expert testimony."

The judge rolled his eyes. He clearly thought the objection, though valid, was a waste of his time. "Sustained."

Blount pressed on. "In your role as detective with the Fall River Police Department, did you have occasion to meet my client, Jaden Sanders?" The attorney pointed at the fidgeting defendant.

Sanders looked as though he'd aged five years since he approached Royo minutes earlier in the peanut gallery. He chewed on his thumbnail, bouncing in his seat as his gaze darted from speaker to speaker.

"Yes."

"Could you describe the circumstances that led to your meeting Mr. Sanders?"

"Sure." Royo scratched his stubble then opened the folder he'd brought with him. He placed it on his lap and scanned the police report inside it. "At approximately 5:40 a.m., dispatch received a call from a person who identified herself to be one Norma Templeton of 307—"

Blount hovered over the witness box. "I'm sorry to interrupt you, Detective, but are you reading from something?"

Royo hadn't made any attempt to hide the fact. Blount could clearly see that he was. He understood the need for things to be stated to be entered into the record, but that didn't make the obvious questions any less irritating. "Yes."

"What are you reading from?"

"This is the police report from the night of the break-in. Officer Stravenski drafted it, and I signed and approved it."

"I'd like to have that marked as an exhibit," Sanders's attorney said.

Laughton stood. "No objection, but we have clean copies—"

"Your Honor..." Blount grabbed his lapels and puffed out his chest. "I would like an exact copy of what he's looking at."

"It's the same as what was provided to the DA, Your Honor," Royo said. "I haven't made any markings on it."

"May I see it?" Sanders's attorney asked.

"Certainly." Royo handed over the folder. He had his share of flaws, but dishonesty had never been one of them.

If only this jackass attorney could figure out I'm on his side. Maybe then he'd ask the right questions.

Apparently satisfied that Royo hadn't made any marks on the report, Blount handed him his copy. "How was this report made?"

"As I said, Officer Stravenski typed it."

"And you reviewed and approved it?"

"That's correct."

"Why did you review and approve it?"

"Because I was the senior officer on the scene."

"And is that standard procedure?"

"Could you please rephrase the question?"

"Yes. Is it standard police procedure for the senior officer at a crime scene to review and approve or deny his subordinates' reports?"

"From that same crime scene, yes, at least at our precinct."

"So, dispatch received a call from..."

"Ms. Templeton."

"Then what?"

"Ms. Templeton cited a disturbance at her address, the Prospero apartment complex at 300 North Street, a possible B and E... uh, breaking and entering." Royo glanced down at the police report and, after pausing briefly to allow for any objections, began to read. "Officer Stravenski and Sergeant Rollins were first on scene along with emergency medical personnel. Upon arrival, they found the defendant... uh, Mr. Sanders, in the third-floor hallway, holding a butcher knife covered in blood. He, too, was covered in blood. He stood over a man later identified as one Morton Tresser, who was also covered in blood and bleeding from multiple lacerations. Sergeant Rollins ordered Mr. Sanders to drop his weapon. The defendant complied and was... subdued."

Blount raised an eyebrow. "Subdued?"

"Tackled to the ground and handcuffed. That being approximately 6:00 a.m., and I arrived immediately thereafter."

"When you arrived, where was my client?"

Royo put the report on the wooden surface in front of him, no longer needing it. He had lived the rest. "He was sitting against the wall, handcuffed and not saying anything."

"Did you make any observations relative to Mr. Sanders's demeanor?"

"He was calm, quiet, and probably in shock. But given all the blood on him, the apparent lack of wounds, and the man bleeding out at his feet, we... I... initially suspected him to be the perpetrator of whatever crime had occurred that evening."

Blount tucked his chin to his chest and paced. Then he stopped and jerked his head up as if he'd had an epiphany. "Did he seem hostile to you?"

"No."

"Aggressive?"

"No."

"Did he fail to comply with any order given by you or Officer Stravenski or Rollins?"

"Objection," Laughton muttered half-heartedly, not bothering to stand.

"I'll strike that." Blount bounced on his toes and continued. "Did my client fail to comply with any order you had given him?"

"Objection," Laughton said, that time not even glancing up from the legal pad on her desk.

Blount seemed to shrink a bit. "Did you give my client any orders?"

"No."

"Did you speak to my client at all?"

"At that time? No."

"At any time?"

Royo sat back and tented his fingers. "When he came by my office four days later."

"Not a single word was exchanged between you and my client on the night he was attacked?"

Royo squirmed. They'd possibly exchanged a word or two, though he couldn't remember having done so. No, he hadn't. He'd spoken to Stravenski, some of the other officers, and many witnesses. "No. Like I said, he seemed to be in shock."

Blount placed a hand on the box and leaned in. "But you're not a medical expert?"

Royo bristled, and his shoulders tensed. "No. I'm not." *But I know what shock looks like, you twat.*

"What happened next?"

"A neighbor—by then, the hallway was brimming with them—told me that the defendant—"

"Objection!" Laughton shot to her feet. "Hearsay. Move to strike."

"He hasn't even finished his answer, Your Honor," Blount whined.

The judge's glare shot daggers at Sanders's attorney. "You know as well as I do that his answer wasn't going to be admissible. Sustained."

A heavy breath whistled through Blount's nose hairs. His lips moved, but no words came out, as if he'd been knocked out of his train of thought.

Royo threw him a softball and answered the unasked question. "I learned that the defendant was the lawful occupant of the apartment." Royo had been called to testify enough times to know he was supposed to wait for a question, but Laughton's objections were slowing things down, and he just wanted to get out of there. He had the feeling he was beginning to know what zoo animals felt like and wanted to get going before the sensation escalated to lab-rat level.

The judge looked as if he might scold Royo. He thought for sure they were in for another objection, but the prosecutor remained silent and seated.

Sanders's attorney pressed on before Laughton could change her mind. "What did you do with that information?"

"I stepped through the broken door of Mr. Sanders's apartment to analyze the scene. The responding officers had already... They'd already checked Tresser for weapons and for a pulse, and finding the latter, they got him a bus. Sergeant Rollins stayed by the man's side until the paramedics came in to do their thing. I quickly cleared the remainder of the apartment with another officer before waving in the EMTs. We found two other gentlemen in the bedroom. They were already dead."

"Mr. Kealan Grady and Mr. Leonard Malden?"

"Yes."

"How did they die?"

"Objection." Laughton stood, a smirk twitching up the corners of her mouth. "As counsel has already pointed out, the detective is not a medical expert."

Blount puckered his lips. "I'll rephrase. Detective Royo, in your nineteen years on the force, in which you investigated hundreds of crimes, does all your experience and skills learned via the academy or on the job grant you the ability to form an educated opinion on what crimes were—"

"Objection!"

"Committed inside that apartment?"

Laughton stood again, her chin out. "Objection. Form, and also Detective Royo is not here today as an expert witness of *any* kind."

Blount bounced on his toes and shoved his hands into his pockets, still managing to puff out his chest like a bullfrog. "Oh, I don't know, Attorney Laughton. I think a seasoned detective might be able to give an opinion—"

Laughton hovered over her desk as if about to pounce. "On the ultimate issue to be resolved by the jury?"

Judge Cullen raised his voice. "Mr. Blount, the witness may offer an opinion on what occurred inside the apartment without offering an opinion on whether such actions on the part of the defendant, Tresser, or the two other deceased individuals constituted a crime. To that extent, overruled." The judge turned toward Royo. "Along those lines, Detective, you may answer."

Blount smiled. "Thank you, Your Honor."

Royo winced. "What was the question?"

Laughton was still on her feet, hovering over the table, ready for a fight. "Objection: foundation."

The judge blinked slowly. "Overruled."

"Speculation," Laughton said, though the inflection on the last syllable made it sound more like a question.

The judge rolled his eyes. "Overruled."

"Form."

The judge's cheeks reddened. He took a deep breath and faced Royo. "Detective Royo, what happened in that apartment?"

"The evidence suggests that the defendant grabbed a pair of knives from his kitchen and hid with them in his bedroom. Or perhaps he was chased in there. What we know for certain is that Tresser and the two decedents kicked in Sanders's apartment door and upon finding Mr. Sanders in his bedroom, converged upon him. As his attackers closed in, Mr. Sanders drove a butcher's knife into Malden's stomach. He then used a paring knife to stab Grady in his side and in one eye. A struggle with Tresser occurred near the door into the apartment, where Sanders stabbed him as well. The confrontation continued into the hallway, where Sanders delivered a final blow."

Blount chewed on the arm of his glasses. "So my client took on three aggressors who broke into his apartment to do him physical harm?"

"Objection." Laughton didn't give a reason for it.

"It certainly seems that way," Royo continued.

"Move to strike," Laughton said.

"Overruled," the judge snapped.

Blount carried on as if he hadn't heard anyone else speaking. "You didn't arrest my client, did you?"

"Nah." Royo sat up straighter. "No."

"Why not?"

"Because I didn't think he had committed a crime."

Laughton shot up. "Objection!"

The judge shook his head, and Laughton sat back down.

"Do you now?" Blount asked.

The judge kept Laughton in her seat with a glare.

"No."

The judge scoffed. "Counsel, you've made your point. Now bring it back to the Fourth Amendment violation."

Blount nodded. "When you arrived at the apartment complex, my client was handcuffed, correct?"

"Correct."

"An officer stood beside him?"

"Yes."

"Was my client allowed to leave?"

"At that point in time? No."

"At that time, had you or anyone else from your department read my client his Miranda rights?"

"I don't know."

"Well, you hadn't, had you?"

"No."

"Why not?"

"Because we hadn't arrested him."

"Does your report indicate whether anyone read Mr. Sanders his rights?"

"It does not."

"If someone had read Mr. Sanders his rights, would that typically be noted in the police report?"

"Yes."

Blount gripped the box and leaned into his hands. "You seized my client against his will, cuffed him, and placed a sentry over him. Isn't that an arrest?"

"Objection." Laughton stood. "Leading."

"Hostile witness, Your Honor," Blount responded.

"Overruled" came the judge's decision. "You may answer, Detective."

Royo didn't think he was being remotely hostile, but he understood the rationale. Still, he'd already said he didn't think Sanders had committed any crime. *If anything, doesn't that make me a* friendly *witness?* He cleared his throat again and shifted in his seat. "No. We detained him for questioning."

"You testified earlier that, on arrival, you thought my client was the perpetrator of some violent crime, correct?"

"Yes."

"And upon that suspicion, you kept my client restrained and guarded. Isn't that the definition of an arrest?"

"Objection!"

The way Laughton exploded out of her chair then sat right back down only to explode up again made Royo think of a CrossFit class he'd once taken. *A lot of burpees.* He awaited the judge's ruling before answering.

"Sustained."

Blount leaned against the witness box with a casual air that made him look too comfortable. "Detective Royo, if you admit to detaining my client on the suspicion of committing a violent crime, depriving him of his freedom of movement, why do you say you did not arrest him?"

"Because..." Royo stumbled. He knew Blount was trying to get under his skin, so he couldn't figure out why he was letting the attorney get to him. "Because..." He was at a loss. "Because we cut him loose. And we never charged him!"

Blount stood taller. "Still, even though you had detained him on suspicion of a violent crime, you did not read him his Miranda rights. Correct?"

"We detained him and did not read him his rights. Correct."

"You had my client come in to give a statement four days later. Correct?"

"Yes."

"At any time from the point you 'cut him loose' to the time he entered the Fall River Police Department four days later, had anyone from your squad read him his Miranda rights?"

"We wouldn't have. We weren't arresting him. I never wanted to arrest him."

"So no?"

"No."

"When my client entered your department the next day, did you have any intention of arresting him?"

Royo shook his head. "No, sir."

"But you knew the commonwealth was considering bringing charges against Mr. Sanders?"

"I knew there was a possibility the state might file something."

"And did you inform my client of this 'possibility'?"

"Yes. Eventually."

"Eventually?"

"At the close of the interview."

"You mean after Mr. Sanders had given his full statement?"

"Yes."

"One more question, Detective. At what point did you finally read my client his Miranda rights?"

"When we arrested him."

"And when was that?"

Royo counted on his fingers. "Another four days, so four days after he gave his statement."

"No more questions, Your Honor."

Laughton rose and strode over with the confidence of a champion gladiator. "Good morning, Detective. Thank you for taking time away from your important work to testify here today—also important work."

"No problem," Royo said softly, unsure how he was supposed to respond, if at all.

"Detective, when was the defendant arrested for murder in the second degree, the crime for which he is presently charged?"

Royo opened the folder in front of him. "August 19, 2022."

"And that was four days after you interviewed him?"

"Yes."

"And at that time, did you read him his rights?"

Royo tapped his chin. "No. Sergeant Rollins did."

"Objection. Hearsay."

"Sustained."

"Were you present when Sergeant Rollins read Mr. Sanders his rights?"

"I was not."

Laughton walked back to her desk and withdrew a thin stack of papers from one of her perfectly positioned folders. "Your Honor, may I approach the witness?"

"You may," Judge Cullen said.

Laughton handed copies of the document to Blount and Judge Cullen then gave one to the court officer to hand to Royo. She kept a fourth copy for herself.

"Detective Royo, do you recognize the document that's been placed before you?"

Royo flipped through the two-page document. "It's the arrest report for the defendant."

"Did you fill out that report?"

"No. That was Sergeant Rollins."

"But you reviewed it for accuracy and signed off on it. Correct?"

Royo paused, expecting Blount to object to the leading question, but the attorney remained seated, his eyes moving like a typewriter back and forth across the report. "Yes."

"Does the report state whether or not Mr. Sanders was read his rights?"

"It does. He was."

"I'd like to add this police report to the record."

"Counsel, any objections?" Judge Cullen asked.

Blount stood. "No objections, Your Honor."

"Detective Royo, you testified earlier that you didn't believe the defendant should have been arrested?"

"I did."

"On what law did you base that conclusion?"

"Not really the law *per se* but my view regarding the intent behind it."

"Your moral code, as it were?"

"I guess you could call it that."

"Let me pose a hypothetical—"

"Objection."

"Your Honor, counsel opened the door to this line of inquiry."

"Overruled."

"A attacks B with his fists, and B draws a knife. A then turns and runs. If B chases A and stabs him in the back, killing A, would you arrest B for murder?"

"Yes, in that very limited scenario, but that's not—"

"Is your answer yes?"

Royo huffed. "Yes."

"So regardless of what you feel is right or wrong, if the scenario I posed to you is what actually occurred in this case, Mr. Sanders would have committed a crime?"

"Yes, but the evidence—"

"And is that crime murder in the second degree?"

"As you describe it in your hypothetical, possibly. We don't know intent."

"No more questions, Your Honor."

CHAPTER 13

Jaden's head spun. The boring tans and grays of the hallway outside the courtroom seemed to swirl together like watercolors. Red crept in at the corners.

He'd allowed himself to believe he had a chance to escape the nightmare. With the detective seemingly on his side, the judge would have had to dismiss the case.

But Judge Cullen had made his decision swiftly, as soon as all the evidence had been presented and arguments made. *Motion denied.*

The case would go to trial, which meant he would miss more work. He was running out of excuses and had pretty much just stopped going. A termination letter was probably already in the mail. "Ugh. Why won't this just fucking end?"

Giles, who'd been rambling on for the last minute, none of which Jaden had processed, said, "We knew this would be the result going into today. It doesn't change where we stand. You haven't lost anything."

"Except a couple of grand for your services." He growled then softened. "I'm sorry. I just... I don't know how much more of this I can stomach." How he wished Cass were there. He wasn't too much of a man to admit he would have done anything to be in her arms then.

But he was not Cass's concern. He should leave her be. *Let her go? Isn't that what Tara has said? How do I do that if I can't even stop seeing her?*

"Have faith," Giles said.

"Huh?" He glowered at his attorney. "Easy for you to say."

"We could see what's on the table and make a deal, if you want."

"What kind of deal?" Jaden clawed at his hair. His eyes twitched, rattling against their sockets. "I refuse to go to jail for killing someone who broke into my home and attacked me."

121

Giles frowned. "Hold on a sec. I'll be right back." He disappeared into the courtroom.

Jaden took the opportunity to run out to his car and grab his phone. With it in his pocket, he sat on a bench outside the courthouse and rested his head in his hands, trying to smooth away the burgeoning migraine. When he thought himself composed enough, he pulled out his cell phone. No calls. He ran down his call history from top to bottom. *Tara. Cass. Cass. Cass. Cass. Mom. Cass. Cass.* Of course Cass was all over the list. She was the best thing he'd ever had and all he'd ever wanted. God, his head was spinning. The world streaked around him.

He made the call.

A man picked up. "Hello?"

"Who's this?"

"Who's *this*?"

Giles barreled out of the courthouse. Jaden hung up, his concentration divided between why some guy had answered Cass's phone and why his attorney was so excited. Split-minded, he was unable to focus on either.

The attorney vibrated with energy.

Jaden again gave in to that folly of all emotions: hope. *What was it Mom said? Something about shitting in one hand and—*

"I've been looking all over for you. I thought you were going to wait for me inside."

Jaden swayed as he stood. "I just wanted to check my phone."

"Never mind that." Giles clapped him on the shoulder. "I've got good news. Now, I couldn't get jail time off the table—"

One hand filled up fast.

"But the DA's offering voluntary manslaughter. The deal's five years, but you'd be out in three or maybe sooner with good behavior."

"No fucking way!"

"That's what I said." Giles again clapped him on the shoulder. "But that's her starting point. I guess she lost a little confidence when her star detective showed dissention in the ranks. I'm sure I could get her down to involuntary manslaughter. You'd do two years, tops!"

Jaden's jaw dropped, and his stomach churned. "Two years in prison... for what?"

"I know it's a bitter pill—"

"No, you don't know. These assholes break into my apartment and try to kill me, and I'm the one who pays for it? In what world does that make any goddamn sense?"

Giles placed a hand on his shoulder. Jaden shrugged it off. The repeated touching had become as nauseating as wet, muddy worms slithering over his skin.

"Jaden... they're dead. And you stabbed one of them in the back while he was already down and out."

"And so fucking what! They got what they deserved. Meanwhile, I'm going to lose my job, my money, my freedom, and my future, all because some criminals kicked in my door? That's crazy!"

"It's a good deal, Jaden. If convicted of second-degree murder, you're facing a minimum mandatory sentence of fifteen years. Worst-case scenario, you'll spend the rest of your life in a cage. If your fellow inmates don't kill you, the boredom and monotony will."

Crossing his arms, Jaden said, "No jail time."

"Jaden—"

"No jail time."

Giles started to pat his shoulder again but stopped himself. "Go home. Think it over. Take your time. Even without waiving our right to a speedy trial, we won't be going forward for another month. I'll be in touch." With that, he turned on his heel and left.

Jaden stood in a busy courtyard, with only his thoughts to keep him occupied. Maybe he would try Cass one more time. Maybe somehow he'd dialed the wrong number or hit the wrong button.

Perhaps he'd called Dr. Clemson by accident. The man who'd answered hadn't sounded like his psychiatrist, though.

"Howdy, neighbor."

Jaden had been so lost in his thoughts that he hadn't noticed the Jehovah's Witness-looking guy from the courtroom standing directly in front of him. Something about his giant alligator grin was off-putting, particularly given the hand Jaden had been dealt only moments prior. He looked up from his seat and had to squint against the brightness. The lanky law clerk only narrowly eclipsed the sun.

Something about the man's greeting was equally off-putting. "Do I know you?"

"I live in the same apartment complex as you, and I also happen to be Judge Cullen's law clerk. I shouldn't be talking to you right now—or at all until your case is over—but I just wanted to let you know that some of us think what's happening to you is wrong."

"Oh yeah? That judge you work for doesn't seem to give two shits about me."

The law clerk chuckled. "Judge Cullen may come off as a crotchety old goat, but he will treat you fairly, especially when he has me helping him research the relevant law." He winked.

Jaden did not find the clerk's words comforting. His whole casual attitude and friendliness put Jaden on alert. Still, he supposed he could use all the friends he could get in that courtroom. "Which apartment is yours?"

"Oh, I'm on the first floor. Haven't been there too long, so I'm not surprised we haven't run into each other or fought over one of the few washing machines that actually work."

"Tell me about it." Jaden sagged on the bench. "Hey, if you see a skinny cat running around, mine got loose. Could you grab him or let me know? I'm apartment—"

"I know. It's 314." He raised his palms. "I'm working your case, too, remember? Anyway, will do." He peered over Jaden's shoulders at the courthouse doors. "Well, I gotta go. Good luck in there." He hurried off.

Detective Royo passed by on Jaden's right. Jaden gave him the finger.

CHAPTER 14

Royo walked up to the first-floor home of the two-story tenement. The grass was high where it wasn't brown and dying. A bike lay tipped over near the front steps, bravely left unchained in a city not known for its charity. The sound of a kid crying came from inside.

He rang the doorbell.

"Oh, for crying out..." a woman inside said. "Stay here! Hold this against it. I know it stings, but keep it there anyway. I'll be right back."

The door swung open, and Tara Morrison stood in the entrance-way, her coarse, sandy hair frizzy and frazzled, as if she'd been caught in the rain. A scrunchie held it up loosely, a few strands falling over her face. Her clothes, a nice gray blouse and a long black skirt, were a wrinkled mess covering what might have been a nice figure, had she not been so hunched by life's burdens.

"Hello?" She fixed Royo with an accusatory stare that said he'd better talk fast.

Royo showed his badge. "Good evening, Mrs.—"

"It's Miss. The deadbeat whose name I share skipped town after our second child. I've got two kids to feed and a thousand things to do before I have to get up and do them all over again, so let's skip the pleasantries. What do you want?"

Royo smiled and decided he liked Tara Morrison.

"I'm Detective Asante Royo. I was wondering if I might have a moment of your time to discuss your brother."

Tara's expression went from stone to pudding. "Why? What's happened? Is Jaden okay?"

"Yes," Royo said softly. "Your brother is fine." *As fine as someone who's going to be on trial for murder can be.*

The color vanished from her face. "He didn't... try again, did he?"

"No, no. Nothing like that." Royo smiled warmly. "Please, may I come in?"

Tara stepped aside and let Royo into a living room spotted with Matchbox cars and action figures. Cartoons played on an older television, the kind with a giant back and a curved screen. At the kitchen beyond the living room, a boy of five or six sat sniffling and holding gauze against his knee.

"That's Damien. He fell off his bike, and we were getting him fixed up, weren't we, Damien?" Tara grabbed a box from the table, removed a bandage from it, peeled the covers off the adhesive ends, removed the cotton balls from her son's hand, and gently smoothed on the bandage. She kissed it. "There. All better?"

Damien nodded. He looked up at Royo. "Mommy, who's that?"

"That's Detective Royo. He catches bad guys and locks them away."

"A real detective?" Damien's eyes lit up. A smile spread across his face.

"That's right." Royo returned the smile, always appreciative of a fan. He extended his hand. "Nice to meet you."

Damien stared at Royo's proffered hand as if it were a cookie he needed his mom's permission to take. But after a moment, he took it and gave it a mighty double shake, laughing.

"Whoa!" Royo waggled his hand, pretending to be in pain. "That's some grip." He whistled. "All right, battle scars! Fell off your bike, huh? When I was your age, I used to fall off mine at least once a week. So tell me—what were you trying to jump?"

Damien looked at his mom with uncertainty then back at Royo. Apparently deciding he'd better not lie to a police officer, he said sullenly, "The curb."

"Yep." Royo chuckled. "Curbs are tricky. You'll get it next time, I bet."

His mother ruffled his hair. "Okay, you. Go watch TV for a bit so that Mommy can talk to Detective Royo. I'll make us some mac and cheese in about fifteen minutes."

Damien extended and curled the fingers on his right hand three times.

"That's right," his mom said.

"Can I ride my bike?"

"In the driveway."

Damien scampered off.

Royo listened to the door swing open then shut. "Brave kid."

Tara huffed. "Short memory." She crossed her arms. "Now, why do you want to talk to me about my brother?" She took a seat, offering him the one across from it.

Royo sat. "He's your brother. I assume he confides in you."

She flicked back a loose strand of hair. "Maybe."

"Look, I know you think I'm the enemy here—"

"Nah, why would I think that?" She tapped her chin, a fire lighting behind her eyes. "My son is no longer here, so we can stop being polite. I know who you are. You're the one who told my brother you weren't going to arrest him, and now he's on trial for murder."

Royo sighed and nodded. "Fair enough, but do you also know I testified at his first hearing that, in my opinion, your brother is innocent of that crime?"

"It's the only reason you're sitting there, Detective." Tara choked up, but she sucked back her tears. "My brother may be a lot of things, but he isn't a murderer."

"Then help me prove he isn't."

"How?" Her palms fell flat against the table. "You already know I wasn't there that night."

"Look, my goal is to find out the good, bad, or ugly truth. I'm not going to lie and say that if I find out he's involved with selling drugs or something worse, I'll turn a blind eye. But if the truth is as you say, that your brother has committed no crimes, then"—he made air quotes—"'the truth will set him free.'" He smiled shakily, hoping she couldn't see the shallowness of it. He'd told her the truth, but he'd neglected the part in which he wasn't just looking into one crime.

"Yeah, a lot of good it's done him so far."

"Well, surely you can answer some of the easy questions. Is he on any drugs?"

"Antidepressants, for sure. Something for his anxiety, too, I'm guessing." She frowned. "You must have searched his place that night and found all of it. So you probably know better than me."

Royo slid a notepad and a pen from his inner jacket pocket and flipped the pad open. "Does he take anything besides the antidepressants and antianxiety meds?"

Tara leaned forward. "What are you getting at, Detective?"

"Painkillers?"

"No."

"You know he tried to kill himself—"

"Yeah, I know." She jolted up and let out a breath. Her hand trembled as she smoothed out the creases in her brow. Giving another long sigh, she sat back down. "I know. I made him promise not to try that again... and to try to beat this bullshit you're slinging at him." With her eyes downcast, she muttered, "He'll keep his promise."

"I'm just saying he had a lot of prescription meds that didn't belong to him."

She frowned, balling her hands up as she met Royo's gaze with a steely one. "I have all sorts of pills, but he didn't get them from me, if that's what you're implying." She blew her bangs out of her eyes. "I know better than to give them to him." She groaned.

"Meds?" Royo asked, chewing the end of his pen.

"Cancer."

"I'm sorry."

"Don't be. I'm gonna beat it. I have to, for my kids... and for Jaden."

"Sounds like your brother could use some of your spirit."

Tara scowled. "He wasn't always like this, Detective. He was happy. Normal, whatever that means. A really good brother. My best friend, even. Then..."

"I just meant—"

She waved a hand dismissively. "Look, I have no idea where he got those pills, Detective. Probably that girlfriend." Tara clamped her mouth shut and seethed, as if she wanted to punch someone.

"Cassidy Branigan?" Royo tapped his fingers on the table. "I investigated her death. Your brother was really torn up when she died."

"That bitch ruined him!" Tara collapsed onto the tabletop, letting her tears flow. She shook her head. "No, no. That's not fair. Jaden, well, he's always been... sensitive. But he fell hard for that girl. I always thought she was bad news. Had too much baggage. You know? But man, did he fall for her. And if I'm being honest, she sure seemed to love him too." She gritted her teeth. "What she did, it tore him apart."

"Sent him to a hospital, didn't it? He downed a handful of oxys when we arrested him. That wasn't the first time he tried to kill himself, was it?"

"That's none of your business." Tara's face reddened. She hovered over the table.

"The girl, then. Cassidy—you said she was 'bad news.' Why?"

Tara pushed herself back from the table. "I think you should leave."

Royo remained seated. "Please, Miss Morrison. You understand that your brother was found in possession of illegal drugs. That's a problem. I might be able to help him if you help me."

"The drugs were hers. Had to be. That apartment was like an opium den, so bad that I stopped bringing my kids to see their uncle.

Cass always had strange men funneling in and out of it, the type of people who when you see them walking toward you, you cross the street. She was definitely using, probably dealing, and maybe even... you know, selling herself. Those people who hung around her were the reason why I didn't want my brother anywhere near her. Yeah, I'm pretty sure she was dealing. She had no job, as far as I could tell, but was never short on cash. Nothing hardcore or anything, at least as far as I know."

Royo winced. "Stolen oxy is no small thing."

"Yeah, well, my brother didn't steal it."

"You sure? We didn't find anything when we searched his apartment the night of the break-in, but then again, we weren't really looking for it. We don't really have a right to go through all the victim's belongings, and we couldn't do a search incident to an arrest, since we didn't arrest anyone at that time. Yet there it was when we did get around to arresting him."

Royo sighed. "But that's neither here nor there. What I want to know is: Where'd he get it? Who's his source? And if it was his girlfriend, where'd she get it? We know the source and who it ended up with, but not the middleman or men. If I find that out, I'm willing to overlook the felony possession charge."

"Like you did the insane murder charge?"

Royo looked away. "Unfortunately, that was out of my hands. This... this *here*... is between you and me. And I have full authority to kick free a small fish who helps me catch a bigger fish."

Tara buried her face in her hands. Through sniffles, she asked, "Can you blame him?" The fire in her eyes returned, and Royo knew the Sanders stock was swayed by passion.

She thrust a finger at Royo. "You have no idea what he's been through. He didn't just lose a girlfriend. He lost his lifeline. His tether to the world. Then... *then* they put him in that awful place to heal, but he didn't heal there. He was tormented by patients and staff alike.

They did horrible things—monstrous things to him at that hospital. I'm not sure what, but I know it was bad. He went in there broken and came out destroyed. He thinks I don't know, but his nightmares... He screams in his sleep. I couldn't even let him stay here anymore because he was terrifying Damien. Isn't that awful? I kicked my own brother out because of the hurt others did to him, because he was too shattered and couldn't put himself back together. He's got no one, Detective, except me, and even I pushed him away. He's the victim here. Why can't you see that?" She cried into her hands. "Why can't any of you see that?"

For a moment, Royo was speechless. Gathering his wits, he said, "If something happened to him at that hospital, we can open an investigation—"

Tara scoffed. "He'll never talk to you, Detective. He won't even talk to me. He's trying to pretend none of it ever happened. Jaden's good at that." She sneered. "Besides, it's not like he has any reason to trust or confide in you."

Royo took a deep breath. "Tell me what his connection is to the oxy, and I swear on my soul, I'll do everything I can to help him."

"I don't know!" Tara shouted then buried her face in her hands again. "I don't know anything about it. I'm just a single mom trying to raise her kids far away from that crap, but you can't take a step in this freaking city without worrying whether a needle's gonna stick you in your foot." She shuddered then slouched.

Royo leaned forward, relaxing his posture and softening his tone. "I believe you, Tara. May I call you Tara? What I'm asking, and I know it's hard, is for you to convince your brother to talk. Give up his supplier. I'm not after him for possession. If he's a victim here, get him to talk to me. I promise you, if he rolls on his supplier, I'll do everything in my power to reduce the present charges against your brother and forgo the felony possession charge entirely." He sat back, his mind returning to how Branigan had looked on that couch. "Unless it turns out your brother is guilty of something far worse."

"Worse?" Tara slammed her palms down on the table. "He's already on trial for the murder of three assholes who kicked in his door and tried to kill him. On top of that, you've accused him of being a drug dealer. What *worse* can you think there could be?"

Royo regretted saying that last bit out loud and smartly resisted the temptation to correct the error in her statement that Sanders was on trial for three murders. He stared at her with all the gravity he could project. "Cold-blooded murder."

Tara froze, searching his face for some kind of read. "You can't be serious."

"Has your brother ever been violent? Discounting the night of the break-in, of course."

Tara stood. "Get out."

Royo rose but made no motion to leave. "I've been going over some of the things he said. I tried to speak to his doctor, but he's not talking. The prosecution has shown me some of the medical records received through pretrial discovery. Redaction only works up to a point. Black marker doesn't hide printed type when you hold the paper up to the light. So we know about the suicide attempt. We know about the periods of... What did the records call them? Disorientation?"

"Get out." Tara gritted her teeth and threw a finger at the door. "Get out! Get out! Get out!"

"You know, Alzheimer's sufferers are often violent during bouts of disorientation. Early-onset dementia—"

Tara slapped Royo. She pulled her hand away, her mouth agape at what she had done, but still balled her hands into fists at her sides. She made no apology. In a voice as low as a growl, she said, "My brother is a good man who has trouble coping with bad turns. And believe me, he's had way more than his share. A father who used to beat him. Schoolkids who used to bully him. Cass. That godawful place they sent him to. It's amazing he's holding together as well as he is. Can you blame him if he's introverted? A little socially awkward?" With a sneer, she wiped a tear from her cheek as if it were the most grotesque thing on the planet. "And when he finally finds someone who makes him happy..."

Tara collapsed into the chair, all the wind blown out of her sail. She ran a hand through her hair, exposing gray roots Royo hadn't noticed before. Her forehead wrinkled with worry. "He needs help, not more torment. Dr. Clemson is a good start, and thank God for his keeping Jaden out of that hospital this time around. He just... gets confused sometimes when the stress and anxiety become too much. Dr. Clemson calls it denial, but that word must mean something more to him than it does me."

She turned to Royo and stared him straight in the eyes. Hers were the big brown puppy dog kind that stabbed him right in the heart. "Please, Detective. Just leave him alone. He hasn't hurt anyone who didn't have it coming. He's a good man." She grabbed his hand and squeezed. "A good man. Are you?"

Royo tried not to let her display of affection soften him, but he found it hard to swallow. Still, he kept his expression flat and, he hoped, unwavering. Before he could stop himself, he slipped. "We have reason to believe that Cassidy Branigan may not have killed herself after all."

Tara's dull, tired eyes slowly widened into a look of wonder and disbelief. For a moment, she was speechless, the weight of the implication behind Royo's words likely slowing down its processing.

"Y-Y-You can't think..." She blinked several times before clarity returned to her eyes. "You don't honestly believe that he had anything to do with that?"

"We're investigating several lines of inquiry."

Groaning, she gazed up at the ceiling as her head fell back on her neck. "You must be out of your freaking mind. Jaden? Kill Cass? That girl was like a light out of the darkness for him. Her death plummeted him deeper into it." She stood and again paced, shaking her head wildly. "And you think..."

She unleashed a glower in his direction so fierce and ugly that he had to look away from it, ashamed and a little afraid.

"Forget Jaden. You're the one who's crazy." She slammed her foot against the floor. "Get the hell out of my house!"

Royo circled the table but paused at Tara's side. "I only want to see justice done, for Jaden and for everyone else involved. Your brother lawyered up, so I can't talk to him. But you can. Convince him to talk to me. My offer stands."

Tara stood with arms crossed and her mouth firmly shut. As mad as she was, she would think about his offer because she loved her brother. He hoped she would come to the conclusion that she should help. Not willing to guess, he showed himself out.

"Mister, look!" Damien said as he pedaled to the curb and jumped off it, nailing the landing.

"Good job, kid!" Royo smiled. "Do us all a favor, okay? Don't ever grow up."

CHAPTER 15

Jaden wished *he'd* never grown up. Life had been so much simpler before responsibilities and expectations and rules crafted to conform behavior to what some faceless and timeless society felt was appropriate. They were hard lines with no give, even when flexibility and common sense should go hand in hand.

Pause. Eyes closed. Breathe.

God, how he wished Cass were there. He'd been sentenced to another month of anxiety, awaiting a trial he might not be strong enough to see through and might not even *want* to see through.

He froze on his apartment steps, closed his eyes, and concentrated on breathing, but neither his heart nor his hyperventilating would slow. The pounding in his head rumbled like a race car's engine as the driver revved it over and over again.

"Cass?" He blinked through the pain. Her platinum hair swirled as she turned to face him, like silk dancing on the wind. She stood at the top of the stairwell with her arms crossed, frowning. Her pink scarf flittered in the same breeze as her hair, though he couldn't feel it.

"It's not my fault. I don't know..."

Jaden shook his head, and her hair whirled about her and became translucent, turning the rest of her translucent as well, like clouded glass seen through a clouded mind.

He pressed his eyes shut. "What happened to you, it's not my fault." He choked on a sob. "You're not real. Oh god, I wish you were. I need you so badly. But *you're not real.*"

When he opened his eyes again, Cass was gone. He looked down the stairs but saw no one. White-knuckling the railing, he climbed one step then another on trembling legs and summoned the tiny reserve he had left to make it to the hallway. He wanted to crash onto his bed and close his eyes forever, safe from the outside world.

And maybe see Cass again. Truly see her.

His was a place that used to be safe, but the world had kicked and battered its way in, and he couldn't wash away the stains. Worse still, a piece of his inner sanctum had gotten out. Jaden's beloved cat, who was a piece of his sanity and sanctity, the glue that had held his tenuous connections, had been missing since that terrible night, and he hadn't held out much hope of ever seeing him again.

But something furry lay outside his door. "Rascal!" Jaden sprinted down the hall, toward the lump of fur and paws curled up at its threshold. He cried with a new kind of joy, finally finding a spark of hope in a season of darkness.

He reached the cat quickly and skidded to a stop then jumped back a step, repressing an urge to scream. The cat didn't respond to his approach. It didn't move a whisker.

Jaden dropped to his knees, his lizard brain registering what his higher functions struggled to comprehend. At first, he thought maybe the stress of being outside had been too much for Rascal. After all, the cat had been very ill. But one look at Rascal's oddly bent neck indicated something far more sinister at play. *What kind of person would kill a harmless, gentle cat?*

Someone with an agenda against me. Someone with a personal grudge. But the only one he'd let down was Cass. *The only one I've hurt—*

Jaden moaned loudly enough to disturb neighbors. Latches clicked as doors either opened for people to ogle his torment or locked to keep out his insanity.

No! He fumbled with his keys, crying freely as he tried to force them into the knob. He dropped them once then again. "That wasn't my fault!"

Despite the supernova blasting through his brain, he got the door open. Cass waited inside, smiling and welcoming him home.

He scooped up his cat, sandy flakes falling like snow from Rascal's fur, and showed his girlfriend—his love and loss.

She sat on his sofa and opened her arms to him. With his head reeling and his thoughts disintegrating, Jaden gently placed Rascal on his kitchen counter. Then he staggered over to the couch and face-planted into Cass's awaiting lap.

She stroked his hair. Part of him understood he was imagining her, but a bigger part, so willing, wanted and needed to accept the deception, if only a little longer. It wasn't healing. *But if what Dr. Clemson wants me to do is, then why does it hurt so damn much?*

"Don't go," he whispered, clinging to her legs and to her memory, like a child who was learning to swim and unwilling to let go of his father's arm. "I can't do this anymore. Not without you." But she was already fading, a throw pillow appearing where her legs had been, soft beneath his cheek.

She was dead, and he couldn't force her to stay. Rascal was too. And all of it was his fault.

CHAPTER 16

"I'm spending way too much time here lately," Royo said, pulling his Charger into the lot of the Prospero apartment complex at 300 North Street.

A straight-backed, plainclothes Officer Costa sat in the passenger seat, soaking up the hot sun through the open window. She smiled at him then forced away the grin. "If it were up to Sanders, I would have been here yesterday too. Did you hear about his cat?"

"No. What happened?"

"According to Sanders, someone broke its neck. The guy was a mess, calling me and demanding I do something. Had to refer him to animal control."

He parked in the fire lane behind a moving van and got out of the car. They walked unencumbered into the building because the movers had propped open both doors. He twirled his keyring around his finger then dropped the keys into his pocket. Waving a hand toward a couch in the lobby, he offered Costa a seat then kicked out the doorstops.

"Whatcha do that for?" Costa asked.

"To make sure no one slips past us."

"We're right here."

"Still, if true... that's pretty messed up, don't you think?"

"What is?"

"Sanders's cat. That someone would break its neck. Isn't that how serial killers always start?"

"I don't know. I'm more of a dog girl myself." Costa scowled. "But if anyone ever messed with one of my babies, I'd want someone to do something too. I'd be afraid of what I might do myself."

Royo grunted. Having no pets, he didn't really understand the fascination with things that crapped, urinated, and shed all over the house. He let out a sigh and focused on the entrance.

"So who exactly are we waiting for?"

"Fletcher's oxy comes through E-Z Scripts, a mail-order pharmacy. All his other meds come from in-house care. He's expecting a delivery between three and four today." Royo sat beside Costa on the couch. "There aren't too many people in the chain of custody. I want to confirm whether he's getting what he's ordering."

"And you don't suspect Fletcher of reselling them?"

"According to his wife, he *needs* the Endocet. The man's in a lot of pain and can't even get out of bed. And she says she can account for every bottle they've received."

Costa raised an eyebrow.

"I understand your skepticism. Even appreciate it." Royo rested his hands on his knees. "Of course, we'll confirm it all for ourselves. But I don't know. Having spoken to her on the phone... I just don't like them for it. Doesn't feel right. I think they're being used somehow. I have my suspicions, but let's see where the drugs lead us. Don't you ever get hunches? Go with your gut?"

"Hunches are based on knowledge and experience." She blushed. "I don't have enough of either yet."

"Don't sell yourself short. I think—"

A buzz came from the entranceway. A young black man with braided hair under a red E-Z Scripts hat stood patiently in the breezeway, his E-Z Scripts red polo tucked into his dark jeans. He held an eight-by-twelve cardboard-colored padded envelope in one hand and a small, rectangular black box in the other. Catching Royo's stare, he offered a nod.

Another buzz, and the E-Z Scripts employee stepped into the lobby. He trotted past Royo and Costa and bounded up the stairs. Royo and Costa followed.

Fletcher's apartment was on the second floor. Mr. E-Z Scripts moved so quickly that by the time Royo and Costa reached the landing, he was taking back the pen to his electronic signature machine as a thick white forearm retreated into Fletcher's apartment. The door closed. Mr. E-Z Scripts gave the officers a once-over, nodded again, and walked toward them.

When he was within a few steps, Royo pulled out his badge. "Detective Asante Royo. This is Detective Megan Costa, Fall River PD." He glanced over to see if Costa reacted to her sudden fictitious promotion. To her credit, her expression remained flat.

"Do you mind if we ask you a few questions?"

The young man tensed. "What about?"

"What's your name?"

"John."

"That it?"

"John's fine until I know why you're asking."

"Okay, John." Royo said the man's name as if his tongue disliked forming it. "Can you tell us what you just delivered?"

"No." John frowned. "I can't. Confidentiality. Besides, I don't know what's in the bags anyway. I deliver what I'm told to deliver where I'm told to deliver it."

"Can you tell me *who* you were delivering it to?"

"Like I said—"

Royo held up his hand. "I know. Confidentiality." He stepped closer to John, who didn't flinch. "How about this, then? I'll say what I know, and you nod if I'm right." He smiled. "No harm in that, right? Confirming what I already know?"

John shrugged. "Maybe. What do you know?"

"I know that you were delivering medication to Edward Fletcher."

John nodded.

"And I know what the medication is for."

John sneered. "I told you—"

"I know. You don't know what's in the bags. I'm not asking you to confirm it." Royo considered the size of the envelope. It had seemed awfully big for one bottle of Endocet. He took a chance. "And I know that package had two bottles of pills in it."

John hesitated then shook his head slowly.

"Three?"

He nodded.

Royo looked at Costa and saw her understanding as the trenches in her forehead smoothed. Three bottles were a heck of a lot of oxy to be getting in one order.

"And Mr. Fletcher didn't sign for it?" Officer Costa asked.

She looked apologetically at Royo, who nodded, encouraging her to jump in whenever she wanted.

John took the question as a statement and nodded.

Royo sighed and *tsk*ed. "I'm afraid I'm going to have to ask you who did."

"I can't answer that." John raised his arm in front of his chest, holding up the electronic signature device, screen out. "He's still in there. Why don't you go ask him yourself?" He tapped the device, drawing Royo's attention to it.

Royo nodded. He read the name still on the screen. "Thank you, John."

John nodded and walked past them then hustled down the stairs and was gone.

Costa shrugged. "I'm guessing you don't suspect our friend John." Costa's mouth curled at the corner. "Seemed kind of suspicious to me."

"Suspicious of us." Although he didn't think ill of Costa, he doubted she would understand. "It's a minority thing."

"But you're a minor—"

"Doesn't matter. A cop is a cop. Hard for some to trust." He tapped Costa on the shoulder and laughed. "But yeah, a white cop is worse."

"White people don't trust us these days either." She smiled uneasily. "Okay, so why not him? A hunch again?"

"What's his motive? Sure, whoever's inside could be giving him a kickback. But we didn't see any such exchange. Everything looked aboveboard in the transfer, and I believe John when he says he doesn't know what's in the bags. He could have delivered three bottles of super-charged Ex-Lax, for all he knows."

"That a thing?"

"Probably." Royo looked down the hall at Fletcher's closed door. "My money's on the signatory. Does the name Dmitri Petrakis mean anything to you?"

Costa bit her lip then shook her head. "No, sir."

"Well, call it in. Get someone to run a check on the name before we—"

Fletcher's door opened, and a man in blue scrubs stepped out. He looked like an Olympic gymnast and had sleeve tattoos running up wiry muscles. A hairless streak ran through the middle of one of his dark eyebrows, as if a scar prevented the hair from growing there. A plastic bag hung loosely from his grip.

His dark-brown marble eyes locked on Royo's, and they held each other's gaze in silence. The man's eyes twitched a little wider.

Royo gasped and reached for his gun as the man turned to run. "Freeze! Police!" He charged after him. "Cover the front!" he shouted back to Costa.

The man in scrubs was younger and healthier and had a thirty-foot-or-so lead on Royo. He was leaping down the stairs, heading for the building's side exit, before Royo had started giving chase. That gave the man three choices: he could circle to the front parking lot, where Officer Costa would cut him off; he could dash straight out from the side door into thick woods; or he could turn toward the back of the building, where a thin line of sparse hedges separated a short lawn from the freeway. Royo didn't feel like wearing thorns and ticks, so he prayed for anything but the woods.

As he reached the top of the stairs, the door crashed open below followed by a metallic clang resembling the sound of a cymbal. He jumped down the stairs, clearing all but the last two. The lip caught his heel and sent him stumbling into the wall beside the door. A little shaken but otherwise unharmed, he burst through the door and slammed into someone, knocking him over.

"Hey!" the stranger whined and stood, dusting the gravel off his palms.

Royo saw no sign of the man in scrubs. Bouncing on his toes and glancing around feverishly, he was barely aware of the person in front of him. "Which way?"

"Why don't you watch where... Detective Royo?"

At the sound of his name, Royo focused on the man: Judge Cullen's law clerk. "What...?" It didn't matter. He seized the clerk's arms. "Did you see him? Which way?"

"Who?" The clerk's eyebrows formed a *V* then flattened. "Oh, that man who just came out? He went around the back."

"Thanks." Royo rushed past a dented aluminum trash can toward the back of the complex. Working on instinct, he checked the can as he passed and caught a glimpse of a plastic bag on top.

Wheezing, he rounded the building and, seeing no one, bent and rested his hands on his knees. He looked around for footprints, but the ground was dry, and the tall grass showed no signs of trespass.

"You sure he went..." he started, heading back to the side of the building, but the law clerk was gone.

Officer Costa rounded the opposite corner. "Where is he?"

Royo shrugged. "Got away, I guess. Just means we have to do a little more work before we pick him up."

"On what exactly?"

He stood tall and strutted with exaggerated swagger over to the garbage can. "Oh, I'd say possession with intent to distribute." He smiled, but as he looked into the bin, his smile fell away. The plastic bag was gone.

CHAPTER 17

Voir dire had started the last week of September, and Heather felt good about the jury selected. Pulled from a community tired of crime and polluted with lowlifes and filth, the jury could easily have consisted of twelve men and women who would have applauded Jaden Sanders's actions on the night in question and equated his vigilantism with justice. *Street justice.* Instead, she had been able to pluck several jurors who didn't flinch at the commonwealth's questions and—although they wouldn't openly admit to it—believed police arrested criminals, and only criminals were prosecuted. Everyone was guilty unless proven innocent. She'd even managed the nearly unheard of and seated a lawyer. They were almost always granted carte blanche not to participate in civic duty or even show up to jury selection, but Heather had fought to keep him on, believing him an early-Justice Scalia, black-letter-law type, like her.

And why not? Heather could establish all the elements of a crime and could show that Jaden Sanders had committed that crime. She could only hope the jury would see this glaring truth and not be dissuaded by muddied water, half morals, or street justice.

Everything had gone Heather's way so far—well, almost everything. She'd won the fight on admissibility of Tresser's affidavit as a dying declaration, which she'd assisted Tresser to write in one of his rare lucid moments. But she'd lost the fight on Sanders's psych records, though she hadn't pressed too hard. The records, if anything, supported an insanity defense. But given Blount's curious adamant opposition to their admission—except to the limited extent they might be used to show *mens rea*—and his assertion that his client would not be pursuing an insanity defense, Heather counted that argument a win too.

Blount had always been a difficult adversary, but he seemed to have truly dropped the ball. Temporary insanity was by no means an easy defense to make but one certain facts tended to support. He hadn't even proposed a jury instruction along those lines.

Under pressure, Heather had even tried to resolve the matter with a voluntary-manslaughter plea. She'd offered a fair deal, lenient enough by even her boss's standards. Sanders had balked at the opportunity, choosing to face life in prison when a few years maximum were being dangled in front of him like the carrot before the donkey.

She glanced at her opponent, who stood straight-backed and poised, either projecting real confidence or faking it well. Blount hadn't even sought a delay on competency grounds. Sanders's mental health was sure to come into play. She would have to skirt delicately around his shaky composition to avoid raising it as an issue at trial. Yet nothing of the sort had come up in any of the pretrial motions or legal arguments. And if Blount wasn't going to raise it, her lips were sealed.

Again, she looked over at the table beside her. Giles Blount stood by his client and offered her a nod. She nodded back, suppressing a smile. She had him.

Do I? Heather frowned as her butterflies momentarily flapped their wings and spread self-doubt. She always went through pretrial jitters, but the current one had her shaken. She was confident she was doing the right thing but not one hundred percent. Then there was Blount. She couldn't read him to tell whether the bravado was genuine or a façade. She'd been in the game long enough to predict an opponent's defense before it was made, pick it apart, and exploit its weaknesses. But Blount's strategy seemed no more complex than to state that his client was innocent.

No backup plan. All or nothing. A roll of the dice.

Which meant she only needed to prove Sanders was guilty. Heather set her jaw and nodded. She knew how to do that.

Before the jury entered, Blount had moved for a directed verdict, which the judge summarily denied without argument. Surely Blount had expected as much, and she would need to reface the motion at the end of the commonwealth's case and again at the end of the trial—a waste of time but all part of the criminal-justice process. Without a deal, the case was going to the jury.

She tucked a strand of hair behind her ear and straightened. She hadn't achieved a 95 percent conviction rate by being timid. And she hadn't done it by only trying obvious winners either. She'd done it by being better, smarter, and sharper than her opponents, letting the old boys club believe their plainly pigheaded view that an attractive blonde couldn't be as bright as or, in her case, brighter than them.

Sanders sat beside her opponent, gnawing on his thumbnail. She felt nothing but revulsion at the sight of him. He was a messy and nervous man hoping to get away with what he'd done. She's seen homeless people better put together than him and more worthy of her sympathy. After the trial, her conviction rate would be increasing to 95.3.

"All rise!" a court officer bellowed as the jury entered the courtroom and filled the chairs in the box to her right.

Once permitted to sit, Heather retreated to her thoughts. As the judge went through his introductory comments to those in attendance—the press, who were out in full, and the jury—she made last-minute tweaks and mental notes on words she should stress or inflect in her memorized opening remarks. Trial was as much about theatre and pageantry as it was about justice and law, sometimes more. She didn't have to be right. She just needed to make the jury believe she was.

Heather received a slight blow when she noticed that the lawyer hadn't been chosen as foreperson. Still, the MBTA driver who'd been selected would serve nearly as well.

A microphone squealed, then the session clerk read the indictment and charges against Jaden Sanders.

"Is the commonwealth prepared to make its opening statement?" Judge Cullen's vulture-like gaze landed on Heather.

She smoothed out her suit as she stood. After glancing down at the bullet points listed on the sheet of paper in front of her, she cleared her throat and approached the jury, leaving her notes right where they were. She didn't need them.

"May it please the court, counsel, members of the jury." Heather strode closer to the jury box, hands folded in front of her. She made eye contact with each juror, noted who made eye contact back, and went to work.

"Throughout this trial, you will likely hear a lot of conjecture—reasons why certain people may have done what they did, not only concerning the defendant, Jaden Sanders..." She waved an arm toward him. "But all other important players that make up the events you will soon learn about. You may hear emotional arguments. You may have personal opinions that may influence how you view the facts. But I caution you not to let them do so. Your job here today is far too important to be influenced by sentiment or bias."

Tucking a loose strand of hair behind her ear, Heather continued, "As the judge instructed you moments ago, you have only one job to do here today: to hear the facts and apply the law to them. All that matter are *facts* and *law*." She accentuated the words by mashing her fist against her palm. "Everything else is clutter, hogwash, bullsh—" She tucked her chin, bit her lip, and grinned, flashing her perfect smile for each member of the jury while pretending to have almost slipped.

"Well, you'll hear it all, and I'm confident you'll know how to separate the wheat from the chaff. The facts from the fluff." She slid her hand along the railing then paused at its end before turning for dramatic effect. "And in applying the facts to the law, you'll have one question to answer: 'Is Jaden Sanders guilty of the crime for which he's been charged?'"

She pressed her lips into a tight line. "Now, certainly, I don't make light of that decision. It impacts not only the defendant but also whether justice is done for the family of his victim. If you remove all the clutter and apply the law as explained to you to the established facts, you may find your decision becomes an easy one. The outcome is clear and simple."

Only one of the jurors, a heavyset African American woman in a sharp business suit, looked disinterested, her eyelids droopy. Two others, with their furrowed brows and flat lips, appeared cynical. Heather mentally checked them off as three she would need to win over before the close of testimony.

"And the facts are simple. What they show is a tale of a hunter becoming the hunted, a series of actions transpiring over the course of one evening that turned the defendant, Jaden Sanders, from a victim of a break-in into a murderer, by every definition of the word."

Heather paused and pulled on the ends of her jacket. "On Thursday, August 11, 2022, at approximately 5:40 a.m., the defendant awakened to the sound of pounding on his apartment door, apartment 314 at the Prospero apartment complex located at 300 North Street, Fall River, Massachusetts. Three men—Morton Tresser, Kealan Grady, and Leonard Malden—were outside the defendant's apartment, unarmed but clearly up to no good. The only evidence of their intent came from Tresser, now deceased, who stated they had gone to the defendant's apartment to beat him up. The commonwealth does not dispute that Tresser, Malden, and Grady were at the apartment with criminal intent and even with the intent to harm the defendant."

Heather paused and scanned the eyes of the jurors. She even had the sleepy juror's attention then. She'd exposed the primary flaw in her case and laid it bare before them at a time she could control how it was delivered, where she could appear honest while minimizing its impact. *Time to bring them into the fold.*

"When the defendant refused to let them in, Mr. Tresser and his companions broke in the door. The defendant grabbed a butcher knife and a paring knife from his kitchen drawer and hid with them in the bedroom. He did not call the police, cry out for help, or attempt to notify anyone of his danger.

"Instead, he lay in wait, concealing his weapons from his would-be attackers. After Tresser, Malden, and Grady gained access to the apartment, they cornered the defendant, who then killed Grady with his butcher knife and Malden with his paring knife in a gruesome fashion."

Heather examined the jury and saw equal parts skepticism and cringing. But the line had been cast, the hook set, and the reeling begun. Her line was sturdy. It would hold. She had no intention of letting any of her twelve little fishies get away.

"The defendant has not been charged with a single crime relating to the deaths of Mr. Malden and Mr. Grady. His sole crime concerns the death of Morton Tresser. The evidence will show that Tresser, out-armed and outmatched, attempted to flee the apartment. It will further show that not only did Sanders chase down Tresser and block him from fleeing, but he also stabbed Tresser, who had not laid a finger on Sanders, a total of twenty-eight times. Finally, the evidence will show that the defendant, after becoming the aggressor and acting with excessive force, willingly, knowingly, and maliciously slaughtered Tresser, *stabbing him in the back*, when he instead may have let Tresser escape, called the police, and allowed law enforcement to do its job. As witnesses will testify, the defendant not only handed out vengeance as he saw fit but was overjoyed to do so... overjoyed to kill a fleeing, unarmed, and totally incapacitated man!"

She pounded on the railing for emphasis then straightened and refolded her hands in front of her. "Some of you probably already see the violent and despicable crime in the defendant's actions, while others likely have formed an opinion that the three men"—she scrunched up her nose—"maybe got what they deserved. Three men, all dead, paid up for their crimes in the most absolute way, while the defendant walked away without a scratch."

That last part was technically untrue, but fighting over a bruised wrist would have diminished Blount's credibility, had he objected. She glanced over her shoulder but saw no movement from the defense table.

"But you must wipe your mind of those initial impressions, whatever they may be. Your civic duty is to hear the facts presented and determine what is truth and what is clutter. You will then be instructed on the law and asked to apply those facts to it."

She spread her arms along the rail. "In doing so, ladies and gentlemen of the jury, you will find that all the evidence adds up to one clear and undeniable conclusion: that Jaden Sanders, after any attack on him had concluded, willfully and knowingly pursued and repeatedly stabbed a fleeing man to death. Under the laws of the Commonwealth of Massachusetts, that constitutes murder in the second degree. I know you will see justice done here in this courtroom, where it belongs. Thank you."

Heather walked light-footed back to her table, where she scanned the jury, divining what she could from their expressions. Then she sat back and focused all her attention on Mr. Giles Blount and the story she would need to show was false.

"Counsel for the defendant?" Judge Cullen called.

Blount stood, his conservative gray suit ballooning over a chest full of hot air. He rested a hand briefly on his client's shoulder then walked silently toward the jury box. All eyes watched him, while Heather studied the watchers.

"Esteemed jurors. You've probably all seen enough TV to know how this works. In every criminal case, the burden of proof is on the prosecution to prove beyond a reasonable doubt that the accused committed the crime he stands accused of. What that means, essentially, is that the prosecution gets to go first in an effort to try to convince you of a story: a recitation of so-called '*facts*'"—Blount made air quotes—"that the state will claim meet each element of the crime charged. Here, that crime is murder."

Blount studied his shoes. "Let that sink in for a moment. My client, Jaden Sanders"—he pointed—"sits over there accused of the big M. At the end of this trial, it will be your job to determine whether he is guilty of that crime or not."

He paced along the railing. "Murder..." Borrowing a page from Heather's book, he turned on his heel and faced the jury. The corner of his mouth turned upward.

"Now, the prosecution is going to lay out certain facts it says show beyond a reasonable doubt my client committed murder. It's going to downplay or outright ignore facts it doesn't want you to give any weight to. Facts you'll likely hear in cross-examination of the witnesses or when the defense has its turn to present its case."

Blount leaned into the box as if he were having a heart-to-heart with the jurors and lowered his voice. "Facts the prosecution calls *clutter*. Facts like... well, how about the fact that three men broke into my client's apartment while he slept, with the intent to cause my client serious bodily harm?" His voice rose. "Or how about the fact that my client was placed in fear for his life? Three attackers against one. But instead of allowing himself to be beaten, to be murdered, he fought back. Exercised his God-given, constitutionally granted right to fight back. And how about one more, like the fact that had my client *not* defended himself the way he did, you might be sitting here hearing a case against three men instead of one, three known criminals engaged in a felonious home invasion, while my client lay dead in the morgue!"

He took a breath. "Now, Jaden Sanders doesn't have to prove a thing here today. No, that burden is all on her."

Heather bristled as she regarded the finger accusatorily pointing her way. Her face heated, but she quickly quelled her rising discontent. "Never let them see you sweat" was a mantra as true in the courtroom as it was in life.

"And she has to prove, beyond a reasonable doubt, that Jaden Sanders was no longer in fear for his life when he stabbed Morton Tresser. That he was no longer acting in self-defense. At the same time, the prosecution will fully admit—in fact, has already conceded—that my client acted in self-defense with respect to the two other deceased criminals."

Blount pointed at Heather again. "She'll want you to believe that at some point during the break-in and attack, Morton Tresser, a career criminal engaged in a terrible and terrifying felony, somehow became a victim."

Blount pursed his lips and shook his head. "The evidence you'll be presented with won't make Morton Tresser into a victim. There is no assembly of the facts that ever would. No, the evidence will show that my client acted in self-defense when he was attacked in his home by three men on August 11, 2022, and that self-defense resulted in Morton Tresser's death."

"Again, the prosecution has to prove that, beyond a reasonable doubt, my client murdered Morton Tresser and that Jaden Sanders was not justified in defending himself. If even only a part of you thinks that my client was justified in defending himself the way he did against three home invaders, you must find him not guilty."

The jurors followed Blount's every movement. They were listening. Heather only hoped they were entertained rather than sold.

"You, the jury, will soon hear all the facts of the case. You will determine how much weight to give each fact and the credibility of each witness. You may... No, you are *encouraged* to view those facts in light of your life experiences and that sometimes-latent virtue I know each of you possesses: common sense. And when you do, I am confident you will return the only possible verdict: not guilty. Thank you."

Blount sat down. Heather felt he'd given as good as she had and maybe even better. But her case wouldn't be won on an opening statement. It would be won on facts and law.

She straightened her notes and prepared to call her first witness.

CHAPTER 18

"The prosecution calls Detective Asante Royo."

Here we go again. Royo plodded through the courtroom to the witness stand, where he was summarily sworn in. He looked up at Attorney Laughton and instantly got a feeling of déjà vu.

Her first twenty questions were the same twenty Sanders's attorney had asked him at the motion to dismiss, doing nothing to alleviate that feeling. He answered them robotically. The low hum of the stenographer muttering into her mouthpiece threatened to lull him into a trance. The dim lighting in that hallowed hall paired poorly with his undercaffeinated and underrested mind.

Worse, Laughton's structured questioning lacked any dynamic. She stuck to a script, one he'd heard a hundred times, throwing him softball after softball and easing him into his testimony to make him comfortable before kicking over his chair. Laughton went through his professional experience, his promotions and accommodations, and his entire resume, almost all the way back to his teens, when he'd served as a lifeguard at a public pool.

With the preliminaries done, Laughton carried a document over from her table: the police report. *Still, no sweat.* She ran through it with him, having him confirm the events described therein without putting any spin on the fact that Tresser and his coconspirators had broken into the apartment and intended harm to Sanders. As far as Royo could tell, Laughton was making the defense's case for it, and *that* forced him to focus. He shifted uneasily, knowing better than to trust a lawyer, even one supposedly on law enforcement's side.

Laughton looked up from a notepad she'd tucked behind the police report. "Did you previously testify in this matter?"

"Yes."

Laughton rifled through the pages of her pad then paused on what Royo suspected was a record of his testimony from the motion to dismiss but decided against using it. He frowned. She was trying to trap him, to see if he would answer something differently than he had previously or make him do so through some wicked trick of the tongue.

He swallowed something bitter and awaited the next question. Only lawyers could make truths into lies.

Laughton tapped a pen against her lower lip. "When you arrived on scene, who did you think had committed a crime?"

"Jaden Sanders."

"Why?"

Royo glanced at the defense table. Sanders looked feverish, beads of sweat carving rivulets down his ashen face. Royo was struck by the irony of how much calmer the office worker had looked immediately after killing three people.

He snapped his attention back to the prosecutor. "Because he was covered in blood that did not appear to be his."

"Did the defendant have any physical injuries?"

"None that I could see at that time."

"Did you see any injuries at any other time?"

"Did I see?" Royo thought about how to answer. He didn't actually see Sanders's injured wrist, but it had been in the report. "No, but I—"

"Did you see the injuries Morton Tresser sustained?"

"Yes."

"Could you describe them to the court?"

Royo turned and faced the jury. "Tresser had received multiple stab wounds about the face and torso. His arms and hands also sustained several cuts, and he'd been stabbed once in the back. He'd lost a lot of blood and was unconscious when I arrived."

Laughton went back to her notepad and retrieved copies of a document she'd tucked within its crease. She handed one to Sanders's attorney and another to the clerk for the judge. "Your Honor, may I approach the witness?"

"You may," Judge Cullen said.

Laughton handed a copy of the document to the court officer, who in turn handed it to Royo. He grumbled quietly as he read the title at the top: Affidavit of Morton L. Tresser.

Sanders's attorney rose. "Your Honor, we would like to renew our objection to the admissibility of this affidavit and our motion to suppress any line of questioning stemming from it."

"Your motion has been heard. Denied. Objection overruled. The document has already been included as an exhibit in the record."

Although the affidavit repulsed him, he hadn't been surprised by it, having received a copy for inclusion in his case files. It was only two pages long, and he had familiarized himself with its contents.

Laughton stepped so close that Royo could smell her lavender skin cream. "Detective Royo, could you please read that document for the court?"

He flipped to the second page. "The whole thing?"

"Why don't we start with the first five paragraphs?"

Royo cleared his throat and adjusted on the seat. "I, Morton L. Tresser, of 736 Highland Road, Fall River, Massachusetts, do solemnly swear and affirm as follows: one, on August 11, 2022, Kealan Grady, Leonard Malden, and I went to the apartment of Jaden Sanders at 300 North Street, Apartment 314, Fall River, Mass-achusetts, with the intent to cause him bodily harm. Two, upon ar-riving at Mr. Sanders's apartment, we proceeded to break down the door. Three, my intent in doing so was to hurt Mr. Sanders, as he was abusive..."

That was not the document he'd been provided previously. It had been edited sometime after being obtained from a quickly dying man and that man's ultimate death. He flipped to the signature page and saw Tresser's signature, which was big, curvy, and zigzagging, as if written with an unsteady hand—just as he remembered it. Assuming it was Tresser's signature, Royo wondered if Laughton could have doctored the testimony after Tresser's death.

"Detective Royo?"

He lifted his head to see Laughton staring at him with an eyebrow raised, one hand on her hip. "Sorry, um... I've never seen this document before."

"You weren't asked if you had. Please, continue."

He scanned the paper, still having difficulty processing what he was reading. After clearing his throat, he read on. "Three, my intent in doing so was to hurt Mr. Sanders, as he was abusive to our mutual friend Cassidy Branigan, who committed suicide in January 2022. I considered him responsible for her death."

Sanders sprang from his seat. The sides of his head were slick with sweat. His lawyer was on him before the judge could throw a tantrum with his gavel, coaxing him gently back into his seat. The attorney whispered through gritted teeth into his client's ear. The muscles in his arms strained, and a vein in his neck swelled as he tried to keep Sanders under control. Sanders's features were contorted into the exemplification of contempt and rage. His nostrils flared like a those of a bull about to charge, his skin was the color of rare meat, and his eyes stared with the full focus of a predator targeting its prey—Royo. He knew that face: the face of a killer.

Royo gulped then cleared his throat and continued reading, his voice trailing off here and there as his mind lingered on the explosiveness of Sanders's anger and how it might relate to that last statement. He'd already suspected foul play in Sanders's girlfriend's death. As it turned out, he wasn't the only one with suspicions. But the only link he'd been able to find between Sanders and Tresser was the dead woman. Perhaps that was link enough.

Why didn't Laughton share this version with me? Did she withhold information regarding an ongoing investigation merely as a play to get a reaction out of me? Royo huffed. *Except Branigan's case isn't actually ongoing... not officially.*

He glanced repeatedly at Sanders as he stumbled through the next two paragraphs. The temperamental man had lost fuel and sat low in his seat, clearly still unsettled, running his hands through his hair and muttering as his gaze darted about.

"Four, we cornered Mr. Sanders in his bedroom, where he was hiding. I could see no weapons in his possession. Five, Mr. Malden tried to pull Mr. Sanders up to his feet. Mr. Sanders revealed a blade hidden in the sleeve of his robe, which he used to stab and kill Mr. Malden before I even knew what was happening. Upon seeing Mr. Malden mortally wounded, Mr. Grady attacked Mr. Sanders. At which point, Mr. Sanders revealed a second blade. He killed Mr. Grady with it, plunging the knife into Mr. Grady's eye."

"Thank you, Detective." Laughton paced toward the jury box then turned.

"Do you have any reason to dispute Tresser's description of events in paragraphs one through five of his affidavit?"

"The events?" Royo shrugged. "Not exactly, but—"

"Please read paragraph six."

Royo frowned and glared at Laughton, who'd cut off his answer one time too many, but he did as instructed. "Upon seeing my friends stabbed and dying and fearing a similar fate, I attempted to flee. Mr. Sanders blocked my path. I pleaded for him to let me by, but he came closer, smiling with the butcher knife raised. Again, I begged for him to let me go, and he said, 'You're not going anywhere.' I backed away and circled toward the bedroom door then backed toward the apartment door, all the while pleading with Mr. Sanders not to attack me. I made no movement of any kind toward Mr. Sanders. Nevertheless, he attacked, pulling me toward him by my jacket and stabbing me over and over again. Every time I tried to block the strikes with my hands and arms, the pain was unbearable, and I had to pull away. This allowed him to stab my body and face. In all, he stabbed me approximately twenty-eight times about my hands, arms, body, and face."

Laughton pressed. "And the next paragraph?"

"I fell, and Mr. Sanders fell on top of me. I managed to buck him off and crawl into the hallway, where I felt his knife stab me in my back."

When he'd finished reading, Royo looked up at the jury. Their faces were awash in horror, their eyes wide and their mouths agape. They were eating up Tresser's rotten sob story, and he'd been forced to feed it to them. He suddenly felt uncomfortable in his skin.

Laughton's chin dipped, and she worried her lip. Royo could tell she was formulating a doozy of a question, probably one she would ask in such a way that he would have no choice but to answer the way she wanted him to. The defense would always be able to clarify through cross-examination, assuming Sanders's attorney was paying attention. He glanced at Blount, who still held his client at bay. They might have looked like a couple, if not for the fact that Sanders was pressing his palms so hard against the table that the blood had drained from them.

Laughton looked up. "Did you see any evidence to support the allegations you read from paragraphs six and seven of Morton Tresser's affidavit?"

"Yes." He did not wait for the follow-up question before adding, "Tresser had defensive wounds indicative—"

"What are defensive wounds?"

"Just as they sound: injuries sustained when an individual is defending against an attack."

"And what sort of defensive wounds did Morton Tresser have?"

"He was stabbed and cut about his arms and hands."

"How does this show defense?"

"It suggests Tresser had thrown up his arms in an attempt to block or deflect the knife strikes."

"Did you find any weapons on Morton Tresser?"

"No."

"On any of his cohorts?"

"Aside from those stuck in them?" Royo grimaced, immediately regretting his sarcasm and anticipating the jab back. "No."

"And those *stuck in* them belonged to the defendant, correct?"

Blount stood. "Objection. Leading."

Judge Cullen ignored the defense attorney, but Laughton corrected her question anyway. "The only weapons on scene... who used weapons that night?"

"Mr. Sanders."

"Anyone else?"

"No."

"Do you—"

"Wait. The answer to the last—"

"Let me finish my question, Detective."

Blount rose. "Judge, can the witness be allowed to finish his answer?"

Judge Cullen, not exactly following procedure, since Royo *had* finished his answer then thought better of it, smiled and seemed to take silent pleasure in disrupting the prosecution's case. "That seems like a reasonable request, counsel." He leaned toward Royo. "Detective, please finish your answer."

Royo nodded. "Grady attacked Sanders with a lamp. He struck Sanders across the wrist." He fidgeted. The point seemed of little consequence after all the to-do preceding it.

"And who did that lamp belong to, Detective?"

"Jaden Sanders."

"Do you have any evidence to dispute Morton Tresser's statement that he was attempting to flee when the defendant stabbed him repeatedly?"

"I don't think the evidence is conclus—"

"And the knife in Tresser's back, is that conclusive that Tresser was trying to flee?"

Blount rapped on the table. "Objection! Argumentative!"

"Withdrawn," Laughton snapped, her words biting with disgust. Frowning, she paused in front of Royo. "Was Tresser stabbed in the back?"

"Yes," Royo answered then quickly added, "Once."

"So let me ask again. Do you have any evidence *to dispute* Morton Tresser's statement that he was attempting to flee when the defendant stabbed him repeatedly?"

Royo sighed. "I don't know."

"When you first saw the defendant that night, all covered in Morton Tresser's blood, did he appear frightened to you?"

"He appeared to be in shock."

"Did he seem afraid?"

"No."

"Did he show any remorse?"

"No."

"Did he show any emotion at all?"

"No. Like I said, he appeared to be—"

"Did you take a statement from the defendant?"

"Of course."

"When did you take his statement?"

"Four days after the break-in."

"Where?"

"At my office."

"Did the defendant say in that statement who he thought was knocking at his door that night?"

Blount stood. "The defense renews its objection to the admiss—"

"Already decided, counsel," the judge stated. "You may answer, Detective."

Royo peered suspiciously at Laughton, wondering if she knew something else she wasn't sharing with him. "Yes."

"Who did he think was at his door?"

"His girlfriend."

"Cassidy Branigan?"

"I believe so, yes."

"Branigan—she's dead, isn't she, Detective?"

"Yes."

"And she was dead prior to the night in question?"

"Yes."

"Why would the defendant lie and tell you he thought his dead girlfriend was at the door?"

Blount sprang to his feet. "Objection!"

"Withdrawn." Laughton leaned into the box. "In fact, Detective, the defendant told you he thought his deceased girlfriend was home, correct?"

"Objection. Leading and relevance," Blount said. He hadn't even sat back down yet.

"Sustained." Judge Cullen shot Laughton a cautionary glare.

"Did the defendant tell you he thought his deceased girlfriend was home that night?"

"Yes."

"Did the defendant tell you why he thought Morton Tresser and his friends had arrived at his apartment that night?"

"He said that at the time of the home invasion, he thought Tresser and his crew had come from Brentworth—the psychiatric facility. But at the interview, he discounted that theory and believed the attack had something to do with a note."

"With respect to the note, can you please elaborate for the court?"

"Sure." Royo tented his fingers and leaned forward, curious as to why she wasn't pursuing the Brentworth angle. "He said that he had received a note on his door that complained about his slamming it. Or some neighbor had previously left a note. Mr. Sanders seemed very confused about it. I dismissed it as irrelevant at the time."

"Did you ever see this note?"

"No."

"Were any notes taken into evidence?"

"No."

"Did the defendant give you any other reason why those three men might have shown up at his door?"

"Other than Brentworth? I can't remember."

Laughton walked to her desk, picked up another stapled document, showed it to opposing counsel, and handed it to the court officer without asking if she could approach. The judge nodded, and the court officer handed the document to Royo.

He scanned the first page.

"Detective Royo, for the record, I am showing you a copy of the transcript of the statement you took from the defendant. Could you please turn to page seven and read paragraph three?"

Royo flipped through the pages, found the paragraph, and read it. "No, but before he kicked in the door, I caved and asked him what he wanted. He started screaming for me to open the door. He said there were consequences for what I had done earlier, and the only thing I could think of that might have upset anyone was how I reacted to that stupid note." He looked up at Laughton.

"Does that refresh your memory as to whether the defendant gave you an alternative reason for the three men's presence at his door that night?"

"Sort of. Mr. Sanders indicated that it might have been an act of revenge for something he'd done, which he thought had something to do with a note."

"How did Mr. Sanders appear to you during this statement?"

"Confused. Nervous. At times, angry."

"Remorseful?"

Royo chuckled then composed himself. "No."

"Did you form any opinion as to his credibility during his recorded statement?"

"I didn't think too much of it at the time. He wasn't being charged, and what he said with respect to the home invasion matched what was known at the time."

"And now? Do you have an opinion concerning his credibility during his recorded statement now?"

Royo scratched his stubble. "His testimony seemed confused."

"Unreliable?"

"Not necessarily." Royo studied Sanders, who stared blankly into space as if reliving that night had reset the shock of it upon him. "I don't know."

"Did you ever see any notes relating to this case?"

"No."

"Did you give the defendant any advice with respect to how to testify?"

Royo furrowed his brow. "No. Of course not."

"Please turn to page eleven, paragraphs two and three."

Royo read the cited portion of the transcript and swallowed. The taste of his saliva was vomitous. Begrudgingly, he raised his head, anticipating a question.

"Does that refresh—"

"I told him not to deviate from the testimony he had already given." Royo slouched.

"Why?"

"Because I didn't think he'd committed a crime, from what I'd seen and the testimony he'd given. I made the comment without thinking. I shouldn't have said that."

"Is it possible that you provided the defendant with a position that would best place him within the confines of the law?"

Blount was back on his feet. "Objection. Speculation."

The judge raised a hand, palm out. "I'll allow."

Royo bristled. "No, he'd already given his testimony at that time."

Laughton cocked her head and *tsk*ed like a parent scolding a child. "Is it possible you confirmed that the position the defendant was taking might be within the confines of the law?"

"Objection."

"I'll allow, but Ms. Laughton..."

Royo sighed. "I don't know. It's possible."

"And you understood at the time that the state could charge the defendant—that the defendant could be arrested and charged with the murder of Morton Tresser?"

"Yes."

Laughton paced. Her fingers fidgeted. After a moment, she took a chance. "And do you still think the defendant committed no crime?"

Royo sighed again, causing a crinkling sound in the microphone. "Now?" He pursed his lips and glanced at Sanders, who still appeared to be off in dreamland. "I don't know."

Laughton closed her notepad. "No more questions, Your Honor."

Blount stood and buttoned the top button of his suit jacket. With empty hands, he walked over to the witness box. "Detective Royo, did my client express what he was feeling at the time of the home invasion?"

Royo scratched his jaw. "Yes. He said he was afraid and felt like he had to kill them, or they would kill him."

Blount removed his glasses and polished them with a handkerchief. "He said more than that, didn't he, Detective? He said he was—" He put on his glasses and walked over to the defense table, leaned over it, and read from his legal pad. "Scared out of his freaking mind."

"Yes, I believe he did say that."

"Afraid for his life?"

"Yes."

"Do you have any reason to doubt that Jaden Sanders was, at all times during the morning when three strangers kicked down his door for the sole purpose of hurting him, in fear for his life?"

Royo nodded. The attorney was finally catching on that he had a friend on the stand. "None whatsoever."

"In your investigation, did you uncover any evidence that would contradict my client's statement that at all times during the three assailants' unlawful home invasion, he was in fear for his life?"

"No, I did not."

"In fact, Detective Royo, your investigation revealed no other statements regarding my client's state of mind at the time of the attack that in any way contradicts his statement to you that he was in fear for his life, correct?"

"That is correct."

Blount walked over to the defense table and smiled at his client. Sanders continued to chew his thumbnail, apparently not reassured by the favorable testimony. The defense attorney dropped off his legal pad and returned to his questioning. "Now, you previously testified at a preliminary hearing in this case. Did you not?"

"I did."

"And at that hearing, you testified that, neither on the night of the incident nor several weeks later at the hearing or at any time between did you believe that my client, Jaden Sanders, had committed a crime. Is that correct?"

"That's correct."

"A moment ago, you were asked if you believe Jaden Sanders committed the crime he's been charged with. The crime of murder for which he's being tried today. What was your response?"

"Objection." Laughton stood. "Asked and answered."

"Overruled."

"I don't know." Royo frowned. "I mean, my response was 'I don't know.'"

"In fact, you could have arrested Mr. Sanders on August 11, 2022, but decided not to. Correct?"

"That's correct."

"Why was that?"

"I didn't think he'd committed a crime."

"Is it fair to say, then, that you have doubts that my client, Jaden Sanders, committed any crime on the morning of August 11, 2022?"

"Objection."

"Overruled."

"That's fair to say."

"Then it's also fair to say that you, an officer of the law charged with enforcing it for the last nineteen years, don't know and, in fact, have serious doubts about whether my client should face any charges whatsoever relating to the death of Morton Tresser?"

"Objection."

"Withdrawn. No more questions, Your Honor."

After a short redirect, which Laughton used primarily to get him to repeat some of his more prosecution-favored answers, the judge dismissed Royo. A court officer led him out of the witness box and through the gate into the seating area, where he showed himself the rest of the way out. Exiting into the hall, he nearly bumped into Judge Cullen's law clerk for a second time that month.

"Excuse me," the clerk said, a broad smile across his face.

He tried to step around Royo and enter the courtroom, but he blocked his path.

"You're Anthony, right?"

"Yes." He extended his hand. "Anthony. Nice to see you again, Detective." He smiled like a clown on speed. "I'm sorry, but I've got to get back to work before Judge Cullen notices I'm missing. The man would prefer I go in my pants than miss a word of the trial."

"How do you think it's going in there?"

"Hard to say." He again tried to squeeze past Royo. "Now, if you'll excuse me..."

Royo stepped aside but held the door closed. "Been meaning to ask you—what brought you to Sanders's apartment complex that day I ran into you?"

Anthony shrugged. "Oh, you know. The judge wanted to get an idea of the layout to help him visualize the case, so, you know, of course he sent me." He bounced like a toddler who needed to pee. "I really have to get back inside."

Royo let him pass, narrowing his gaze on the young man. Anthony disappeared into the courtroom, leaving Royo to wonder why the law clerk had just lied.

CHAPTER 19

That's it? Jaden couldn't believe he'd had to sit through more than an hour of the detective's testimony without comment or defense, much of which he'd lost to a swirling pain and jumbled thoughts, only to have his lawyer ask like three questions when it was all over. *What about my side of the story? What about my rights?* Bewildered, he stared at Giles as the attorney sat back down beside him.

What was worse was the prosecution continued. Jaden's skin crawled as he listened to the medical examiner go through her report, describing how that sicko Tresser's wounds could only have been obtained while defending himself against Jaden's violent attack, as if the man who'd kicked in his door were some kind of saint. His stomach turned as he heard neighbor after neighbor testify to how he'd looked in the hallway. They said he'd held the knife while covered in blood, raving about slamming his door hard enough. He couldn't remember any of that. They'd all heard someone cry out for help and seen Jaden stab a downed man in the back. A psychologist opined on the mental state indicated by such an act—what he equated to bloodlust—and showed the jury how it was all corroborated by circumstantial evidence.

The worst part was that Jaden could deny none of it. The time following his hiding with the knives in the corner of his bedroom remained a blur, though his brain retained enough snippets of the action, playing it back as if via a slideshow behind his eyelids, that he could piece together the gist of what he'd done.

A paramedic followed the psychologist, echoing the intruder's apparent statement as he carted Tresser off to the hospital. "I tried to get away, but he wouldn't let me." Even the paramedic who'd treated Jaden on the scene testified that Jaden had said he'd killed his three attackers. And he had *killed* them, but he hadn't *murdered* them. *I'm not a murderer.*

All the evidence the commonwealth presented made him look like he was some sort of maniac. With his heart pounding, he stewed, simmering in his own sweat.

Under a microscope, with all eyes on him, Jaden suffered in silence. One of those stares belonged to that scrawny law clerk, the one who'd professed to be his friend in there. His eyes seemed to smile, like he enjoyed watching Jaden squirm. But seeing law at work was apparently more intriguing to him than the life at stake.

Then there was the judge—a cold, indifferent codger. He glared at Jaden as if he were a pesky obstacle standing in the way of an afternoon tee time. The session clerk was indifferent out of sheer obliviousness. His blank expression revealed either a spacy or an empty mind. In the stenographer's eyes, Jaden saw a monster reflected.

And worst of all was that prissy, perfect prosecutor. She reminded him of a Baptist preacher straight out of a comic book, all fire and brimstone, her righteous indignation having the power and will to see him burn.

Shifting from her condemning gaze, Jaden searched for a focus point somewhere between her and the judge. His eyes again landed upon the law clerk, who was sitting in his own special galley as if granted a box seat across from Lincoln at Ford's Theatre—so content to lounge in his seat on the sidelines, thinking himself above Jaden and the turmoil his life had become.

Jaden scowled. *You're not better than me. You're not so important.* He looked down at the table, letting out a breath as he ran his fingers through his hair. If the law clerk wouldn't help him, he would have to help himself. *Concentrate on what is important. Like your own testimony. What did you say to Royo about Cass? And the note? What did you say about the note?* He needed to get that straight. Of course, Cassidy was dead.

Cassidy...

Jaden flexed his fingers, and the pounding in his head dulled. Blinking, he tried to focus. He *had* gotten a note. He'd gotten one from Cassidy that had spawned their relationship, but he'd found another, too, an identical one, long after her death. *How? Why?*

He must have imagined the second note. Dr. Clemson had tried to sift through his confused mind. Jaden knew Cassidy was dead, no matter how much it hurt him to admit it. Still, he saw her sometimes, and she looked so real.

Felt real.

God, he missed her. He would have done anything to have her back. *Does it really matter if she isn't real, so long as she's there? Does it—*

That fucking law clerk! Still sitting alone in the otherwise-unused box, grinning like a hyena over crippled prey, he seemed purposely placed there to provoke Jaden. His features—high cheekbones, narrow face, and military-cut brown hair—were infuriatingly familiar, though Jaden wasn't sure where he might have seen the man before his arrest. If he'd had a rock, he might have hurled it at him and maybe knocked out some of those tombstone teeth.

Jaden grabbed his pants over his thighs and crumpled the material in his fists, taking his anger out on the fabric. He turned to the session clerk, the stenographer, then the court officers. Each avoided eye contact, as if he'd suddenly become contagious. And he knew what must have changed in his face to shift their gazes away: anger hardened his features, contorting them into something menacing and evil. Even the jurors wouldn't look at him. No one would. *No one except that fucking clerk.*

A headache reemerged behind his eyes, and his pulse beat in his skull.

He was vaguely aware of his attorney making some motion for a directed verdict, whatever that was, but soon, too, his voice faded out. All that remained was the *beat, beat, beat* of his heart and the locked gaze of that sniveling, lily-white, over-privileged law clerk.

Hands pulled him to his feet. "Get up!" Giles hissed.

Jaden blinked and scanned the courtroom. Everyone was standing, and the jury was leaving through a back door.

"We're done for today," his attorney whispered. "We'll present our case tomorrow, though we shouldn't have any case to present."

Jaden tried to shake away the cobwebs. "What are you talking about? All those things"—he nodded at Laughton, who stood oblivious to his reproach—"implied about me through her questions... I have to address them."

Giles grimaced. "Sometimes less is more. You may not think so, but we should have this case won. You don't need to convince all the jurors of your innocence, just one who won't cave under pressure. And I think we've got at least half of them. You risk everything by going on the stand. The state is begging for a chance to tear you a new one. Don't give it to them."

Jaden only half listened as the courtroom emptied. The law clerk winked at him then picked up his folders and followed the judge into his chambers.

Giles sighed. "We'll talk more outside. Come on."

He followed his attorney into the hall, where Giles gripped him under the arm and led him over to a quiet alcove. "You're dead set on testifying tomorrow, aren't you? As your counsel, I can't stress how strongly I advise against it."

"How else is the jury going to hear my side—"

"The jury doesn't need to hear your side!" Giles let out a breath and grabbed Jaden's arms. "They don't need to hear your side if the state can't prove its side first."

"If that hasn't happened, then why are we still going?"

Giles flinched then said, "It's standard bullshit. The judge doesn't want to have to make a call on something he can push on someone else."

Jaden squinted. Giles's answer left him wanting, but the pause before spoke an entire encyclopedia. *He's not confident we'll win.*

"Okay. Sleep on it. If you do decide you have to speak, despite my counsel, which is based on the many years of experience I have doing this, I'll be ready. Answer only the question I ask as it is asked. Don't explain or offer more than asked."

He crouched lower so that he was eye-to-eye with Jaden, almost close enough to kiss. "The same goes for every question Laughton asks. Just like we practiced. You got that?"

Jaden nodded.

"You'd better. She is going to try to twist every answer you give. Let her. Don't fight her. Don't argue any point. If something needs cleaning up, I will ask you the necessary questions. Be patient. Wait for them to come from me, or better yet, don't testify at all."

Jaden shook his attorney's hand and headed home to no one and nothing. He felt distracted by his attorney's admonition, that snotty law clerk's stare, and his own confusing prior testimony. He certainly hadn't meant to lie. He'd been doing so much better since he started seeing Dr. Clemson. *How could the attack not have rattled me? Or what happened to my cat? Or Cass?*

His breath hitched. *The jury will get that. They'll understand.*

He ate a light dinner and went to bed early. The hours ticked by slowly, and Jaden spent them staring at the cracks in the ceiling.

CHAPTER 20

Officer Costa smiled as Royo approached her desk. Somehow, she was still happy to be a cop.

Though her contentment wasn't quite infectious, it did take a little of the edge off Royo's surliness. He figured he must subconsciously like her uncalled-for optimism, since she'd become his go-to staff when he needed assistance. That, and she was proving competent beyond her years and experience.

"Good afternoon, Detective," she said, glancing up from her computer as she clickety-clacked away at her keyboard.

"What are you working on? Anything important?"

Costa stopped typing, sat back, and folded her hands on her desk. "Nothing that can't wait. You need me, sir?"

"Something came up at trial today—more evidence that Sanders might have had something to do with Cassidy Branigan's death. Tresser signed an affidavit stating that he went after Sanders as revenge for the way he abused Branigan. He suspected Sanders was somehow involved in her death."

Costa cocked her head. "I thought Sanders killed all three guys."

"He did. It's a long story. Well, it's a short story, but it doesn't matter. My point is the two cases are definitely connected. I'd like to try to get Branigan's medical records, if possible. At the very least, let's check the autopsy report again. All those old bruises and breaks, maybe they aren't that old after all, or maybe Sanders knew her longer than he's letting on. He certainly has a temper and may be prone to violence. His reaction to the break-in definitely shows he has it in him to deal out some hurt."

"I'll get on that right away, sir."

"Nope, that can wait until we get back. Grab your coat."

Costa did as ordered without question.

After stopping at his desk for the case file and walking out to the parking lot, they got into his Charger and headed off.

On the way to Sanders's apartment complex, he filled her in. "We asked Sanders's neighbors if they'd seen Morton Tresser and his goons around before. Some witnesses thought they had, but we never really locked down when or with whom they might have seen them. If they were Branigan's friends, that would bolster Tresser's testimony and cast a more negative light on Sanders's relationship with her. It's all one man's word against another's right now—something Sanders is quite familiar with—and it seems more likely that even if he'd been involved, he may only have driven Branigan to suicide, not actually killed her himself."

"Except..."

"Go ahead."

"Except for the bruise on Branigan's cheek."

And the placement. Royo remembered how Branigan had lain on her couch with one sneaker still on her foot, the other dangling off. He still couldn't put a finger on why that had bothered him so much—just one of those things at a crime scene that made it seem wrong and gave it the scent of foul play. Everything she needed to kill herself sat right beside her. Everything was so neat and tidy.

"Heck," Costa continued, "he might have slipped the oxys into her drink."

"True."

Royo headed up the drive to the apartment complex, still picturing Branigan's feet and, from there, widening to the whole tableau of her final state. He pulled into a spot in front of the office. "Let's find out what we can about Branigan first. Knowing how long she'd been here will at least give us a time frame for our investigation."

"Assuming Sanders met her here."

"Yes, assuming that." He shouldered open his door. "Let's go."

Climbing the steps to the office's entrance, he froze. "No, not the feet," he muttered.

"I'm sorry, sir?" Costa halted beside him.

A picture came into his mind as clearly as if he'd been transported back in time to Cassidy Branigan's crime scene. The dead woman lay flat on her back, her arms straight against her sides and her legs straight over the arm of the couch. An alarm sounded in his brain.

"It's like you thought, Costa, and what's been nagging me since we left that scene. By focusing on her feet, I keep missing the forest for the trees. People who overdose don't die like Branigan did, so neatly and peacefully. Ordered. She was like a doll on display. That's exactly what it was: a display, a staged scene. Her positioning was off in that it was too perfect."

Costa smirked. "So... suicide's off the table?"

"What are we doing here if we ever really thought it was on the table? But we certainly don't have enough to trump the medical examiner's findings. Let's keep digging." He hurried into the office with a renewed bounce in his step.

Inside, Royo's senses were bombarded. The smell of nicotine laced with his grandmother's perfume saturated the upholstery, while the number of phone lines ringing and going unanswered reminded him of a call center. Flashing lights indicated left messages.

He showed his badge, which was hardly necessary, given that Costa was in full uniform. He had yet to change out of the brown suit he'd worn to court. "I'm Detective Royo of the Fall River Police Department," he said to the middle-aged woman standing behind the counter. She wore slacks and a sweater, and her glasses hung on a chain over her bosom beside a name tag that read Maggie.

"What can I do for you, Detective?" she asked.

"We're looking into a former tenant of yours: Cassidy Branigan."

Maggie frowned. "The suicide? Apartment 315. Kind of a hard one to forget."

"Anyone living there now?" Royo asked. "We'd like to take another look around, if that's not a problem, and talk with some of the neighbors."

"No problem with me, Detective." Maggie muttered something to herself then added, "Can't rent that apartment anyway."

"Oh? No one wants it because of the suicide?" Costa asked.

"No. People around here don't care about any of that so long as the price is right." Maggie tapped her finger on a thick binder closed on the counter between them. "That apartment's been paid for through the end of the year. The state frowns on double leasing."

"Paid in advance for an entire year?" Royo gave Costa a quizzical look. "That's not normal, is it?"

"Not. At. All," Maggie said. "Though it's certainly welcomed. We have a hard time getting some people to pay at all." She shook her head. "Nope, the gent who's been paying the rent for that apartment comes by each January. He always pays the bill for the year."

Costa asked the question circling through Royo's mind. "Someone else was paying Branigan's rent?" She looked at Royo. "Didn't we look into that at the time?"

Royo swiveled his neck slowly. "There wasn't any reason to. Neighbors confirmed Branigan rented the apartment. If we were going to investigate it beyond that, we were cut short by the medical examiner's conclusion."

They both turned to Maggie, apparently with intensity enough to cause her to take a step back. She recovered, flapping a hand dismissively. "That girl never paid a dime for the place. If you ask me, she had herself a sugar daddy. Seemed like she had it pretty darn good. Can't understand why a sweet young thing like that would go and do what she did to herself, particularly if she had a man doting on her like that."

She batted her eyelashes at Royo. "I wouldn't mind a nice fine-looking man coming by and helping *me* with the rent." She wiggled the fingers on her left hand, exposing the absence of a ring.

But Costa was a dog chasing a hare. "Who, then? Who leases the apartment?"

Maggie leaned forward conspiratorially. "Well, now, I'm not so sure I should be sharing that with you. Confidentiality and all. But seeing as you two are cops, and I know I can trust you..."

The real estate manager's face lit up, and Royo immediately knew her type: the kind who took pleasure in the misery of others and were gossips. They were bad for his temperament but good for his business. He plastered on the most genuine smile he could manage.

Groaning as she bent over it, Maggie opened the binder and flipped through it. Her finger underlined the words on the page. "Let me check the records here. Hmm. That's funny."

"What's funny?" Royo asked.

"Looks like we never took down his name. Everything's under Branigan." She slouched against the counter. "Just know he said he was a relative of the dead girl—a brother, I believe—but I never bought it. He didn't look like no brother." She straightened, her stomach sliding off the counter like a beanbag chair slipping over a cliff.

"So you don't know who you're leasing that apartment to?" Costa asked, the words singed with surprise more than disbelief.

Maggie frowned. She peered down her nose at the open binder. "Cassidy Branigan, as far as I'm concerned. Don't matter who's paying for it. The lease has always been taken out in Branigan's name. I'm sure the gent will come by soon, and we can get the whole matter straightened."

"Can you tell us how long the apartment has been rented on Branigan's behalf?" Royo asked.

She slumped back down on the counter, nearly out of breath, and pointed at her computer. "It's all in there, of course, but I'm old-fashioned." She flipped the folder back toward its front until she landed on the page she apparently wanted. "Yep, just as I thought. The leases in the woman's name go back to 2018."

"And before that?"

"To a Rex Billings, but he isn't the one who rents it for the girl, if that's what you're thinking. He's one of those folks I mentioned that we had enough trouble getting to pay their rent."

Royo smiled as flirtatiously as he could muster. "Can I get a copy of the lease documents?"

The woman blew a raspberry. "Sure, but I'll have to redact some of Ms. Branigan's personal information—her Social Security and bank info and whatnot—but otherwise, I don't see why not."

"Are you sure the financial info is Branigan's?"

"They got her name on them. Looks like he paid, but she filled out the paperwork."

Royo tugged the stubble on his chin. "Was rent paid by check?"

Maggie whistled. "Cash, it seems."

"You accepted cash?" Costa sounded incredulous.

Maggie scoffed. "Honey, we take it any way we can get it."

"Great." Royo smiled again and handed her his card. "It's got my email and fax number on it. Thanks again for your help, Miss—"

"Maggie's fine."

"All right, Maggie. Mind if we take a look around the complex?"

She picked up a keyring loaded with keys then put them down and dialed a number preprogrammed into the handset. "Manny, come by and open 315. The police are here, and they want to take a look around."

"One more question," Costa blurted. "Was the guy across the hall from Branigan footing the bill?"

"Sanders?" Maggie scowled. "No, but if you see that guy, tell him he owes me for the new door."

***

As they walked toward the apartment complex, Royo spotted the maintenance man, Manuel, who'd helped him into Branigan's apartment previously. Manuel stood in the foyer, shifting from foot to foot and looking as guilty of something as he had the last time. He gazed across the parking lot as if he were debating whether to run.

"*Buenos dias*, Officers," he said overly cordially as Royo and Costa approached. He laughed then laughed more when he smoothed out his face to stop himself from laughing.

Eyeballing the curious man, Royo extended his hand. "*Buenos dias*. I'm not sure if we caught your name last time. I'm Detective Asante Royo. This is Officer Megan Costa. We're here to take a look at apartment 315."

"*Si*, uh... yes, sir." Manuel nodded at Officer Costa. "Ma'am. Right this way, *por favor*." He turned, opened the outer door, and stepped into the entranceway. When he pulled his keyring, which was fastened to his belt by a lanyard, up to the lock, his hands were shaking.

Royo exchanged glances with Costa but said nothing of the man's failure to state his name. They moved across the lobby and began climbing the stairs to the third floor. "I've seen you again, haven't I? I mean after the woman in 315 died?"

Manuel continued onto the second landing without slowing. "I don't know, sir."

"Yeah. You were watching the night of the break-in then again when we returned here to talk to witnesses. It looked like you were carrying a cat."

Manuel froze. Royo and Costa fell silent behind him.

"Not again," Royo whispered.

Manuel dashed up the stairs.

"Wait!" Royo called as he shot forward. "Why does everyone have to run?"

He caught Manuel as he reached the top of the stairs, clawing his fingers down his back and closing them around his shirt. The maintenance man lost his balance.

"I got you." Royo propped the man up, circling his arms under his shoulders. "If I let you go, do you promise to have a seat?"

White-faced, Manuel said nothing, but after a moment, he nodded and sat on the top step.

"You have some explaining to do," Royo said. "That was Sanders's cat, wasn't it? That cat was found dead."

Manuel looked up, his eyes shimmering with tears. "I no hurt that cat!"

Royo sighed.

Costa put her hands on her hips. "Listen, you—"

Touching her shoulder gently, Royo said quietly, "Let me try. Call it a hunch."

Costa stepped down a stair.

Royo did as well so that he could be at eye level with Manuel. "What's your name?"

"Manuel Rodriguez," he said, rolling his *R*'s with pride. But the moment was quickly lost. "Please... I have a family."

"How long have you been a maintenance guy here, Manuel?"

"Like I tell you before, three years... close." He wrung his hands. "It's good. Good job."

"And let me guess: if I were to look up your paperwork, I probably wouldn't find much, would I? Paid in cash each week, I bet."

Manuel opened his mouth, but words were slow to come. "Please. Please, mister. I have a family. The cartels, they kill my brother. My uncle. We come here. Be safe."

"Mexico?"

Manuel nodded.

Royo sat beside the man. "We aren't here for that, Manuel. In fact, if you cooperate with us, I'll do my best to make sure no one ever comes here for that. Or if they do, I can tell them how you helped us with an investigation, which might go a long way toward keeping you here. In fact, I'll do my best for you whether you decide to help us or not." He handed Manuel a business card. "Call it if you ever need to. Of course, I'm hoping you'll do the right thing and talk to us."

"I no kill that cat!" Manuel shook his head rapidly. "I only wanted to care for it for that man, you know, till he comes back. I go to return it when you see me. I panic and run. But I no hurt that cat. It got out, then I find it again, dead at that man's door. Its neck was broken. I think, 'Who would do such a thing?'" That seemed to turn Manuel's stomach, but he pressed on. "I leave it, so he know, and I'm afraid he blames me."

"Can I talk to you for a second?" Officer Costa asked Royo softly.

He rose and walked down the few steps to where she stood.

She cupped her hand over her mouth and whispered not softly enough, "He has access to the apartment and was last seen with the cat. Shouldn't we be treating him like a suspect?"

Royo nodded. "Just... one second."

"The cat had sawdust all over it. We found sawdust in Sanders's apartment." She waved a hand at Manuel's feet. His work boots were speckled with wood shavings. "Just look at his boots."

"I no kill that cat!" Manuel glared at Officer Costa.

Royo turned to face him. "Manuel, I believe you." He waved off the protest Costa was preparing to mount. Shrugging, he showed Manuel his palms. "But you've got to help us fill in the blanks. You don't trust us, and I get that. More than you know. My family came here when the army started spreading a too-wide net on guerilla movements in Tegucigalpa, sweeping up leftists whether involved in the movement or not. Some of them weren't here with the government's blessing either. Funny thing—my dad was about as far right as they come, but my mom... Guess you can't stop love. Anyway, they just wanted to live a life of peace, away from the violence, and give me a chance for something better. I'm sure that's all you want for your children, right? How old are they?"

Manuel squinted at him. "Pablo, he's seven, and already, he's growing. My little Consuela, she's four only." He took a deep breath. "My brother... *pendejo*... he steals from the cartel. They kill him and my uncle, who did no wrong. They try to kill me and my family, too, but we escape to here, make a new life, hiding from the cartel and the government." He set his jaw and looked Royo in the eye. "We go back, we die."

"So, Manuel Rodriguez," Costa said. "That's not your real name, is it?"

Manuel hesitated then shook his head. "New life, new name."

Royo smiled. "And it's a good name." He stepped closer and leaned against the banister. "I know it seems like you don't have any friends here, but we would like to be. My offer stands: no matter what you tell us, I'll do what I can to legitimize your immigration status. But I can tell you know things. You've seen things here that might help us investigate the death of that poor woman who lived in apartment 315 and the break-in that occurred across the hall."

"That woman, she was a nice lady. Always very kind to me."

"Can you tell us anything that might shed light on her death?"

"I don't know." Manuel scratched his head. "One day, she alive. The next..." He shook his head. "She seemed so happy. That man from next door, he and she, they happy together." He pushed his fingertips against each other.

"Do you think he had something to do with her death?" Costa asked.

Manuel frowned. "That man, I no like him, but *he* like *her*. I no think he hurt her. And when he come home and see, he go crazy. Police take him."

"He wasn't home when the woman was found dead?" Royo asked.

"No." Manuel shrugged. "Maybe. I don't know."

"Was he with her earlier that day or the night before?"

"I don't know. I see people come and go, but I no watch every time."

"Did you see her with anyone else that day?"

Manuel grimaced and looked toward the ceiling. "I... I don't know. That day... I don't know. But I see her with those *hombres* who kick down the man's door."

Costa, who had out a notepad, stopped writing and peered up.

"You think the man next door hurt the woman?" Manuel asked.

"We don't know," Royo said.

"And..."

"What?"

"It's no polite to speak ill of the dead."

Royo nodded. "If it could help us get to the bottom of what caused her death, I'm sure she would want you to."

Manuel huffed. "The woman... those three men... they always smoking drugs. Neighbors below complain—the smell. You see them, sweating, shaking, scratching, giggling... You can tell. I see it with my brother. Not just weed. They all doing it."

"Do you know where they were getting it?"

"No, but I see this man, he come here sometimes. He wears those... What are they called? Looks like sleep clothes. He a nurse or something, so I think maybe he gets it."

"Scrubs?"

"*Si*." Manuel tried out the word. "Scrubs. Yes, it is this. He comes often, like once a week. Another man, too, mean looking, always mean to the woman, but he no stay long."

"The man in scrubs, what did he look like?"

Manuel tilted his head back. "White, like her." He pointed at Costa. "And about the same height. Good shape. Tattoos all up his arms."

"Scar?" Royo slid a finger over his eyebrow. "Right here?"

"I... I don't know, but maybe you see him. He come same day you were here. I no get so good a look at his face."

"Anything else you can tell me about him?"

"*Si*, he go see apartment on the second floor before he go to third floor. Still goes. I see him outside 315, talking to someone *inside*. I think probably the mean man. But when I look, I find no one." He clenched his jaw. "No one should be in there."

Royo scratched his stubble. "This other man, what does he look like?"

"White. Skinny." He pointed at Costa. "Young, like her. Always smiling but not friendly."

"Any tattoos or other distinguishing features."

"I don't know... Glasses."

"He wore glasses?"

"*Si*."

"And it isn't the man from 314?"

"No. He always nice to the girl. He no deserve this. So I take care of his cat."

Costa met his stare. "Did you and the man from apartment 314 ever have any arguments?"

"No. I never speak to this man. I think maybe I should bring the cat back, leave it inside, but I don't know when the man comes home. I think, I care for it till then."

Costa leaned forward, crossing her arms over her knee as she shifted her weight to her forward foot on the stairs. "But you said you didn't like the man. Why not?"

Manuel sighed. "I don't know. He talks to the air. Seems... little crazy. But I feel bad for him. Not fair for me to say bad things."

"Well, has he ever said or done anything in particular that made you not like him?"

"No." Manuel twirled Royo's business card between his fingers. "And he treat the nice lady nice. He just sad, so sad. Makes me sad. Alone, no one to look out for him. And I think, 'What must he have done to have the world treat him so?' Maybe nothing. I don't know."

Royo turned to his partner. "Do you have any more questions?"

"Not at the moment."

"Well, Mr. Rodriguez"—Royo extended his hand—"we thank you for answering our questions. I meant what I said about helping you, if I can. We'll be in touch, but in the meantime, if you get into any trouble, you call me."

Manuel nodded. "*Gracias.*"

Royo stepped onto the third-floor landing. "Now, if you'll just open apartment 315 for us, we'll send you on your way."

Manuel headed down the hall and opened the door to the apartment, nodded curtly, and hurried away.

"Do you believe him?" Costa asked once Manuel was out of earshot.

Royo smirked. "Every word."

"Why?"

"Not only guilty people run from police, you know."

"But he *is* guilty, or he's at least hiding something. He's here illegally."

"Yeah." Royo chewed on the end of his pen. "And you want to do something about that?"

Costa furrowed her brow. She paused before saying, "No."

"Good." Royo patted her arm. "I don't either. But as for his truthfulness, I can't fathom a motive as to why he would hurt Branigan."

Costa raised an eyebrow.

His mouth curled up at the corner. "You think he might have had a thing for Branigan and maybe force-fed her enough pills to kill a hippo because he was jealous of what Sanders had?"

"He did seem awfully fond of Branigan and didn't really have a good reason for disliking Sanders."

"Okay, I see your point. Still..." Royo scratched his stubble. "Nah. I just don't like him for it. Which isn't to say I'm ruling him out." He took in the apartment. At first glance, it looked exactly how it had the night they'd investigated Branigan's death, sans the dead body, pills, and alcohol. The faint scent of mildew permeated the air.

"Come on." He closed the door behind them and locked it. "Let's give this place another look."

"And what exactly are we looking for?" With her hands on her hips, Costa scanned the room.

Royo followed her gaze. The apartment still offered no obvious clues or links among three of his cases. "Manuel said he'd seen people in this apartment since Branigan's death. We're looking for anything that might help us determine who those people were and anything we might have missed on the first two go-arounds."

"Are you sure we're not dealing with a suicide, a home invasion, and drug trafficking, each separate and distinct from one another?"

"No, but... we have Fletcher's drugs showing up in three different apartments here. We have a dead woman with injuries suggesting abuse. She dated a man clearly prone to violence at least as an answer to violence. We have three dead users who appear to have been friends with Branigan and who attacked Sanders for the reason, if one believes Tresser's dying declaration, that Sanders abused Branigan."

"So there's the linkage," Costa said. "Branigan was dealing. Selling to her friends, Tresser and gang. She was dating Sanders, who probably uses too. Sanders roughs up Branigan over the course of their relationship and maybe breaks her down so far that she kills herself, or he escalates from abuse, pinning her down and plugging her with pills until she ODs. The three friends, suspecting Sanders's part in Branigan's death or just not happy with the way he treated her before her death, seek revenge against Sanders, kick down his door, and end up dead." She raised her hands and smiled. "The end. Case solved."

"Not a bad theory, but a minute ago you were liking the maintenance guy for it." Royo chuckled. "That's the problem. Both scenarios are plausible, but they only fit some of the facts and some of the evidence. The rest, you're filling in with conjecture, which is a dangerous but sometimes necessary part of the analysis. Too often, it can lead you astray. We need to think of the scenario that fits all the facts and all the evidence."

Costa frowned. "Which fact is missing from that scenario?"

"Evidence of abuse stems back to well before we think Branigan and Sanders met."

"So?" Costa snorted. "Some women go from one bad relationship to another to another, like they're gluttons for punishment."

"You make it sound like it's their fault, like they ask to be abused." Royo frowned. Maybe he'd misjudged Costa. "You can't really think that."

Costa looked away. "I... I know a woman like that. And sometimes her man doesn't just *beat* her." She scowled then softened.

Royo didn't know what to say. He didn't know much about Costa, only that she was a good cop and a good person. Though he didn't agree with her position, he considered where it had been birthed. *Her mother, maybe?* Royo certainly had no intention of asking. He thought of his own mother, still so loving, nurturing, and accepting, especially after his father had passed, and wondered how different he might be if not for her.

He decided to lighten the air. "Also..." He smiled softly. "You forgot about the cat."

The corner of her mouth twitched. "Anyway, I'm betting it was Tresser and his cronies who that maintenance guy saw. She's been dead for months and them barely one—plenty of time for them to continue using in their usual drug den."

"True, assuming they had a key. I don't believe one was found on any of them."

"The maintenance guy has a key. Maybe he was using with Branigan and her friends. Maybe they've been using the apartment since."

"You flip-flop more than a politician." Royo scratched his stubble. He didn't think it had been Tresser and his boys in the apartment, and Manuel seemed confident, consistent, and genuine in his account and hadn't exhibited any of the telltale signs of a liar, despite being under what had to be enormous stress. "If Tresser had access to this apartment, he could have waited here for Sanders to leave. He wouldn't have had to break down the door with the whole complex hearing him do it."

He tapped his chin. "Then again, the fact that he so audibly forced his way into Sanders's apartment suggested he cared little who heard him."

"Plus," Costa said, "they were probably high at the time."

"True, but only marijuana was found in their systems. It's not even illegal to use anymore or known for producing violence, but it may help explain why Sanders was able to take them down. Still, I doubt it would have impaired their judgment to the point of taking such an unnecessary risk."

Costa turned and stared at him. "Sir, don't you think you're giving those three high-school dropouts a little too much credit?"

Royo grunted. He examined the walls and carpet, not looking for anything in particular. The smell of fresh paint was underscored by cigarette smoke hanging in the air. Since he hadn't really reopened Branigan's case, he should already have kicked the investigation into the apartment's recent occupants over to vice. The drug angle was all that remained, since Sanders's attackers were dead and accounted for and Branigan's death had been stamped a suicide. But pieces of those cases were still missing. Royo couldn't let them stay that way.

Costa slapped her thighs. "So... do you think he's dumb enough to come back?"

"Petrakis or our mystery man?"

"Both," Costa said.

After their last visit, he and Costa had needed less than an hour to determine the identity of the man in scrubs: Dmitri Petrakis, a registered nurse and part-time PCA for Edward Fletcher, managing his personal care, including the ordering and administering of pre-scription drugs. Royo had him dead to rights on a host of drug- and fraud-related charges. He'd scammed the pharmaceutical companies for additional oxys and used Fletcher's health insurance and purport-ed need to do so, all for the purpose of selling the drugs, spreading addiction, and spitting in the face of his Nightingale Pledge. Royo had held off on bringing him in, instead returning to the apartment with the hope that Petrakis's buyer might also be revealed. He'd let a few weeks pass to allow the nurse to relax and resume his routine.

Royo tapped the face of his watch. The nurse's shift with Fletcher was nearly over. "We should know soon enough. Petrakis is definitely here. I saw his Toyota on the way in. Even if he suspects we're on to him, he's gotta keep up appearances."

A knock came at the door, and Royo raised a finger to his lips.

"You in there?" came a man's voice, hushed and anxious. "Let me in."

Royo didn't move. A few feet from the door, he held his breath as he moved his hand toward his holster then flicked the thumb break. His Glock fit his hand as if it had been custom made for him. He raised it and stepped softly toward the door. He couldn't see her but heard a creak in the floor and knew Costa was at his back.

Another, louder knock came. "Come on, man. The cops are here. They haven't seen me, and I need a place to hole up until they leave." The door thudded. "Let me in!"

Royo swung the door open and held his gun held high, the muzzle only a foot from Petrakis's face. The nurse kept his hands by his sides. A plastic bag was gripped in one of them, and the other was empty. His face and posture took on that clichéd but so common deer-in-the-headlights expression most criminals had just before they bounded off.

"Don't," Royo said. "Unless you think you can outrun a bullet."

A smile crept up Petrakis's face. "You're not going to shoot me." He turned and ran.

"This is getting ridiculous!" Royo groaned as he sprinted after him.

Costa's footsteps headed rapidly the opposite way then down the closer stairwell leading to the side of the building. It was a less direct route to where Petrakis was likely heading, the front doors, but she would have one fewer door to push through.

Petrakis was fast. He careened down the stairs and out of sight before Royo had reached them. He heard a bang, and someone cried out below. To save time, Royo hopped over the railing down to the lower flight of stairs then again to those leading down to the first floor. He landed on the side of his shoe, and his ankle twisted. Tears sprang into his eyes as he fell. After forcing himself up, he continued down the last few steps, his ankle exploding with pain. He limped hurriedly through the lobby, passing a downed woman with a toddler standing beside her. Her grocery bags were strewn across the floor. The collision must have slowed Petrakis, because he was in the breezeway, pushing through the outer door when Royo saw him.

"Freeze!" Royo shouted.

His voice seemed to echo, but when he saw Costa with her service pistol raised come into full view under the front door's awning, he realized they'd shouted the word almost in unison.

He shifted his weight onto his left foot and took zombie steps toward the breezeway, smiling as his young protégé covered their suspect. Petrakis's momentum had carried him through the door and onto to the pavement, but he was already rising to his knees.

"Stay down!" Costa ordered. "Hands behind your back!"

Petrakis did place his hands behind his back, but he did not stay down. The smile fell away from Royo's face. The glint of metal raised alarms as Petrakis pulled something from his waistline. "Megan! Look out!"

Royo fired, shattering the glass of the first door and spider-webbing the second. Petrakis spun and fell. Costa dropped to her knee then flopped to her side, her face white with fear.

The mother was consoling her child, who had his hands over his ears and was wailing.

"Call 911!" Royo shouted at her. "Now!" She nodded and hustled her boy into the hallway, leaving her groceries where they'd spilled.

Outside, Petrakis started to rise again and reached for his weapon. As Royo stepped through the shattered doorway, he shot Petrakis again. The bullet took out the remaining glass and hit Petrakis squarely in the shoulder blade.

Royo hobbled over to him with his gun trained on the slumped form. Petrakis squirmed but made no effort to rise. Royo kicked his weapon, a standard kitchen knife, out of reach before crouching over his fallen comrade.

"Fucker... got me in the leg," Costa grunted. Spit flew through her teeth as she hissed with pain. She clutched her thigh, and warm blood sluiced through her fingers.

Too much blood. "Let me see."

Costa shook her head, unwilling to let go of her leg as if she alone could hold in the life that was slipping away. The pigment seeped from her skin. Then her hands fell away, and her head lolled back. "Sir... am I..." She fainted.

"You're going to be okay."

Royo was no doctor, but given how much blood Costa had lost so quickly, he assumed Petrakis had punctured or nicked her femoral artery. He tore off his jacket, slid it under her leg, then crossed the sleeves and tied them tightly together.

"Officer down!" he shouted into her handheld. "Bus needed at 300 North Street *stat*!"

But he already heard sirens in the distance, coming closer. The woman must have called 911 as he'd instructed and, in doing so, might have saved Costa's life. As he hugged her leg, squeezing it as hard as he could while keeping an eye on Petrakis, he could feel the blood pumping more slowly. He hoped that his makeshift tourniquet was responsible for that, but he knew better. Likely, the only life that would be saved belonged to a cop killer.

Royo simmered with anger as he glowered at Petrakis, bear-hugging Costa's thigh as if her life depended on it, and it might not be too late to save her. "You're going to be okay," he mouthed, resting his head on her hip. "You're going to be just fine."

With blood smearing his cheek, he winced at the metallic taste of a lie.

CHAPTER 21

For the last month—the last nine months, really—sleep had been unkind to Jaden. When it had come, it was in fits filled with nightmares. He saw Cass's face, mannequin-smooth like when he'd found her, except her eyes were aware and staring at him accusatorily, like her death was all his fault.

She said in his head, "You did this to me, Jaden. You did."

If only he'd come home earlier. If only he'd been smarter and seen the signs of what she'd been planning.

If. If. If.

Crawling out of bed to an alarm that wouldn't quit, he felt the weight of her loss like a cannonball on his chest. If a heart could truly be broken, he wished his would break already. Cass had been his first true love, and it had taken him more than thirty years to find her. He had no doubt she would be his last. For an introverted loner, the prognosis was fatal.

And why not? I killed her, didn't I? From what his sister had told him after the creep showed up uninvited at her house, Detective Royo sure seemed to think so.

Detective Royo, Jaden scoffed. He plodded into the bathroom and observed the state he was in. He laughed, low and sporadic at first, then it built into something loud and more than a little unnerving and uncontrollable. It matched his look: his was hair disheveled, his eyes were red-streaked and gowned in a heavy purple, and he had dry, white-flaked lips. His skin looked like the cracked edges of pounded dough before being rolled and smoothed. His body felt as if he'd fallen from space onto granite.

Even he thought he looked like he belonged in a madhouse. He could only imagine what the jurors must have thought. Snickering in place of a sob, he thought of Jack Nicholson in one of those old Batman movies. *Wait till they get a load of me.* He would have to check the parking lot for white vans and men holding straightjackets before he got out of the car.

With every step forward, a new development knocked him two steps back. Rascal's death was more like eight or nine. In a steady state of hopelessness, Jaden went about his grooming. He ironed his best suit—the lame two-year-old charcoal, not-so-Egyptian cotton one he'd worn the day before—sprayed it with deodorant, and hung it up while he shaved and showered. Then he brushed his teeth, got dressed, fixed his tie and his hair in the mirror, and headed for the courthouse, caring more for an end to life than an end to the trial.

I promised I would try. He was halfway to the courthouse when he realized he'd forgotten to take his meds. Checking the clock on his dashboard, he decided against turning around for them. He drove into the parking lot and pulled a ticket from a mechanized dispenser, wondering how much of a parking fine he would accrue if he ended the day behind bars. *Did I leave a light on? Would my lease auto-renew?* At least Rascal wasn't in any more pain.

Funny what crossed his mind when facing imprisonment. He could picture his mom asking if he'd worn clean underwear that day in case he went to the slammer.

With practice, security had become a mild inconvenience. He marched through it with his belt off and his pockets empty then readied for the supposedly random yet somehow obligatory pat down he received every time. He picked up his things and headed for the courtroom, where he met his sister outside.

"Good luck today," she said, hugging him tightly.

"You don't have to be here." He smiled, fighting tears and truly appreciating that she was. "I'm sure you've got enough on your plate."

"Don't be stupid. You're my brother, and I love you... no matter what happens in there. Okay?"

Jaden nodded, his tears winning.

Tara sniffled. "Do you think it'll end today?"

"I don't know. Probably, if I don't testify. My lawyer doesn't think I should."

Tara held his arm. "You should listen to your lawyer."

"We'll see." Jaden shrugged. "Did you hear them yesterday? Acting like I was the bad guy, not just with that Tresser guy but with Cass too."

"Don't listen to them, Jaden. It's all bullshit. Don't let it get to you. In the end, only one thing matters: you were attacked and did what you had to do to defend yourself. Never lose sight of that."

"I won't." But hearing the words leave his mouth without any conviction, he knew he'd failed to convince his sister.

Tara patted his back. "Let's go in. I'll be sitting right behind you, like yesterday, if you need me."

They separated at the gate, Tara taking a right to sit behind her brother's table and Jaden heading through the gate to sit with his attorney.

Giles sat huddled over a legal pad, his fingers cupping his scalp and his thumbs pressing into his temples. A pencil was tucked behind his ear. "Have you come to your senses?" he asked without looking up.

"If you mean have I decided not to testify, no. I still want to go through with it. I've seen the looks those jurors gave me... when they're not too sickened to even look my way. They think I'm guilty or-or-or crazy—or worse, some kind of monster, but I'm a person just like them. I have to tell them my side."

"I strongly advise you to re—"

"If we lose and I didn't, I'd always wonder what would have happened if I tried." Jaden glanced over his shoulder at his sister and smiled softly. "And I promised someone I would try." He sat up a little straighter. "So save it. I heard you."

"Yet you don't listen." Giles scoffed. "Of course not. Why would you listen to the guy you've hired to represent you?" He slowly exhaled. "Well, since you refuse to follow the advice of counsel, I've come prepared. I hope you have too. And remember: I will always do what is in the best interest of my client."

"What the heck is that supposed to—"

"All rise!" a court officer boomed.

The jurors filed in.

From his chamber door, the judge entered and walked briskly to his bench. "Please be seated."

He fixed his eyes on Giles. "Is the defense ready to call its first witness?"

"I am, Your Honor."

The judge raised an eyebrow then sighed. "Proceed."

Giles stood. "The defense calls Jaden Sanders to the stand."

Jaden took a deep breath and stood. He smoothed out his suit before walking to the box. His palms were clammy. His collar felt so tight that he couldn't swallow the lump that had formed in his throat. Eyes—every one of them in the courtroom—were on him, condemning him.

As the gate closed behind him, caging him into the witness box like some zoo animal to be emasculated and exhibited, he immediately regretted his decision. His attorney was right. He should never have taken the stand. And of all the days to forget to take his meds. His head throbbed, and his pulse quickened. *Where is Cass? Where is—*

A court officer approached and raised his hand. "Do you swear that the testimony you are about to give is the truth, the whole truth, and nothing but the truth?"

Jaden nodded then a second time more firmly. "I do."

Giles approached. "Please state your full name for the record."

"J-Jaden Adam Sanders." *Pause. Eyes shut. Breathe.*

"How old are you, Mr. Sanders?"

"Th-Th-Thirty... Thirty-five."

"And what do you do for a living?"

"I'm a, uh, contract negotiator for DSC. Been there for about five years."

"And before that?"

"Uh, more of the same. Different companies."

"Excepting the current charge against you, have you ever been arrested for a violent crime before?"

"No."

"Have you ever been arrested for any crime before?"

"No."

Jaden swallowed, finally working the lump down. The questions were exactly the same ones Giles had asked during a practice run over the weekend. He sat back in his chair. The thump of his heartbeat pulsing through his head lessened.

"Let's take you back to August 11, 2022. Do you remember what happened early that morning?"

"Of course." He chuckled nervously. "How could I forget it?"

He glanced over at the jurors to see if they were amused, but each stared back with a gravity he shrank from. They were seeing him for whatever he was. And since their gazes were fixed, he might have settled for prison to escape them. *Prison but not that other place.* And in glancing away, his eyes fell upon that law clerk with his hyena grin and a gleam in his eyes. With the temperature rising, he looked down and twiddled his thumbs.

Giles tapped the box, a predetermined trigger that told Jaden to focus on Giles and Giles only. "Why don't you, in your own words, walk us through what happened that night."

"Okay." Jaden squinted at the ceiling, thinking of how best to start. "Well, I was sleeping in my bed when I heard a knock at the door."

"What time was that?"

"About four o'clock. No, five... five o'clock, almost six. I don't know exactly because my alarm clock was blinking."

"Please continue. What did you do when you heard the knock?"

"Nothing at first. I wasn't sure I'd heard anything. I was still half-asleep. But when it came again—much louder, banging—I got out of bed and went to the door. I walked quietly so that I could peek through the eyehole and see who it was without them hearing me."

Giles tapped the railing again. "What happened next?"

"The man, uh, Mr. Tresser, said he knew I was there. He asked me to open up. I didn't say anything, but they wouldn't go away. Eventually, I asked him what he wanted."

"Did he tell you what he wanted?"

"Yeah, he said to talk. And to let him in. I told him we were talking already. He got angrier and angrier and said if I didn't open the door, he'd break it down." Jaden swallowed. He knew he was speaking at a hundred miles an hour, but he couldn't slow his heart or his mouth. Giles wanted short, direct answers, and Jaden felt he was trying but failing to comply.

Giles nodded. He took a deep breath, a signal for Jaden to do the same. "Please, continue. What happened next?"

Pause. Eyes shut. Breathe. "I told them if they didn't leave, I would call the cops. That's when they really started on the door. I looked around for my phone, but it was charging in my bedroom. I didn't feel like I had a lot of time, so I grabbed the next best thing."

"The knives?"

"Yes."

"Mr. Sanders, what was going through your mind when you grabbed the knives from your kitchen?"

"I was terrified. I thought those men were there to hurt me. Kill me, even. They were breaking down my door. I didn't know why they'd come or what they wanted, but I tried to hide, and they still came for me."

"When they entered your bedroom, did you believe they meant to harm you?"

"Yes. Why else would three strangers break down my door?"

"Why indeed?" Giles posed to the jury before turning back to face Jaden. "And where were you when they came into your bedroom?"

"Trapped in the corner with no way out but through them." An idea occurred to Jaden. "A-A-And they still attacked me, even after I showed them the knives. One of them hit me with my lamp. I thought he broke my wrist."

Giles frowned, and Jaden knew he was offering too much.

"After you fought off the first two attackers, what happened with the third, Mr. Morton Tresser?"

"He stood between me and the exit, and he wouldn't let me out. When I tried, he attacked me."

"Were you still thinking he might harm or kill you?"

"Yes, and he would have, had I not killed him first."

"Was there ever a point when you thought Mr. Tresser was no longer trying to harm or kill you?"

"No. Never."

"And that's because..." Giles held his chin. "Strike that. Why did you at all times believe Mr. Tresser was trying to harm or kill you?"

Jaden looked at his attorney then at the jurors, who seemed to be hanging on his every word. Meeting the foreperson's gaze, he said, "Because when three strangers kick down your door and threaten to hurt you, you'd better believe they mean it when they get inside and gang up on you. I thought they were there to kill me, and I did what I had to do to protect myself from them."

"Thank you, Mr. Sanders." Giles turned to the prosecutor. "Your witness."

Laughton stood, smiling at Jaden. *Why is she smiling?* The law clerk, the judge, and all the spectators leaned forward. The lump in Jaden's throat returned.

"Mr. Sanders," she said as she stepped closer. "Who did you think was at your door when you first heard a knock?"

"I..." Jaden froze. His mind went blank. He couldn't remember what he'd told the detective or anyone. He stared at nothing until his eyes began to blur, then he blinked them clear.

"Mr. Sanders?" Laughton leaned forward on her toes.

Jaden fumbled for an answer. "I-I-I didn't know who was at the door."

"Let's try it again, Mr. Sanders. I didn't ask you if you knew who was at the door. I asked you who you *thought* was at the door."

"I—"

"Objection." Giles stood. "Argumentative. Also, I don't think that was a question."

"Withdrawn, Your Honor." Laughton's smug smile wormed its way across her face again.

Why does she keep smiling? Jaden rubbed his temples until he realized what he was doing and forced himself to stop. *Pause. Eyes shut. Breathe.*

Laughton faced the jury then turned back to Jaden. "Mr. Sanders, who did you think was knocking on your door that night?"

"I had no idea. I didn't think anyone in particular."

"Really?" Laughton made a show of flipping through the document in her hands, only to land back on the same page she'd started on.

Jaden shifted in his seat, stretching his neck to try to see what she was reading.

"Did you tell Detective Royo you thought it was Cassidy Branigan?"

Giles stood. "Objection."

"Grounds?" Judge Cullen asked.

"Relevance?"

Jaden didn't know if his attorney meant it to be a question, but it certainly came out as one.

"Your Honor," Laughton began, "if nothing else, the line of questioning is admissible for impeachment purposes. But the commonwealth argues it is admissible for all purposes."

"I see no reason why it wouldn't be. Overruled."

Giles sat down, his suit suddenly looking too big at the shoulders. He looked as if he'd been punched in the gut, and somehow Jaden was feeling it too. He wasn't sure why, but he felt like a tremendous blow to their case had been delivered—or was about to be. He chewed his thumbnail.

"Mr. Sanders?" Laughton pressed. "You may answer the question."

Jaden rubbed his temples. The drumbeat behind his eyes was back and growing to a crescendo. "What was the question again?"

"Did you tell Detective Royo you thought it might be Cassidy Branigan at your door that night?"

"No, I..." Jaden shook his head. "I don't know. I might have."

Laughton looked down at her notepad. "I was in bed when I heard a bang. At first, I thought I had dreamed it. But when it came again, I put on my bathrobe and went to see who it was." Tapping a pen on her pad, she looked up. "Are those your words, Mr. Sanders?"

"I believe they are."

"From the statement you gave to Detective Royo?"

"Yes."

Again consulting her pad, she said, "Detective Royo then asked you: 'Did you think it might be anyone in particular?' Do you recall your response to that question?"

"I... I don't recall."

"According to the recorded statement, you answered, 'Yeah, Cass. She's my girlfriend.' Does that help refresh your memory that you thought it might be someone named Cass at your door?"

"I... I don't remember. If you say I said that to Detective Royo, then I must have."

"Who is Cassidy Branigan?"

Jaden shook his head then buried his face in his hands. The lights seemed to burn into his retinas with blinding flashes, and he had to squint as the pain behind his eyes amplified quickly. "She is... She *was* my girlfriend."

"She's dead, isn't she?"

"Yes?" Still squinting, Jaden looked up. He blinked repeatedly. "Yes. Yes."

"And in fact, she's been dead since January, eight months before the night in question, correct?"

"Y-Yes."

"So why would you tell Detective Royo that you thought your girlfriend was at the door when she had died eight months prior?"

"I..." Jaden bit his lip, trying to steel himself through the pounding in his head. Blurriness returned to his eyes. "I get confused sometimes."

"You were confused about who was at your door?"

"Yes. Maybe."

"Were you also confused when you stabbed Morton Tresser more than thirty times?"

Giles rocketed out of his seat. "Objection!"

Laughton didn't wait for the judge to respond. "Tresser tried to run from you. Didn't he, Mr. Sanders?"

"No, I—"

"In fact, you stabbed a fleeing man over and over again. Didn't you, Mr. Sanders?"

"Enough, Ms. Laughton," the judge warned her.

"No, he wasn't—I didn't—" Jaden couldn't focus or form sentences.

"Twenty-eight times, you stabbed him, didn't you? A bit excessive, no?"

"Ms. Laughton!" Judge Cullen snapped.

The prosecutor leaned into the box. "Were you confused when Tresser tried to run, or did you just not care?"

"Objection!" Giles shouted.

"I don't know!" Jaden tore at his hair. "You weren't there! Those people... The people from the hospital, the things they did to me, trying to put their filthy fucking hands on me. They had no right! And Cass... I loved her! You don't know! You don't know anything!"

The judge rapped his gavel repeatedly. "Order! Order!"

Everyone fell silent.

"Another burst of theatrics like that out of you, Ms. Laughton, and it's automatic contempt. The same goes for you, Mr. Sanders. Am I understood?"

"Yes, Your Honor." Laughton finally wiped the smug grin from her face.

Jaden slumped in his seat, burying his face in his hands while peeking through his fingers. He couldn't catch his breath or slow his heart or his thoughts. Tara was watching him. *Is she humiliated? Ashamed of me?*

The law clerk sat with a hand covering his mouth, his body shaking. *Is he coughing or laughing?*

And Cass stood in the center of it all, her soft glow calling to him and reaching out from the void to welcome him home.

Giles, still on his feet, leaned forward on his palms. "Your Honor, the defense would like to call Mr. Sanders's psychiatrist, Dr. Horace Clemson, once Mr. Sanders's testimony is complete. His testimony should clear up any confusion brought about by the prosecution's grandstanding."

Laughton grabbed her lapels and straightened her jacket. "Your Honor, we stipulated that Mr. Sanders's competency to stand trial was not at issue—"

"And we don't challenge that, Your Honor. We would like to amend our defense to conform with the testimony presented and to be presented, as the prosecution has clearly opened the door to testimony regarding my client's mental stability at the time of the break-in and a possible verdict of not guilty by reason of temporary insanity."

"Your Honor," Laughton said, raising her voice, "counsel stipulated that he would not be raising an insanity defense. The commonwealth has had no chance to obtain expert—"

Judge Cullen banged his gavel. "Sidebar!" The judge tried to lower his voice, but all he managed through his anger was a low, gruff growl that was loud enough for Jaden and, he assumed, the jurors to hear. "It appears you haven't given him much choice, now, have you, Ms. Laughton? This matter should not be argued in front of the jury." With a scowl and the veins in his thin vulture neck bulging, he banged his gavel again. "This court is in recess."

"Simon," he said to one of the court officers, "escort the jury out and get them some lunch." With his face reddening like a pimple about to pop, he locked eyes with the prosecutor. "Counsel, my chambers. Now!"

Firm but gentle hands escorted Jaden from the witness box. He sat in his chair behind Giles, who was hurrying away from him. His mind went blank as he stared at everything and nothing at all—until he found Cass again.

CHAPTER 22

Since Royo hadn't slept a wink after spending the night in the ER, he stepped into his office late the next morning and found a message waiting on his desk.

Detective Royo:

This is Maggie from the Prospero Property Management. I have some information relating to what you were asking about yesterday. I'll be in the office all day, if you want to stop by. There's something I'd like to show you.

Royo rolled his eyes. No one could ever just tell him the important information in the message itself. That would be too efficient. Instead, he was left to guess whether the info might actually be useful or a complete waste of time. That apartment complex was the last place he wanted to be after his part-time partner had been stabbed there. She remained in the ICU, barely clinging to life. He would have stayed if he could have remained beside her. He figured the best thing he could do for her instead was to crucify the guy who'd hurt her.

Remembering Prospero's carnival-of-lights phones and deciding against a simple call back, he threw on an old leather jacket. He'd tossed his bloodstained regular one in a dumpster. Though he had hoped to catch the end of Sanders's trial before returning to the hospital, swinging by Prospero seemed a more likely step toward avenging Costa, if vengeance could be had. Petrakis was in the hospital, too, and a full and speedy recovery was anticipated. If he walked out and Costa didn't, well, then Sanders's brand of justice seemed all the more inviting.

You can't think that way. That's not your way. Recalling how his fellow officer and friend had been as white as a sheet and drier than a raisin, he again reconsidered what exactly was his way. For what it was worth, it wasn't Costa's way.

As for the trial, it was likely over anyway, since Sanders probably wouldn't take the stand, and the jury would soon be out to deliberate. With any luck, he could catch the verdict before checking in on Costa, if the doctors would let him near enough to see her.

Stepping out of his office, he scanned the precinct for someone to replace Costa. He frowned, finding mostly empty desks. The few who were present were unknown to him. *Not everyone works twenty-four, seven like you,* he heard Rickie's voice chiding. It wasn't like Stravenski and Rollins didn't have other assignments. He considered taking one of the unknowns but only briefly and was heading to the parking lot a moment later.

After getting back into his car, he sipped a coffee he'd left in his cup holder. Bitter and lukewarm, it instantly unsettled his stomach, but he drank it anyway as he contemplated the many questions still surrounding Branigan's death. *Who was Branigan's mysterious benefactor? Was he the same person Petrakis had gone to apartment 315 to see? Sanders moved into the complex a few years after Branigan, and Maggie confirmed he hadn't been making the payments, but is that enough to rule Sanders out?* He might have made payments through a proxy.

Royo shook his head. That seemed too far-fetched and overly complex. *Form the theory of the case from the evidence, not the suspect, unless the evidence conclusively determines the suspect.* Sanders had no reason, as far as Royo could see or even imagine, to keep up the act of paying Branigan's rent in secret. And that much was clear: whoever was making those payments had gone to great lengths to keep them secret.

Then there were the allegations of an abusive boyfriend, made by a dying man with a strong motive to implicate Sanders. That said, and crediting Rodriguez's statements linking Tresser, Grady, and Malden to Branigan, the abusive-boyfriend theory worked as a motive for Tresser's attack. *What was it Sanders claimed Tresser had said?* "He said there were consequences for what I had done earlier."

Or Tresser could be trying to pin his own abuse on Sanders. Royo sighed. He didn't feel as though he was getting anywhere. Too many questions, not enough answers.

He pulled into a spot near the complex's office. Tresser was a criminal, sure, but for some reason, Royo couldn't dismiss the ring of truth in his allegations. The lines of abuse were written all over Branigan's body. She had a litany of old wounds healed without proper treatment, fractured bones, and burn marks. The woman had been mistreated and, by the looks of it, for the better part of her life, well before any connection between her and Sanders could be established. She was a product of a sometimes-wicked foster care system, where the emphasis wasn't always on care.

Costa had been looking into that angle, tracking Branigan's past through DCF records. But Royo had known she wouldn't find many answers there. Branigan would have changed foster homes repeatedly over the course of her juvenile life, and her medical records and the medical examiner's report both dated her injuries so varyingly that it would have been impossible to have been the work of one foster parent. It was as if her abuser had followed her through the system. *Perhaps a social worker?* That was possible but unlikely, as records showed little lag in placements with foster homes. *A caregiver?* No one individual provided long-term treatment for Branigan's many ailments. That left Royo with only one remaining credible conclusion: the wounds had been self-inflicted.

Probably the reason the ME so easily ruled her death a suicide. The ultimate act of self-hate after a lifetime of self-loathing.

As he walked into the leasing office, he began to feel silly then terrible for acting on a hunch, wasting both his time and Costa's and possibly getting her killed. *Suicide? Not suicide? Sanders? Not Sanders?* Still, he would only be lying to himself if he tried to let it go. He couldn't stand not knowing the answers but loved the act of trying to find them. No greater disappointment in life existed than a case not solved. He owed it to Costa, if not himself, to solve it.

"Detective," Maggie greeted him as he stepped up to her counter. She wore a broad smile and a broader dress that cinched just below her breasts. "I was hoping you'd come."

Royo managed a smile. "Good morning, Maggie. Forgive my appearance. I spent the night at the hospital."

"Oh, yes, I heard about your partner." She *tsk*ed. "Absolutely tragic."

"Thank you." Royo nodded. "You said in your message that you had some information for me?"

"I do. I do." She tossed a newspaper onto the counter in front of Royo: the previous day's *Fall River Herald News*. On the front page, a wide-angled, almost panoramic view of Judge Cullen's courtroom, with the Sanders trial in progress, filled the space. The photograph had been taken from the back-right corner of the courtroom. Over the heads of a crowd comprising mostly journalists, Sanders stood dead center.

Maggie smiled wider. "Right there's the gent who rents apartment 315. What a stroke of luck, huh?" She tapped an acrylic nail on the photo.

Royo sighed. "That's Jaden Sanders, Branigan's neighbor. I thought you'd said he wasn't leasing the apartment."

Maggie leaned in conspiratorially. Her breath reeked of egg salad. "Not him." She placed her finger over Sanders. "That's the gent from apartment 314."

She moved her finger up and to the left. "Him."

CHAPTER 23

Howdy, neighbor!

Please remember not to let your door slam closed when you leave your apartment. It is very disturbing to the rest of us in the hall.

Much obliged!

Jaden couldn't believe someone would complain about him. He was the ideal tenant—quiet and kept to himself. Well, Rascal meowed once every leap year. So the door slammed shut sometimes, when his hands were full, and he couldn't catch it. That was hardly the end of the world or something to get angry about.

He crumpled the note and threw it into the garbage. As he petted Rascal, the cat slid his body against him, walking back and forth along the counter. Jaden tried to push out the anger with calming strokes and cleansing breaths.

But something about that note wormed its way under his skin. It was a little thing, but the little things were becoming less and less tolerable as he spent more and more time alone. His cheeks flushed, and he slammed his palm onto the countertop, scaring the cat, who jumped off and scampered into the bedroom. Jaden stormed over to his wastebasket, picked out the note, and ironed it flat with his palm. Sneering, he stepped out into the hall.

Before he could reconsider, he pounded on the door across from his. It had been a long day at work, and coming home to that note had sent him over the edge. He wasn't violent, but he needed an outlet for his frustrations, and by God, he was going to give his trouble-starting neighbor, whomever he or she might be, a giant piece of his mind.

"Hello?" A blonde in a T-shirt and sweatpants opened the door, her emerald eyes half-open, as if she'd just awoken. Her wavy hair was mostly tied back in a ponytail, errant strands hanging loose over her face. She smiled faintly, a crooked front tooth appearing between her parting lips.

"Uh, hi," Jaden muttered, scratching the back of his head. The fire inside him had been smothered. "I found this note on my door." His cheeks flushed with warmth, and he turned away. "Anyway, I wanted to say that I'm sorry."

"You live there?" The woman pointed across the hall.

"I, uh... Yeah, that's me."

She opened the door wider. "Well, come in." She smiled. "We're neighbors, so shouldn't we get to know each other? Here, I'll start." She extended her hand. "I'm Cassidy. Friends call me Cass."

Jaden forgot all about the note as he took her hand.

***

"Jaden?"

"You died, beautiful, and... I miss you so much. But I have to let you go now. Is that okay?"

But her hand was in his, and he felt it as surely as he could feel the wood beneath his buttocks and the floor under his feet. When he looked up and saw the shape of a woman beside him, her hair vacillating from deep brown to shimmering blond, he allowed himself one more slip into the fugue. "Cass?"

Tara's frowning face came into view as the fog behind his eyes cleared. Jaden took in his surroundings: hard tile floors, a corridor with four sets of dark, wooden doors, and numbered rooms. He was in the hallway outside his courtroom, sitting on a bench. The last thing he remembered was being on the witness stand, doing poorly.

"Is it over? Did I win?"

Tara, someone true and real and sturdier than a redwood, squeezed his hand. "The court is in recess. How much do you remember?"

"I remember that prosecutor trying to confuse me."

"Yeah, well, it looks like she succeeded." Tara's words came out harshly, and Jaden must have shown it, because she quickly apologized. "Your lawyer's in with the judge now, saying you're not fit to stand trial or... maybe... that you're, uh..."

"Insane? I'm not insane!" Jaden wrung his hands then curled up his fingers. He pouted and knew he must look like a baby to his sister, but what he was going through... He was entitled to pout.

"Then stop acting like it!" She pounded her fist so hard against the bench that it had to have hurt, but Tara showed no sign of it. She looked around, no doubt checking to see what attention her outburst had drawn, then lowered her voice. "You have got to pull yourself together already. I've watched you stumble and stumble, and sometimes, I swear, you're purposely tripping over your own feet. Cass is dead, Jaden—"

"I know."

"I know that's not what you want to hear, but goddamn it already. She's been dead for—wait. What did you say?"

"I know." Jaden looked his sister straight in the eye. For what seemed like minutes but was probably only seconds, they held each other's gazes.

Tara threw her arms around him. "That's good, Jaden," she said as tears dampened his shoulder. "That's... That's just... You know what I mean."

Jaden gently pushed her away. "I know." Choking up, he searched for a change of subject. A chill ran through him as he considered what Tara had told him. "Temporary insanity? What will that mean for me exactly?" Jaden had a fairly good idea. He focused on the trial aspect. "You realize that if Giles succeeds in having me declared un-fit, I may have to go through this all over again?"

"What about double jeopardy?"

"I don't think that's how it works. Besides, I won't be retried. This trial might get put on hold." He collapsed against the wall, his stomach roiling. The logical conclusion entered his brain no matter how hard he tried to fight against it. "And if I'm found unfit or in-sane, I'll probably have to go back to that place." He ran his hands over his face. "I can't do it, Tara. Not that. Not prison either. I just want it to be over."

Giles came around the far corner, spotted Jaden, and hustled toward him with disheveled papers tucked under his elbow. He stopped in front of the bench and remained silent.

After a moment, he opened his mouth. "The trial will continue the day after tomorrow. I will present Dr. Clemson's testimony. The prosecution will then present their expert."

"For what?" Jaden sat up. "Dr. Clemson only knows what I told him." Giles started to say something, but Jaden cut him off. "I know what you're trying to do, and I already told you, I'm not crazy. I don't want you to argue that I am. Got it?"

Giles shifted on his feet. "My job is to represent you to the best of my ability—"

"Your job is to advocate for what's in my best interests. That men-tal hospital is *not* in my best interests." Jaden stood, looking Giles straight in the eye. "I'm not crazy. I won't say that I am."

Giles smiled. "You won't even need to testify." He patted Jaden on the shoulder. "Nine a.m. Thursday." He turned on his heel.

Jaden watched him walking away. "I'll remove you as counsel if you don't do as I ask."

"Nine a.m. Thursday," Giles repeated without looking back.

"Do you believe this guy?" He turned around to find Tara clutching her chest. A sheen of sweat covered her brow, and her eyes were wide with fear.

"What's wrong? What is it?"

"Not sure," she said between labored breaths. She groaned and hunched over then curled up on the bench.

Jaden called 911.

***

"Matthew, do you mind taking your brother to get a candy bar from the vending machine? I want to talk to your uncle for a minute."

Seeing his sister unable to reach her purse from her hospital bed, Jaden pulled out his wallet and gave his eldest nephew five dollars. When the boys had left the room, he sat at his sister's side. "What's up? Something I can get for you? I'm sorry if I did something—"

Tara groaned and slapped the mattress. "You didn't do anything wrong, Jaden!" She took his hand. "Except maybe being your own worst enemy."

"Are you sure? I seem to have enough of them out there."

He smirked, and he could tell she was trying not to laugh, but it came out anyway. He laughed, too, a genuine one. The sound of it seemed strange to his own ears.

"Seriously. I wanted to thank you."

Jaden snorted. "You? Thank me? I think I owe you like—"

"Will you be serious for a second? You really came through for me here. And I don't mean calling the ambulance. Anyone could have done that. But picking up Damien from the bus stop? Getting my kids and bringing them to my side? You came through when I needed you."

"Tara, how many times have you been there for me? This is—"

"It's not nothing! It's the... the Jaden... the *brother* I remember."
She looked away. Her cheeks were rosy. "Anyway, you were there
when I needed you. Thank you."

As awkward as it made him feel, the praise felt good. "I guess I'm
just better at coping with other people's problems than my own." He
scratched the back of his head. "Anyway, so how long do you need to
be in here?"

"The infection should be treatable with antibiotics, but they're
keeping me overnight for observation. It's not the first time it's happened around where they put the port. Can't do reconstruction until—"

"Not the first time? Why is this the first I'm hearing about it?"

Tara looked away. "You had so much going on—still do—I
didn't want to bother you with this."

"With cancer?" *Just how self-absorbed have I been that my own
sister didn't feel comfortable sharing her illness with me?* He wanted to
crawl under her bed and hide or maybe find a bedpan and curl up
with the other pieces of shit. "Tara, I'm your brother. I just wish you
had told me, but... I get it. I'm a terrible brother. And a terrible uncle.
But—" So much inside him wanted to come out. "If I get past this
trial, I'm gonna be better. Hell, even if I don't, when I get out, I'm
gonna be better. I'm sorry for all the times I wasn't."

"You're a good person, Jaden. The problem is you don't know it."

"Maybe." He wiped his nose with the back of his hand. "So...
what do the little hellions like to eat? I'll take them out, stay the
night at your place, then bring them back in the morning."

"You don't have to do that. I can call Mom—"

"It's already done. Anything you need, don't hesitate to call."

CHAPTER 24

Since Detective Royo had come directly to the courthouse from 300 North Street, he only caught the tail end of Sanders's testimony, but he'd seen enough. The man was like a car accident—a total yet captivating mess. He hid behind his arms, running his hands through his hair, muttering and rocking. His sister was trying to get his attention behind him, just outside the gate. But Sanders seemed lost to the world, his one-man chattering certainly making him appear crazy.

And maybe he was. But that didn't mean he deserved any of what was happening to him, especially since Royo had a sense of something darker at play.

Why, Detective Royo, are you actually feeling bad for the guy? Royo snickered at the thought, though it made him uncomfortable. A detective with a bleeding heart was no good to anyone.

Royo steeled himself and scanned the nearly empty courtroom. Sanders had exited with his sister, the poor schmuck hardly seeming to know where he was. Royo doubted Sanders had even noticed him. But he wasn't there to see the man he'd begrudgingly arrested or his sister. He was there to close a case he'd once thought he already closed.

The bent collar of a white button-down in need of starch underlined the short-cropped hair of Anthony Marinelli, who sat in the front row of the gallery. As Royo turned the corner into the first row, Anthony's eyes were closed as the beginnings of a smile came to his face. He was a man at peace.

"How are you? It's Anthony, right?" He took a seat beside the law clerk.

Anthony jolted upright, the corners of his mouth turning downward. "Detective Royo. Oh, uh, hi. Sorry, you startled me."

"You got a second?"

"Sure. What's up?"

"We've been looking into the death of Jaden Sanders's girlfriend, Cassidy—"

"Branigan?" Anthony's smile was too big. "My former sublessee." He tented his fingers. "So sad what happened there. She was way too young."

Royo frowned. He'd expected to surprise Anthony with the knowledge he'd gained from Maggie over at Prospero, not have his new person of interest volunteer it freely. He studied the young man's all-American smile and clean-cut face, searching for fissures in the mask, but found none. He wondered if Anthony had offered the information out of innocence or to appear innocent by offering something he knew Royo already knew. Whether purposeful or not, the comment shifted the dynamic in Anthony's favor. "Sublessee?"

"Yeah, I rented my place out to her." He removed his feet from the barrier and tucked them under his chair, leaning forward to rest his forearms on his bony knees. "But your people already know that. I went over it months ago, when it all went down, with one of your officers."

The punch knocked Royo further off-balance. "Do you remember who you spoke with?"

Anthony sucked in a breath. "Hmm. No. Sorry. That was months ago. I'm sure whoever it was took down my statement in writing. He seemed to be writing down every word I said. It's all probably in a police report somewhere."

"How did you know Ms. Branigan?"

"Through a friend. She needed a place, and I had a place. Worked out well for a while. I needed somewhere to study without distractions, and... you know, there were a lot of drugs going in and out of that complex. I didn't want any part of that, but I couldn't afford to break my lease."

"But you've been renting it for years."

"On her behalf, sure. She liked the apartment, so I've been fronting her the cash. She always paid me back when she could." He shifted on the bench. "What's this all about, Detective?"

Royo decided to play it cool. Petrakis could have been looking for Anthony at that apartment, or he could have been there to meet Sanders, Tresser, Branigan, or any number of drug-den junkies who might frequent the place. Something about Anthony's smile seemed a little too cool and too rehearsed. Wide and toothy, it was like an alligator's. Royo might have had Costa researching Anthony's background already, had she not been clinging to life. He would have to enlist someone ASAP or hit the books himself. Maybe he was wasting time, talking with Anthony with only a suggestion of a link to his cases, but his desire for answers drove him to speak. And some good had come out of it. Anthony had given him a story with facts that could be verified, locking himself into that story.

He smiled just as easily. "Oh, probably nothing. Just trying to get some things straight in my head. This Sanders guy is a real piece of work, isn't he?"

"Sure is." Anthony leaned in closer. "Between you and me, though, I'm not so sure I'd hang him for what he did. But this case sure has been a fun one to watch." That too-big smile, full of teeth, returned to his mouth.

Royo squinted. His nature was to be skeptical of everything everyone said—he would question a priest telling him it was hot in the desert—but something about Anthony wasn't adding up. He was way too close to Sanders to be sitting in that courtroom and whispering in Judge Cullen's ear, even if that relationship was only with the defendant's dead girlfriend.

But he was investigating a death even the medical examiner had ruled a suicide, wasting the people's tax dollars. *Who am I seeking justice for?*

Not justice. The truth.

"One more thing," Royo said, starting to rise. "What brought you to the complex the other day when I bumped into you?" He'd asked Anthony the same question earlier and recalled his answer, but Anthony had failed to mention that he rented an apartment at the complex at that time. He studied the clerk closely, watching to see if a lie would form.

Anthony looked up and to the left. "This case, actually. Judge Cullen wanted a full description of the complex, and I didn't trust my memory not to mess something up."

Royo nodded. The answer matched his previous one, and it took into account the new information. If Anthony was a liar, he was a good one.

"Well, if I don't see you before all this is over, let me know how it goes the next time I do. It's always good to get the perspective of someone in the know." Still faking a smile, he turned to leave.

"Will do, Detective."

CHAPTER 25

Jaden watched the man with whom he'd shared his most private thoughts traipse up to the witness box. The judge had admonished Giles not to even try to argue Jaden's competency to stand trial at that late stage of the proceedings, but he'd allowed an insanity or temporary insanity defense to be made. Jaden found prison preferable to doctors and that hospital where he'd been treated like a plaything for the support staff and crazies and a guinea pig to indifferent doctors. But his claims of mistreatment had been seen as the fabricated ramblings of an unsound mind. Jaden had objected and even pleaded with his attorney not to present the argument. *Where have doctors ever gotten me? When have they done less harm than good?*

Dr. Clemson had seemed to be the one exception. A shaky trust had formed from reluctant beginnings. And he *had* eventually trusted Dr. Clemson and allowed himself to believe the one familiar, friendly face was somehow different from the rest of his brood. But there he was, taking his money on his lawyer's request to lie under oath—to claim Jaden was insane and send him back to the place he feared and loathed most.

Only a true sadist would prescribe such torment. *Is anyone on my side?* Neither his lawyer nor his doctor was looking out for him.

A hand fell on his shoulder. He turned to see his sister and let out a breath. No matter how alone he felt, he knew he wasn't, as long as Tara was around. He shuddered as he thought of her hospitalization, and her hand weighed heavily as he considered his selfishness.

He'd done so little for her, yet she'd thanked him. He could and *would* do better, for her sake and for her kids' sake. He'd been too wrapped up in his grief. *Is that what's led me to this predicament? If I could have just let go—let* her *go.*

Though it would be hard, it needed to be done. He could handle prison, maybe, for a little while, then maybe reconsider the plea deal.

He still had time. Sometimes it seemed as though time was all he had. Not only was committing more of it to his family the right thing to do, but the thought of it made him feel a little better about himself, too, like he wasn't totally worthless and might still have something left to offer someone. And Tara had thanked him.

Just... please, God... no more setbacks.

The court officer swore in Dr. Clemson, then Giles went through the rigmarole of establishing the good doctor's credentials.

"How long have you treated Mr. Sanders?" Giles asked, finally getting to the meat of things.

Dr. Clemson pushed his glasses up to the bridge of his nose. "Oh, just under a year, I think. Yes, since January."

"In layman's terms, if possible, can you describe the circumstances upon which Mr. Sanders was directed into your care?"

"Jaden suffered a complete mental breakdown and attempted suicide. He was treated at Brentworth Hospital, where... he continued to decline. The hospital consulted me because of my specialties."

"And what are those specialties?"

"Well, they're more areas of practice, I should say. I care for patients with severe treatment-resistant depression as well as several forms of psychosis."

"Do you know what spawned Mr. Sanders's breakdown?"

Dr. Clemson shifted in his chair. "The apparent suicide of his girlfriend."

Giles started. "Apparent? Why do you say apparent?"

Dr. Clemson appeared distracted. He was looking across the floor at the law clerk, who seemed to be leering at the doctor as much as he had Jaden. Perhaps that was the clerk's way of showing interest in the case—staring in an uncomfortable and off-putting way—and it hadn't been only Jaden that he'd watched in such a way. The doctor stammered and narrowed his gaze on the clerk, expressing something close to a look of recognition or suspicion. *How does it feel to squirm?*

"Doctor?" Giles said.

"Uh, sorry. What was the question?"

"You used the word 'apparent' to describe the suicide of Mr. Sanders's girlfriend. Why did you choose to use that word?"

Dr. Clemson cleared his throat. "I didn't investigate the matter and was not privy to all aspects of it, which might have been helpful to Jaden's care."

"But certainly you don't think—"

Laughton jumped to her feet. "Objection."

Giles huffed. "Do you think Mr. Sanders had anything to do with Cassidy Branigan's death?"

"No!" Dr. Clemson sat up. "No. I'm sorry. I didn't mean to suggest or imply anything of the sort. Her death crippled Jaden, and we're still working to bring him back to a healthy place."

Without a doubt, Dr. Clemson was violating his doctor-patient confidentiality, and Jaden couldn't understand why. *Don't I have to waive that right?* Giles had said something about his head state coming into play if they pursued an insanity defense. But he hadn't wanted to pursue such a defense. *Should I fire Giles? Can I at this point?*

As he watched lawyer and doctor do their dance, his anger mounted. Without the corresponding migraine, it kept Jaden focused. He glared at his betrayer. *Do I look crippled now?*

"How had he been, to use your term, crippled?"

"Jaden suffers from severe depression and anxiety and, beyond that, a flaw in his coping mechanisms the likes of which I've not personally seen before, though there have certainly been similar documented cases. He is firmly rooted in the denial stage of grief and cannot move past it, so much so that at times of extreme stress, his mind simply cannot accept Cassidy Branigan's death. His brain has created a false reality in which she still exists, remains his girlfriend, and lives across the hall from him. We've made considerable progress to pull him out of this fantasy, but sometimes—again, particularly when the depression and anxiety are at their peaks—he falls back into his deception. At these moments of confusion... delusion, even... he is prone to wild shifts in mood and even hallucinations."

"Can he be violent?"

"Conceivably, but I've not witnessed it. Like any symptom of post-traumatic stress, its manifestations can be somewhat unpredictable. But Jaden is a sad case. He is more likely to be prone to feelings of worthlessness, grief, guilt, or loneliness. He's far more of a risk to himself than to others."

"Dr. Clemson, when Mr. Sanders suffers the delusions and mood shifts you've described, does he suffer from temporary insanity?"

"Most certainly."

"And you can say that with a reasonable degree of medical certainty?"

"I can."

"And these delusions Mr. Sanders suffers, they come at peak moments of depression or anxiety?"

"Yes."

"Are you familiar with the events that occurred in the early morning of August 11, 2022, at Mr. Sanders's apartment?"

"I am."

"Are these the sorts of events that are likely to trigger Mr. Sanders's delusions and mood swings?"

"I'd say, to a reasonable degree of medical certainty, that Jaden was suffering from such an episode that morning."

Giles removed his glasses and shook them in Dr. Clemson's direction. "And during these—" He folded his glasses and tapped them against his mouth. "We'll call them bouts of insanity, is Mr. Sanders in control of his actions?"

"In control?" Dr. Clemson frowned. "Somewhat. He gets confused and may not interpret the circumstances in which he finds himself accurately and thus may react based on this confusion."

"So for example, in this case, he might perceive a fight for his life as ongoing even after he obtained an upper hand?"

"Objection!" Laughton shouted. "Calls for speculation."

Giles paused and turned to the judge, taking the opportunity to put back on his glasses. Jaden was waiting for him to chew on the end. The lawyer theatrics added to his revulsion with the whole line of questioning.

"Overruled," Judge Cullen said, not even acknowledging the prosecutor with a glance.

"Yes, that seems most likely."

"And it would be your opinion, to a reasonable degree of medical certainty, that Mr. Sanders was temporarily insane the morning of August 11, 2022?"

"Yes, that would be my opinion... to a reasonable degree of medical certainty."

Giles pointed a finger at Jaden. "Is Mr. Sanders insane now?"

"I think it's very likely Mr. Sanders has reverted to his fantasy at some point during this trial, if not now then at multiple other times. He likely did so as he offered his testimony. Mr. Sanders is not well and should be remitted to my care."

"Do you feel he is competent to stand trial?"

Judge Cullen rolled his eyes but remained silent.

"No. I do not." Dr. Clemson met Jaden's gaze despite the contempt Jaden must have been projecting. "He should be remitted to my care."

Giles nodded, paused, then nodded again. "No more questions, Your Honor."

Jaden softened but only a little. Remittance into Dr. Clemson's care might not mean going back to that hospital. That might not be so terrible. He could resume life... maybe.

Life alone.

Laughton stood and approached the witness stand. "Dr. Clemson, I won't waste your time or this court's, so let's get right to it. Shall we? When the defendant suffers these delusions you've described, does he still understand the consequences of his actions?"

"You see, he gets confused—"

"Dr. Clemson, it's a yes-or-no question: does Mr. Sanders still understand that when he stabs a man, it will harm that man?"

After a moment, he replied, "Yes."

"During these so-called bouts of insanity, does Mr. Sanders still understand right from wrong?"

Dr. Clemson sighed. "Yes."

"Is there ever a time his condition prevents him from understanding the difference between right and wrong?"

"No, but—"

"No more questions, Your Honor."

CHAPTER 26

Scanning Officer Costa's desk, Royo felt a lump in his throat and a hollow pang in the pit of his stomach. A framed photograph showed Costa with three other women, all her age and with matching climbing gear strapped around their waists. A beautiful sunset cast a corona of color around their heads as they conquered some unknown peak. Next to it sat another photo of a German shepherd almost as big as Costa. Her desktop monitor showed the department's home page and a prompt to enter her username and password. The desk was clean and orderly and in all ways representative of a woman who was proud to be in law enforcement.

Royo didn't relish the thought of going through her things, and he smiled wanly when he realized he didn't have to. A file labeled Cassidy Branigan sat at the center of her desk—exactly what he was looking for. He suppressed a cough as his throat tightened at the thought of the doctors struggling to keep his fellow officer and friend alive. Several blood transfusions and constant care had kept Costa breathing so far, albeit in the ICU with a faint pulse, drastically low blood pressure, and not a single period of consciousness. Every time he received a call, he hesitated before looking at the number, offering a short prayer that it wouldn't be the hospital with bad news.

"Still helping me even when you can't be here." He sighed heavily, sat in her chair, and opened the file. "Let's see what you dug up."

"Cassidy Branigan," he read aloud from the DCF records. "Birth parents unknown. Abandoned at a local church as a toddler and taken in by St. Mary's Orphanage. Adopted only a few months later by Thomas and Willa Branigan." He flipped the page. "Cassidy Branigan, twelve years old, readmitted with her adopted brother to St. Mary's after adopting parents died in a house fire. Brother—Anthony Branigan, ten years old—traumatized when separated from his sister. Recommend all future placements keep them together."

"Brother?" Royo rubbed his forehead, not knowing what to make of that. He turned the page and found a sheet of notepaper with neat, curvy handwriting he recognized. When he read the first line Costa had written, he laughed. *Brother?*

He shook his head, chuckling as he skimmed the summary. Costa had looked into Branigan's brother. She'd written a note in the margin, reminding herself to ask around about the fire. Cassidy was twelve and Anthony ten at the time. St. Mary's had had little trouble placing them in foster care, but the foster parents never kept them long, and they were in and out of homes over a dozen times throughout their teenage years. When pressed for explanation for the frequent placements and re-placements, the nuns at St. Mary's wouldn't comment.

Any arrests made in relation to the fire? Royo closed the file and stood, walked over to his office, and sat down in front of the computer to which he did know the password. He cross-checked the date of the Branigan children's return to St. Mary's with the Branigan name in the department's database and quickly found a police report detailing the fire. It had started sometime in the early hours, October 26, 2003, at the Branigan home at 84 Halloway Street. The cause of the fire was unknown, and the only surviving witnesses were Cassidy and Anthony Branigan. The fire had started in Thomas and Willa's bedroom and spread quickly as they slept.

He heard Costa's voice inside his head. *I know what you're thinking, but investigators found no evidence of foul play.*

"Anthony Branigan," he said, trying the name out. "Anthony Marinelli."

Again, Costa's voice sounded in his head. *Lots of people are named Anthony.*

"Yeah," Royo answered. "But how many Anthonys would rent an apartment for Cassidy Branigan?"

He tapped his fingers across his keyboard then slouched. Anthony Marinelli had no record and was as clean as a baby's diaper still in the box.

"Wait..." *He does have a record!* The sparse information on the screen noted a juvenile record that was sealed up tighter than a bank vault.

Any detective worth his salt knew half a dozen ways to get the information in a sealed record. *Sealed* just meant he had to dig a little deeper. He would start with newspaper articles from Anthony's teenage years, though neither Anthony nor Branigan would likely hit. Since Anthony had been a minor, Royo would probably need to get creative. He scratched his chin, hoping he wasn't plummeting down a rabbit hole. But his gut told him otherwise. Something about Anthony stank. Even from afar, Royo could always sniff the rotten apple out of the bunch. Jaden Sanders didn't have that stink.

I could always talk to him again and show him our cards to see if he squirms. Royo debated his next steps. No matter how he chose to proceed, a trip to city hall to check whether Anthony had always been a Marinelli was in his near future.

"Well, he's definitely hiding something," he said, slapping the file. "Why else would he fail to mention he and Branigan had lived under the same roof for half their lives?"

Still doesn't link him to any crime, Costa chided in his head. But the real Costa would have been all over the information. The voice was merely his own overthinking in Costa form.

Royo grunted. *None of this makes much sense. He might have lied because he wants no part of a criminal investigation. He probably changed his name for a similar reason: to distance himself from his past. He's a law student. You have to go through a background check and all that to get into law school... and maybe to sit for the bar too.*

"Wouldn't know it from the practice," he murmured, thinking of his recent time in court. *Anyway, everything we have so far links him to Cassidy Branigan, not to Jaden Sanders. I'd like to see justice for that poor girl, if she truly didn't take her own life, but even the medical examiner ruled it a suicide. What am I really doing here?*

Frustrated, Royo turned the case over and over in his mind but saw no clear motive for the break-in and no known relationship between Anthony Branigan or Anthony Marinelli and Jaden Sanders. *Except that they are both—or all—linked to the same woman, who was found dead in her apartment nine months ago. With the close personal relationships each had with Cassidy, either could have had any number of motives for killing her.*

A piece of string began to form between seemingly disconnected events. *Relationships.* He repeated his thought aloud. "With the close personal relationships both Anthony and Sanders had with Cassidy, their motives for killing her could be many."

He remembered the woman's scars, her long history of abuse, and how it had seemed to follow her through the foster system. He hammered his fists against the desk. "Yes! That makes sense!" After kissing the file, he stood and grabbed his coat. "Costa, you're a genius."

CHAPTER 27

The rest of the trial went by in a blur as Jaden's head reeled and his stomach churned. In an obvious show of confidence, the prosecutor hadn't even offered up expert testimony, and Jaden had been rooting for her in that regard. Giles didn't push the matter of Jaden's competency, and the judge skirted it. He did, however, permit Giles to enter an insanity defense, which mostly relied on Dr. Clemson's testimony. With the lawyer refusing to call Jaden back to the stand and the prosecutor evidently wary that Jaden might lose it again and thus prove Dr. Clemson's claims, Jaden was relegated to the sidelines in a battle that would determine his fate. He had no way to explain to everyone how sane he was. He knew what was real and what wasn't, and anyway, Cass seemed to be gone. Despite the justice system's contriving every way it could to pull him apart, Jaden was holding himself together. Retreating to what Dr. Clemson called his fantasy world, he'd spent most of the trial lost in his head. Now that he was finally ready to face the trial and whatever outcome might happen, he had no means to do anything about it.

Eventually, closing arguments were made. Giles renewed some motion Jaden didn't understand and no longer cared to, which Judge Cullen promptly denied. The judge banged his gavel, gave the jurors another half hour's worth of instructions, and sent them away to deliberate, minus the two alternates. Passing Tara and Dr. Clemson, who'd apparently decided to see the thing through with Jaden, he exited the courtroom and headed for the restroom.

Standing in front of a urinal, he closed his eyes and let his mind drift. As he urinated, his muscles relaxed, and the tightness in his chest vanished. The ordeal was over. He didn't have to do another day in court, and sure, the jury would do what it was going to do, but hallelujah, he was done. He would do his time and keep on living. And that almost felt good. The notion seemed queer to him, yet there it was.

A shadow fell over him, and the tightness returned. Without opening his eyes, he knew someone was using the urinal next to him. With no separators, there were a line of them to choose from in an otherwise empty bathroom, yet some guy had decided he needed to be inches away from Jaden while they did their most private of activities.

"You killed her, you know."

Jaden's breath hitched. He opened his eyes and saw the toothy grin and gaunt face of the law clerk. Their shoulders were less than a few inches apart. "W-What did you say?"

"You killed it." The clerk sniggered. "I don't want to get your hopes up or anything. I certainly can't predict juries. But I know I wouldn't convict you based on that evidence." He slapped Jaden on the back with his unclean hand. "Me... Some of the others... We're all still rooting for you. Fingers crossed they just send you to Brentworth for—"

Without zipping up, Jaden grabbed the clerk by the front of his shirt and sleeve and drove him against the far wall. "What do you know about Brentworth? What do you mean I killed *her*?"

The clerk threw up his hands. "Hey, man. Take it easy! I'm on your side."

Seething, Jaden cocked his fist back.

"Pause. Close your eyes. Breathe," Dr. Clemson said from behind him.

Without lowering his fist, Jaden did just that. When he opened his eyes again, he looked into the anxious eyes of a possible friend, one he'd surely alienated.

He let go of the clerk's shirt, smoothed it out, and stepped back. "I-I'm sorry. I thought you said something you didn't."

"Whatever, man." The clerk hurried out of the restroom without washing his hands. At the door, he paused just long enough to say, "Crazy assholes like you belong in Brentworth."

Jaden flinched as a hand landed on his shoulder, but he relaxed when he realized it was only Dr. Clemson's. "You did well there, Jaden. You lost control, but you found it again and fairly quickly. Did you... see her again?"

"No." Jaden scanned the restroom for Cass or anyone else who might have entered. "I think she's gone. Maybe for good."

"That's good, Jaden. Really good." Dr. Clemson glanced at the door. "Who was that young man?"

"Judge Cullen's law clerk. Other than seeing him at the trial, I don't know him. He says he lives at the same apartments as me, though. Small world."

"I guess." Dr. Clemson squeezed his chin. "What did he say or do that set you off?"

"I thought he said I killed her. You know, Cassidy." Jaden took a deep a breath. "Anyway, I heard him wrong."

Dr. Clemson stared blankly at Jaden's open fly, prompting him to zip it. But the action didn't affect the doctor's gaze. He was lost in thought.

After a moment, he seemed to remember where he was. He grunted. "Well, you did well there not to strike him. Let's head back, shall we? You should be with your support structure when the verdict comes in."

"Are you part of that, Dr. Clemson?" Jaden's voice squeaked. "I mean, you were just up there telling everyone how delusional I am. And you know I can't go back to Brentworth."

Dr. Clemson clasped his shoulder. "I am one hundred percent on your side and will do everything I can to keep you out of Brentworth. There is a possibility you may be sent there initially, but I will insist that your care be carried out under my supervision elsewhere or at the very least that Brentworth has proven antithetical to your treatment. I am well respected among my peers and have some connections. I will be beside you every step of the way, if need be."

Jaden searched Dr. Clemson's face for a lie. Seeing none, he said, "Thank you."

"That's what I'm here for." He waved his arm toward the door. "Shall we?"

Jaden studied the man closer. "Don't you have to go? You must have come in here for a reason. Unless you were just following me."

"Actually, I... Never mind. Well, I'll leave you to wash your hands and head back in. See you inside, and remember, I am there if you need me."

Jaden stared at his trusted doctor as he scurried from the restroom. His vague suspicions were aroused, first about the law clerk and second about his doctor. He wondered if treatment for paranoia might be in his near future. *One more thing to add to the list.*

He returned to the hallway and sat on a bench. His sister and his attorney took seats at his sides. No one spoke as they waited for the verdict to come back.

"For what it's worth, I don't think you deserved any of this."

Jaden looked up to see Detective Royo staring down at him. He had no power to reply. Nothing was left in him to lash out or cry foul. The last of his fight for the day had been spent irrationally on a law clerk in a courthouse bathroom. *What has Royo done—really and truly done—to prevent the nightmare I'm going through? Isn't he part of the ass-backward system that put me there in the first place?* Everything Jaden might have wanted to say came out silently on the breath between his lips. His gaze fell to the floor. He was exhausted but alive and would begin the fight anew the next day.

"New evidence has come to light," Royo continued. "I just came from city hall, and... Well, I can't really say much right now, but I'm beginning to believe someone else has been playing you and me for fools since this whole thing started." He sighed. "Since before that, even."

Still Jaden stayed silent.

Giles leaned forward. "Detective, if you have additional evidence that might exonerate my client—"

"In due time, counselor." Royo let out a long, labored breath then sucked it back in. "Do you mind if I ask your client a few questions?"

Giles sneered. "Wasn't it your questions that got him into this mess in the first place?"

Jaden waved off his attack dog. He'd heard enough arguing to last a lifetime. "Let him ask his questions, Giles. If you think I shouldn't answer them, I won't."

"Thank you," the detective said. "I'm sorry to say that they're about your—about Cassidy Branigan. I'm not sure how to ask them delicately, so... Did you ever notice her having any strange or unexplained injuries?"

Giles put his arm across Jaden's chest like a driver protecting his passenger. "Where are you going with that question, Detective? What exactly are you investigating here?"

"It's all right, Giles. I—"

"I don't trust him." Giles frowned then sighed. "Jaden, he may be trying to implicate you in her death somehow, making you responsible."

Jaden slammed his head back against the wall and groaned. "I *am* responsible! Don't you see? I didn't help her. I wasn't there for her. She needed me, and... and... and... I wasn't there! The signs—so many signs!" He ran his hands down his face. "How could I have been so fucking blind?"

Pause. Eyes shut. Breathe.

He faced the detective, his head heavy with shame and guilt, but he found strength somewhere inside him to own it and bear it. "Yes, Detective. Once, she had a burn mark on her arm, a perfect circle.

It looked like someone had pressed one of those car lighters into her skin. She said it was from the stove. Another time, she limped for days. Refused to go to the hospital. That time, she said she'd stubbed her toe on the footboard. Tons of lesser things—a bruise here, a cut there. Nothing alone that seemed suspicious. But when you add them all together..."

The weight became too much, and Jaden's head fell into his hands. He laughed morosely through tears. "You know, she used to joke that she was accident prone." He shook his head. "I was so blind. So stupid."

Tara threw her arm around him. "I think that's enough, Detective."

"Okay." Royo straightened. "This isn't your fault, Jaden."

Jaden sneered up at him. "Tell that to the girlfriend I let die."

Royo sighed. He opened his mouth to say something then stopped. After a moment, he said, "Have faith, Mr. Sanders. Justice will be done... eventually."

"Thank you, Detective," Tara said then shook his hand.

Jaden made no move to shake it. He listened to Royo's footfalls echoing in the corridor as he walked away. *Thanks for nothing, Detective.*

Time seemed to freeze. He looked around for Cassidy, expecting to see her though knowing she wouldn't be real. It didn't make him want to see her any less. But except for those occupying his bench and the occasional soulless photographer snapping pictures of one man's fall, the corridor was empty. With the courthouse otherwise closed for the day, no one was there to care about justice for Tresser and his crew. The prosecutor had elected to camp inside the courtroom, smiling for the many cameras, which were powered on and ready to roll.

The sun was setting when the door beside them opened. A court officer stood in the cracked opening. "The jury's back. The prosecutor is already inside."

"Let's go in," Giles said, as if Jaden needed to be told.

As he plodded to the defense table like a witch to the gallows, Jaden averted his eyes from all those upon him: a courtroom full of them, most behind or beside zooming-in lenses. The only safe place to look was down. He remained standing while a court officer left and returned with the jury.

Once the jurors were seated, all except their foreperson, Judge Cullen asked, "Has the jury reached a verdict?"

"We have," a stout African American woman said. She glanced at Jaden then quickly averted her eyes. His stomach turned as if on a spin cycle.

Judge Cullen went about the process as if it were a boring routine, indifferent to the fact that what would be said next would liberate or condemn a man. "Madame Foreperson, would you please hand the verdict to the session clerk."

The juror did as instructed, and the clerk walked back to his desk and stood behind it.

Judge Cullen sat up. "The jury has reached a verdict, which Mr. Ralston will now read. Will the defendant please rise?"

Jaden had never sat. He bit his lower lip to try to keep it from trembling. The clerk stared down at the verdict in his hands. Jaden held his breath. He'd been praying for his trial to hurry up and finish ever since it started. As he was moments from it ending, he wanted to stall it. Everything was happening so fast that his head was spinning, and a fog had come over him.

"On the charge of murder in the second degree, the jury finds the defendant, Jaden Sanders, not guilty."

Giles clapped Jaden on the back, but the celebration was premature. He flinched with every strike.

The session clerk continued with the lesser crimes of voluntary and involuntary manslaughter, all let in with the insanity defense. The words *not guilty* echoed off the walls.

Giles hugged him. "We did it, Jaden. It's over."

Jaden's jaw dropped. "Over? What about the insanity defense?"

"You're not guilty. The jury found you not guilty. No defense needed. You didn't commit a crime, as far as they're concerned, the law is concerned, and *you* should be concerned."

The judge banged his gavel. "Mr. Sanders, having been found not guilty of the crimes for which you have been charged, you are hereby free to go as you please. This court strongly suggests and advises, however, that you continue to seek the counseling you so clearly need."

As the judge thanked the jurors for their civic service, Jaden allowed his sister to cry over his shoulder. He felt nothing except the sense of loss and grief he always felt. He looked around again for Cass, hoping for one more chance to see her smile and say goodbye.

But Cass wasn't there, and a part of him knew that maybe that was for the better.

CHAPTER 28

After leaving the courthouse, Royo drove directly to the hospital. He first paid a visit to Officer Costa's room. The prognosis as to when she would wake, *if* she would, was all over the map, but her condition was stable. The steady beep of her heart monitor was a cadence symbolizing the marching forward of time and a reminder of how precious time could be. More than half the department had given blood, with officers—even the shady ones—still filing in, and for the first time in a long time, Royo felt proud of his shield. He was part of a team.

He took Costa's hand and held it for several minutes, making all sorts of promises to her he wasn't sure he could keep as he studied the bruising around her IV port. Color had returned to her skin. She looked content, resting peacefully as her attacker slept equally peacefully nearby.

Royo stood, a scowl contorting his mouth. He would have to do something about that. *If you had arrested him right off, this would never have happened. But you had to play a game of cat and mouse.* The thought came with the realization that no matter how angry he was with Petrakis, it paled when compared to his anger with himself.

Less than two hundred yards away, Dmitri Petrakis lay handcuffed to his hospital bed, healing from a gunshot wound through his shoulder: Royo's second shot. Although he'd been aiming for center of mass, his first shot had carved a trench in his cheek that would leave a scar but had been nowhere near lethal. After what Petrakis had done to Costa, Royo wished he'd been a slightly better shot—but only slightly.

He nodded to the guard outside Petrakis's door and stepped inside, closing himself in the room alone with his suspect. He approached Petrakis's bed, making no attempt to be quiet. Still, the nurse-turned-drug-dealer slept. Royo slapped him hard on the side of the head, careful not to hit the stitches in Petrakis's cheek.

"What the fuck?" Petrakis whined. His head rocked to the side, and his eyes rolled until his gaze landed squarely on Royo. "You."

"Me."

"What do you want?"

"I want to talk."

"Really?" Petrakis smirked. "I want my lawyer."

"Yeah?" Royo snapped. *I've lived by the rules for so long, and where have they gotten me? Gotten Costa?*

Before he could rationalize his actions, he cupped one hand over Petrakis's mouth while driving a knuckle of the other hand under his back, into the bandages over the bullet wound. "You lost that right when you stabbed a cop."

Petrakis screamed then bit Royo's hand, for which Royo punched him in the teeth. He started to shout for help, but Royo punched him in the mouth again. The cop outside looked in through the window, nodded, and walked away.

"No one's going to help you in here." Royo grinned. "It's just you and me." He wriggled his knuckle into warm, wet gauze.

After a moment, he stopped, and Petrakis quieted.

Royo removed his hand from his mouth. "Don't say anything. Just listen."

"Oh, my lawyer is going to hear all about this. He's gonna sue your ass—"

Royo shot his hand back under Petrakis but didn't touch the wound. "Just listen."

Petrakis glowered at him, but he kept his bloodied mouth shut.

"Here's how this is going to work." He drew his gun and pressed it to Petrakis's temple. "You're going to tell me what I want to know, or I'm going to kill you."

Petrakis licked the blood on his lips and grinned. "You aren't going to shoot me."

"Oh yeah? You said that before, and how'd that work out for you?" Royo pursed his lips. Petrakis was right, of course. Royo wouldn't shoot him. He wouldn't have even been threatening to, had he not put a cop in the ICU. He held up the gun with both hands, using the second one to keep the first one from shaking. Royo kept to procedure ninety-nine percent of the time. His rare departures had only come when things got personal, and he was feeling Costa's pain deeply. *But not like this. This isn't me. This is—*

"You know what? Fuck it." He yanked a pillow out from under Petrakis and pressed it over his face then drove the pistol into the middle of the pillow. Yeah, he would never fire the gun, but Petrakis didn't need to know that. *And anyway, who am I trying to convince I wouldn't shoot?*

Petrakis squirmed, making muffled grunts.

Royo pulled off the pillow and tossed it on the floor. "You ready to talk?"

"You're crazy!"

"That's not what I asked." He raised his Glock.

"Okay!" Petrakis jerked up his hands for protection. One caught against the handcuff and rattled its metal against the rail. "What do you want?"

"Who's in room 315?"

"I don't know."

Royo picked up the pillow.

"No, man, I really don't know. Skinny guy with glasses. He never gave his name. I give him the oxys, and he pays me. That's it."

"Bullshit."

"That's it. I swear! He doesn't know my name, and I don't know his."

Royo dug his thumb into the soft flesh under Petrakis's collarbone. "If that's so, how'd you meet him?"

"All right! Lay off! I met him through this dealer I know from back when I was doing clinical shifts at Brentworth. This guy was always overdosing on his own goods. I approached him to see if I could unload some oxy on him and make some extra cash, you know. He hooked me up with the girl in 315. He and his friends were always hanging out with the girl who lived there. She was my buyer until she died, and the skinny guy showed up."

"What's this dealer's name?"

"I don't know," he said. But before Royo could pick up the pillow, he added, "But he goes by the nickname Waldo. I think his last name is Walder. Check the hospital records. The guy's in here like once a month. Might even be here now."

"If you're lying to me..." Royo hit him in the head with the butt of his pistol. "And if that officer you stabbed doesn't come through her injuries as good as new, you'll be seeing me again."

He walked to the door, opened it, and left without looking back at Petrakis. He might have asked him additional questions, but he was having a hard time keeping his anger in check and was afraid he might seriously hurt the man.

It didn't matter. Every cop in Fall River knew Waldo, and Royo knew where to find him.

***

About an hour later, Royo was watching a handoff. A dime bag slipped through a handshake to some college brat one of the officers around the corner would pick up. He got out of his Charger and walked toward the dealer, a low-level thug named Grisholm Walder.

Waldo's gaze lingered coldly on Royo before he turned and ran—directly into Officer Stravenski's clothesline.

"Police brutality!" Waldo shouted from the ground as Stravenski rolled and cuffed him.

Royo trotted up. "Shut it, Waldo." Royo helped Stravenski lift the criminal to his feet. "Selling drugs right in front of us, and you know there's a day care center around the corner? I think that constitutes a school under the law. What do you think, Officer Stravenski?"

"Not sure, but..." He patted the man down.

"I wasn't selling nothing."

Stravenski pulled four dime bags from Waldo's pocket. "Look what we have here."

Waldo scoffed. "Personal stash."

Royo grabbed him by his shoulder and dug his thumb into the soft spot under the bone, the same way he had done to Petrakis an hour earlier. "Relax, Waldo. Today's your lucky day. We need information. If you provide it, maybe, just maybe, I'll give you a pass."

"I ain't no snitch, pig!"

Royo grabbed him by his shirt then pushed him back into Officer Stravenski. "Everyone's a tough guy. You haven't even heard our request yet. We're looking for info on a guy you used to run with: Morton Tresser."

"What you want with him? He's dead."

"Exactly. So you see, you won't be snitching at all, and you have my word, if your information's good, I won't arrest you."

Waldo slouched. "What you want to know?"

"The night Tresser died, he broke into an apartment. Do you know anything about it?"

Waldo lit up. "Yeah, yeah. He was going there to fuck up some punk who'd messed with Cass, this girl we knew... before she killed herself. Wanted me to go with him, but I was in the hospital."

"You pussed out?"

"I... Whatever. I ain't gonna go fuck up some dude I don't even know, risking my neck for some whore who died. Shame, though. The things that girl would do for oxy." He whistled. "But from what she used to say, that dude was whack. Fucked in the head. You know what I'm saying? Dangerous like Anthony Perkins, you know? Shit, I don't need that kind of crazy."

Stravenski shook him. "Explain."

"You know! Look what he did to M.T. and his boys! Cass would ramble when she got wasted. The shit she told us he'd do to her: put cigarettes out on her neck, cut her, and... worse shit. Shit you don't want to know about. Fucked her up for years while telling her how much he loved her. Abusive love shit. He's the guy you should be arresting, not me."

Royo glanced at Stravenski then turned back to Waldo. "You said 'years.' Branigan knew this guy who was abusing her for years?"

"Yeah, they went way back, like they were fooling around as kids, man. I think he even killed his parents or some shit. I'm telling you, the whole thing was beyond fucked. I didn't want nothing to do with it."

"All right." Royo patted the dealer's cheek. "Thanks, Waldo." He walked away as Stravenski pushed Waldo toward his squad car.

"Wait!" Waldo shouted. "You said you'd let me go!"

Stravenski said, "He *is* letting you go. Me? I'm not so forgiving."

CHAPTER 29

Trying to come to grips with Cassidy's death had been like walking until collapse, but Dr. Clemson was helping Jaden cope. He didn't like the increase in medication, but he had his biweekly appointments, his mood swings seemed to be leveling out, and he had Tara to help him through it. *And Rascal.*

Jaden couldn't hold back his tears when he realized his slip. It had only been a week since the trial ended, and his mind was still in the earliest stages of healing, moving past denial to acceptance. At least that was what Dr. Clemson had said. But with the trial past Jaden, he was ready to face reality and find a way to be a whole person again.

No. No Rascal. He opened the door to his apartment complex and climbed the stairs to the third floor, thinking maybe getting another cat might do him some good.

Living across the hall from the woman he'd loved, who'd been taken from him, was hard. *How?* Since Royo had planted a seed of doubt with "Someone else has been playing you and me for fools," he no longer knew what to think about Cass's death. He was finding it hard enough to accept her absence regardless of its cause but was still trying. Thinking someone else might be to blame alleviated some of his guilt. *Some.*

Suicide, though, made no sense. They'd been so happy together. *Weren't we?*

Yes, Jaden was sure of it. His mind wavered between two extremes. Half the time, he condemned himself for her suicide, and the other half, he contrived ways to mete out justice to anyone else who might have been responsible. He wasn't a murderer, at least not in the eyes of the twelve jurors, but he was a killer, and not a moment passed when he felt even a tinge of remorse for taking the lives of three men. If he was honest with himself, he knew what sort of person he was—not all good, not all bad, and feeling too much when he shouldn't and too little when he ought to.

But he didn't want to be that way, and he'd gotten help. Dr. Clemson had discontinued the Haldol, and already he was doing better, with none of the withdrawal symptoms he was told to expect. He'd finally learned to tolerate himself and, more surprisingly, to look for reasons to try.

A small part of him still wished he wouldn't. Not feeling was so much easier than feeling, than trying, than... *Love?* But Cass, she had loved him back. They were happy. He knew they were.

So then why? Or if Royo was right, then who? He wanted more than justice. He wanted vengeance of a kind that overshadowed the crime. He would be fine with doing what he'd done to those three junkies to anyone who might have hurt Cass. No, he would be fine with doing much worse.

Dr. Clemson had said not to dwell on it. If anyone could understand what made someone suffering from severe depression do what Cass had done, it should have been Jaden. He wasn't to blame, just as she wouldn't have been had he decided to the same thing.

He grunted, though all he wanted to do was scream. *Why do I still feel so guilty and dirty, like the weight of her death is on me as surely as it would have been had I fed her those pills myself?*

I should have seen it, but I was too blinded by my feelings to notice hers. Didn't I make her happy? He sniffled and shook his head as he stepped out of the stairwell. *No, there were no signs.* He shriveled beneath her imagined stare. *Except for all the bruises, the breaks, the burns...*

Jaden froze, and his body began to tremble. "No..." Down the hallway, a note hung on his door.

He turned and started walking away. "I can't deal with this. Not now." He paced and took out his phone, torn between calling his psychiatrist and his sister as he clawed at his hair.

He paused, closed his eyes, and took deep breaths. "It's just a notice about the building." *What else could it be?* It was logical. It made sense. He laughed, but it came out high and shrill. He stopped, chewed on his thumbnail, and stared at the note.

"It's just a note. She's dead. It's just a note." With shaky confidence, he strode to his door, tore the folded paper off it, opened it, and read.

Howdy! That's what you get for slamming doors, asshole.

A smiley face punctuated the sentence. As if an outsider looking in, Jaden was aware his lips were moving, but he couldn't hear what they said or know if they said anything at all. The corner of his left eye twitched incessantly. A god-awful migraine chiseled at his forehead and temples.

He roared. Someone was messing with him. They'd been doing it all along.

"Who are you?" He slammed his shoulder into the door across the hall. "Why are you doing this to me?" He hit the door again and again, pounding it with his palms and batting it with his fists.

Wood cracked, and the door loosened in its frame. Jaden froze.

"Cass?" The thought echoed through his rampaging mind. Maybe whoever was behind that door knew something about her death. Perhaps the same person who was screwing with him had done something to Cassidy. Yeah, Cassidy was dead. He could admit that now. But it didn't mean he had to like it.

And so help me, if whoever's behind that door had anything to do with it... He charged at the door and burst through it. Stumbling into the apartment, he nearly collided with a man.

Jaden heard the blast and knew he was falling. He hit the floor, surprised by how cold it was. He didn't feel anything except that cold carpet and the contrary sticky warmth spreading over his hands.

A man stood over him. The gun wasn't in his gloved hands then, but something else that shone. He crouched and put something in Jaden's hand.

"I... I know you... from court."

He lifted the object in front of Jaden's eyes.

A blade.

"Wh-What?" His eyes rolled back in his head. "Why?"

The man crouched beside Jaden and spat in his face. "You took what belonged to me." He sneered. "And now I've taken everything from you." He laughed. "All's fair in love and war."

CHAPTER 30

Detective Royo took in the wiry young Anthony Marinelli in his waiter-white button-down and navy suit pants. Its accompanying jacket was draped over the back of the hard plastic chair. As uncomfortable as that chair was, Anthony settled into it with all the ease of a pig in slop.

"Sorry to see you under these circumstances, and such a shame, too, after he was just found not guilty and all." Anthony frowned. "A tragedy, really. I just feel terrible for what I was forced to do."

"Yes." Detective Royo tapped his pen on his desk then slid his tape recorder forward. "Do you mind?"

Anthony smiled. "Not at all, Detective. Anything I can do to help."

Royo pressed the record button. "Statement of Anthony Marinelli, October 14, 2022. My name is Detective Asante Royo. In the room with me I have..." He waved a hand toward Anthony.

"Oh. Anthony Marinelli."

"Officer Megan Costa, also present," Costa said.

Not yet back from medical leave, she'd nevertheless wanted to sit in on Anthony's statement. Royo was more than happy to oblige.

"Thank you, Anthony. Could you describe your relationship with Jaden Sanders?"

"We were neighbors, apparently. He lived across the hall from the apartment I sublet. I had never met him personally before this."

Royo clenched his jaw. "Could you describe your relationship with Cassidy Branigan?"

Anthony leaned forward. "Beyond what I already told you? She sublet my apartment from me."

Royo lowered his voice, speaking in barely more than a grumble. "Records are never truly sealed, Anthony, if you know how to look or who to ask."

Anthony scowled. "Excuse me?"

"Was your name ever Anthony Branigan?"

Anthony's purple worm lips twisted into a smile. "Yes. That's a matter of public record. I'm not sure what you are referring to when you say sealed—"

"In fact..." Heat rose in Royo's cheeks. "Didn't you change your name when you turned eighteen, to distance yourself from your adolescent crimes and psychiatric treatment?"

"I'm not sure what you're getting at, Detective." Anthony smiled again, beaming with the same smugness to which Royo had grown accustomed.

Costa, who'd been listening quietly at the door, had apparently heard enough. The stitches in her thigh hadn't even come out yet, but that didn't stop her from charging at Anthony with all the pride of the righteous. "We know what you did to Branigan, you twisted son of a bitch!" She heaved over him, her heavy breathing inflating and deflating her like a furious beast. "Doctor-patient privilege only goes so far. Did you know a psychiatrist can tell us pretty much everything you tell him if he thinks it relevant to stopping his patient from committing a crime?"

Anthony didn't flinch. "I don't have the faintest idea what you're referring to. Are you accusing me of something? I would remind you that false allegations of a crime do form a rather concrete base for a defamation claim against your department."

Royo laughed. He had no desire to hold Costa back, but he took a cooler approach. "Defamation, huh? You wouldn't be the first. But we know all about what you did when you were ten—what you did to your parents and your sister, for fuck's sake. Dr. Clemson gave—"

"Dr. Clemson had no right!" Anthony flushed but sat back, folded his hands in his lap, and cleared his throat. "What happened when I was a child... I was cleared of any wrongdoing in that fire." He glared at Royo. "And she wasn't my sister by blood."

Costa slapped her palm against the desk. "And that made it okay for you to abuse her for how many years?"

Anthony remained in an infuriating position of relaxation. "I haven't a clue what you might be referring to. My sister was a troubled woman, and I miss her deeply."

Taking Anthony's words as genuine when he smiled like an alligator while saying them was difficult. He seemed to enjoy the game—the thrill of the chase—and obviously felt assured he would outsmart them. He was a true narcissist, just as Dr. Clemson had told him over the phone. If only Dr. Clemson had gone to the trial and recognized the law clerk sooner. He'd been appointed by the courts as Anthony's therapist after the fire and through his early teens. But Anthony had grown into a man, not immediately recognizable but a whole lot more dangerous. But he was still a boy in some ways, one who didn't take kindly to others playing with his toys.

Royo eyed him with disgust. "And we know what you did to Jaden Sanders."

Anthony laughed. "What are you talking about, Detective? Surely you can't be suggesting I in some way provoked his attack. He broke through my door and came at me with a knife. If Jaden wasn't found guilty for what he did, I can't imagine I'd be convicted. It was self-defense, as clear as day."

Royo gave a vengeful chuckle full of loathing and scorn. "As clear as mud, Anthony." He nodded at Costa, who pressed Anthony down against the desk then pulled out her cuffs.

"We know you put a note on his door to provoke him. Have the whole thing on video and much more, but you'll find all that out in due time. Let's just say you shouldn't have killed the cat. Your sister was bad enough, but I really think it was the cat that nabbed us our star witness."

Costa laughed. "Like you said, no one ever notices the maintenance guy."

"But don't worry." Royo smirked. "You'll get your day in court."
He read Anthony his rights.

ACKNOWLEDGMENTS

The author would like to thank Attorney Adrienne Catherine H. Beauregard Rheaume for her invaluable criminal law expertise, Chad Parkman for his also invaluable correctional officer expertise, and Tarrah Parkman for her medical and social work knowledge, all of which greatly helped ground the story in reality. The author would also like to thank Frank Spinney for his most appreciated early content read, Sara Gardiner for her brutal but masterful content edit, Susie Driver for her fantastic line editing, Erica Lucke Dean for her cover and copy assistance, and all the other great folks at Red Adept Publishing who helped push this book out to the world. As always, thanks also go out to Carrie for her help and support and to the author's two dogs, Dakota and Ryder, for keeping him sane... relatively speaking.

Also by Jason Parent

Cycle of Evil
Speaking Evil
Seeing Evil
Hearing Evil

Standalone
Unbalanced

Watch for more at authorjasonparent.com.

About the Author

In his head, Jason Parent lives in many places, but in the real world, he calls Southeastern Massachusetts his home. The region offers an abundance of settings for his writing and many wonderful places in which to write them. He currently resides with his cuddly corgi, Calypso.

In a prior life, Jason spent most of his time in front of a judge... as a civil litigator. When he tired of Latin phrases no one knew how to pronounce and explaining to people that real lawsuits are not started, tried, and finalized within the 60-minute time-frame they see on TV, he traded in his cheap suits for flip-flops and designer stubble. The flops got repossessed the next day, and he's back in the legal field... sorta. But that's another story.

When he's not working, Jason likes to kayak, catch a movie, travel any place that will let him enter, and play just about any sport (except for the one with that ball tied to the pole thing where you basically just whack the ball until it twists in on knot or takes somebody's head off). And read and write, of course. He does that too sometimes.

Read more at authorjasonparent.com.

About the Publisher

Dear Reader,

We hope you enjoyed this book. Please consider leaving a review on your favorite book site.

Visit https://RedAdeptPublishing.com to see our entire catalogue.

Don't forget to subscribe to our monthly newsletter to be notified of future releases and special sales.

Made in the USA
Las Vegas, NV
09 April 2022

47159352R00156